ALIBI
FOR DEATH

ALIBI

FOR DEATH

G.L. Barbour

ARPress
ILLUMINATING IDEAS
EMPOWERING VOICES

ARPress
45 Dan Road Suite 5
Canton MA 02021

Hotline :1(888) 821-0229
Fax: 1(508) 545-7580

Ordering Information:
Quantity sales. Special discounts are available on quantity purchases by corporations, associations, and others. For details, contact the publisher at the address above.

Printed in the United States of America.

ISBN-13:	Paperback	979-8-89356-527-0
	eBook	979-8-89356-529-4
	Hardback	979-8-89356-528-7

Library of Congress Control Number: 2024902558

Other Books by G. L. Barbour

<u>Academic</u>

Quality in the Veterans Health Administration
Redefining a Public Health System

<u>Fiction</u>

The Ron Looney Series 

Death Unexpected
One, Two, Three Times a Murder
A Twisted Death
A Researched Death
Naked Death

<u>Other</u>

Montana in the Rearview Mirror

Contents

CHAPTER 1

Hector Richmond was a happy man. His wife had packed him a wonderful meal for his midnight lunch break. Her meatloaf sandwich on Italian bread with mayonnaise and onion was all a man could hope for - well, after a strong cup of coffee and a smoke, anyway. Hector's meal break came at eleven pm, a third of the way through his twelve-hour shift as a night watchman at the Railway Building. Hector intended to save the apple turnover and the Butterfinger candy bar to snack on later. He had another break in the early hours of the morning; but he couldn't wait to get at the meatloaf sandwich, his mouth began watering before he had it unwrapped.

Hector had been doing the night watchman shift at the Railway Building in Cincinnati for more than a year. He knew every hallway and office owner in the building like the proverbial back of his hand. And he knew his 'rounds' of the building well enough to complete them blindfolded, as he liked to say. Hector clock in time was seven PM on the weekends; he chose the weekends because of the extra pay, although the work was the same as during the week. Weekend nighttime watch tours meant an empty building most of the time. This night, however, he was scheduled for Thursday night in a swap he made so Andy could spend the weekend in Cleveland celebrating his daughter's marriage. The schedule change meant little to Hector; the job requirements were the same every night of the week. He would patrol the five stories of South Railway, clocking in once on every floor and then doing it again and again. His simple responsibilities were to assure that the unoccupied offices and labs were locked and that anyone working late had protection.

Hector had often told his wife he didn't know what he was protecting anyone from since the access to the building was tightly controlled with keycards restricted to physicians working in the adjacent New City Hospital. At least that was true for the south end of the building where he patrolled. The north end held professional offices and medically related activities such as the dialysis unit of New City. The north end was not his responsibility, though.

Hector finished the sandwich and got up for his post-meal walk. When he resumed his seat in the small break room on the third floor, he poured a second cup of coffee from the thermos, and checked his watch. Eleven-twenty; he had another twenty minutes on this break. Hector reached into his bag and pulled out the Zane Grey novel he was currently reading. He leaned up against the wall and found the dog-eared page where he had ended last time. He began reading, moving his lips just a little with the words as he enjoyed the mental picture of the western United States decades earlier. Hector wanted to visit those areas someday. A nice vacation for him and his wife. He liked thinking about that.

At eleven-forty-five, Hector picked up his book, carefully turning down the corner of a page to mark his progress. He packed the paperback and the remainder of his lunch in his carryall bag and put the apple turnover on top where he could easily find it at the next break. He stood and stretched then carried his bag over to the small counter and put it in the corner. Then he adjusted his belt and headed for the toilet. Minutes later, he was on his way to the elevator bank to start his next round of patrolling. In the elevator, he hit the button for the fifth floor, and cracked his knuckles as the elevator silently and smoothly rose to the top of the building.

He was on the fourth floor checking that doors were locked and secure when his Motorola two-way radio came on with a buzzing sound and one of the hospital guard's voice said, "Hector, this is Jack. Come in."

Hector pushed the response button. "Hey, Jack. This is Hector. What's up?"

"Everything all right over there?"

"Man, the building is sound asleep. Why?"

"I just got a call from Mrs. Abbate. The cancer doctor's wife."

"Yeah?" Hector remembered Dr. Abbate's office on the third floor.

"She says he's late coming home."

Hector nodded. "Well, I know he's been here. I saw him in his office right after I got here and the light was still on last time I went by there."

"She wants him to call her. She says he's not answering his phone, office, or mobile." Jack said, with a little tinge of annoyance in his voice.

"Yeah, that's odd. I'll go check. That's down one. I'll find him and tell him to call her."

"Okay. Thanks, man. Over."

"Roger. Over." Hector took his finger off the response button and shook his head.

Hector went back to the elevator bank and summoned a car. He didn't use the stairs even on his rounds because of pain in his knees. Besides, there weren't any doors on the stairwells to check. He went down one floor and headed in the direction of Dr. Abbate's office. Hector knew that the doctor spent Thursday evenings in his office almost every week doing something. On the other times Hector had worked a Thursday night Abbate was usually finished and gone by the time Hector started his rounds after his first break, though, so this call was definitely different.

He found the office door locked, as it had been earlier. Through the glass portion, he could see the doctor's desk, well lit by a small LED lamp. Hector could not see the doctor in the room. He knocked on the door and got no response. Knocking more loudly was no better. Hector pulled out his master key ring and unlocked the door. He opened it and called into the room, "Doctor, are you in here?" He waited for a response.

There was no answer. Hector decided to look around and entered the room, and walked toward the desk, again calling out, "Hey doc, are you here?" As he approached the desk, he saw the doctor, lying on the floor behind the desk, screened from view by a low credenza at the right end of the desk. Abbate was sprawled on the floor on his back; his head turned to the left and bathed in blood and gore. His sightless eyes stared off into the distance. Hector stood transfixed for several seconds before he was able to react. He had never seen a dead person before, let alone one that had been killed like that. For a few moments he felt numb, then he noticed his legs were trembling and he had forgotten to breathe.

Hector took several deep breaths and swallowed the bile rising in his throat, willing himself not to vomit. He recognized the area as a crime scene and carefully retraced his steps back to the doorway. He pulled out his two-way and engaged it, saying, "Jack. Jack, We gotta call the cops."

Jack came on immediately, "What's that, Hector?"

"He's dead, Jack. Call the cops."

"Are you sure, Hector?" Jack said, with a trace of doubt in his voice.

"Oh man, I am very sure. Somebody beat him to death."

"Hold on. You mean somebody killed Dr. Abbate?"

"He sure didn't do this to himself, Jack. Call the cops."

"Okay. Gotcha. Are you all right?"

"Hell, no, Jack. I'm about to puke. Get the cops."

"Right. I gotta call the Director and then …"

Hector yelled into his two-way, "Call the cops right now! Over." He jerked his finger off the talk button and stood frozen in place for a few seconds. He dropped his two-way trying to reattach it to his belt. He leaned against the doorframe and slowly sank to a sitting position in the doorway still willing himself not to vomit. That's where he was when the other security officers and police found him when they arrived at the Railway building twenty minutes later.

CHAPTER 2

Tom Bolling was heading down I-75 at three in the morning at a speed that slightly exceeded the legal limit. He wanted to go even faster but restrained himself with the awareness that the traffic was very light and he was making very good time. He had been awakened by the call from New City only fifteen minutes previously and had piled into his clothes and then into the F-150 within seven minutes, no shaving, no coffee, no breakfast. As an orthopedic surgeon with two years active duty at Bagram, Tom knew how to awaken immediately upon hearing the phone. And he knew how to respond to an emergency by dressing within minutes.

Tom was the chief of staff at New City, the senior medical executive in the hospital and he felt it necessary to be early on the site of the murder in the Railway building. As he drove he recalled the history of the Railway Building as part of the medical care offerings in Cincinnati. The original building, five stories high, red brick and only fifty feet wide, was initially a hospital for railroad workers and their families. After the war in 1945, the medical care picture changed in Cincinnati and the nation. Academic medicine became married to the Veterans Administration, a national exuberance with the 'science' that ended the war began to attract patients to medical care, hospitals became sites of 'cure' rather than a place to die, and the recently expanded Railway Hospital was purchased by Regents Health System and converted to a for-profit center. The current complex in the rail yard area spanned eastward from the Railway building to the 1950s addition and up to the spiraling ten-year-old New City Hospital with its prominent Research Tower and broad access to its Emergency Department Area just off the Interstate. Unlike its beginning in the narrow Railway building, New City Hospital was visually arresting and visible from Interstate 75 by commuters going north and south.

Tom's short tenure at New City had already been marked by two murders that had facilitated his deepening of a prior relationship with one of Cincinnati's homicide detectives, Ron Looney. Tom, an orthopedic surgeon and retired brigadier general in the United States Air Force, met Master Sergeant Ron Looney years before when they were both on active duty. Their wives became friends, and the presence of the Looneys in Cincinnati was a factor in Tom taking the job at New City when he retired from active duty. Tom and Ron Looney had worked together on those 'New City murders' with results that kept the hospital out of the newspaper and maintained its accreditation with the Joint Committee for Accreditation of Healthcare Organizations. That accreditation was important for New City to maintain its profit status and its academic programs. Tom was hoping he would find that Ron Looney and his partner, Gene Novalchek, were working on this new murder on the grounds of New City.

As usual, as Tom drove his six-year-old Ford F-150, he enjoyed both the elevated height over the rest of the traffic and the quiet interior. The truck's height gave Tom a long view of the traffic ahead and offered ample time for him to adjust to changing patterns. The quiet time allowed him an opportunity to think about things he would face in the day ahead. Now, as he drove, Tom centered his thoughts on the minimal information he had about the apparently brutal murder of one of the staff oncologists at New City, Alex Abbate.

Tom remembered Alex as a moderately intense practitioner, often found in the hospital at odd hours, and a favorite teacher of the students and residents. He could not call to mind any incident where someone had expressed anger at Abbate or his actions. Patients and families were consistent in their praise of his communication and manners. Nurses in the Chemotherapy Infusion Unit said he was the most sensitive of all physicians that worked there. Why would anyone want to kill him?

According to what he had been told, the murder involved a brutal bashing of Abbate's head. Tom could not imagine anyone who could carry out such a vicious attack.

The traffic remained light all the way down I-75 to the Western Hills interchange and the 2B exit. Tom pulled left, navigated the 270-degree turn and exited onto Western Hills, then immediately turned north on Spring Grove to the New City Hospital complex. He decided to park in his reserved spot in the main parking deck rather than driving around to the Railway parking lot, since he would likely be staying at the hospital for the remainder of the day. He engaged the access card reader at the gate and hurried to his marked parking space adjacent to the walkway over to the hospital. He descended from the truck, reached back and grabbed his go-bag, locked the truck, and strode quickly to the hospital entrance at the end of the walkway. The door was locked at this time of day, so Tom used his access card, and quietly walked through the darkened lobby. He did not go to his office or pause at the deserted coffee kiosk but continued to the hallway toward the rear of the main building from where he could access the sidewalk to the Railway Building.

Tom did not meet anyone as he walked through the 1950s building, now converted to laboratories and administrative space, although he could see some light down one of the corridors where the chemistry lab was. He took the exit to the Railway building and chose the path to the left that brought him to the south end, the medical office side and a key access door. It opened before he got there, however, and he was greeted by one of the security guards.

"G'morning, Doctor."

"Albert. Where is everyone?"

"They's all up on three, sir. In Dr. Atbee's office there."

"Thank you, Albert."

Tom punched the Up button on the elevator and waited only a few seconds before one opened. He exited on the third floor and started down the hall toward Abatte's office where he was met by a Cincinnati police officer guarding the central hallway at that point.

"Hold on there, buddy. You can't go in there. This is a crime scene." The officer held up a white-gloved hand like a traffic cop.

Tom controlled his voice, smiled at the officer, and said, "I'm aware of that. I am Dr. Bolling, chief of staff here at New City. I was called about this . . . circumstance. I want to speak to the detective in charge."

"Do ya, huh? Well, it's me that you'll be talking to. The detectives are busy."

"Yes, well, of course. And I know that, but would you just ask one of them to step out?"

The officer braced his shoulders as if insulted and was about to say something when Dr. Darringer appeared in the doorway with her large black bag. She tried to move past the man in the doorway and placed her hand on his shoulder saying, "Excuse me." The officer looked quickly over his shoulder, recognized the Medical Examiner and moved to allow her to pass.

Tom recognized her and said, "Dr. Darringer. Can you tell me what's going on?"

Darringer looked up and replied, "Tom, I wondered why you weren't here. I hope you don't mind that I didn't call Monique about this but I thought ..."

"No. That's not a problem. I'm sure she would appreciate not being awakened. What happened?" Tom asked, disregarding the glowering look from the officer.

"Bloody mess, and I'm not reverting to the King's English."

"Is it Alex Abbate?"

"No ID on the body. Is that whose office this is?"

"Yes. Should I identify him?"

The Medical Examiner thought for a second then turned to the officer barring the door and said, "Would you ask Detective Knudson to step out here for a moment?"

The officer looked at Tom as though he had not heard the request. Then he shrugged, pointed to the crime scene tape in the doorway, and ducked under it into the room. Darringer smiled at Tom and headed for the stairs. Moments later, a stocky fellow in a plain brown rumpled suit with a loosened tie appeared in the doorway. He stared at Tom for a long second and then asked, "Yes?"

"I am Tom Bolling, chief of staff here at New City. I got the call about the incident and came to help."

"Uh-huh."

"I know the deceased and his work here."

"Okay. Tell me about him."

Tom hesitated and then asked, "And, who are you?"

"Oh, yeah. I'm Rocky Knudson, Cincinnati Homicide Division."

"So, you know my friend, Ron Looney?"

"Walker? Yeah, I know him."

"Is he here?"

"No. I'm in charge here. Who is this guy?" The detective asked this question while indicating with his head that he meant the dead man in the room behind him.

"This is the office of Dr. Alexander Abbate. He is one of the oncologists here at New City. I cannot identify him from this distance, of course."

Rocky smiled at Tom. "You're a smart one aren't you, doc?"

Tom looked steadily back at him.

Rocky asked, "You want to come in? To identify him, of course."

"I don't wish to intrude. I only want to be certain this is Alex before I talk to his wife."

"Oh, ho. Now you're the notifier, too? Let's not get into that, doctor. It was his wife that called the police about a missing husband. I'll be the one talking with her. And I can always get her to do the identification."

Tom's look remained steady as he said, "And if it isn't Alex, will she know who it is? I know all the other people who work around here."

Rocky sighed, "All right, doc. Put on the booties there at the door and keep your hands in your pocket. Walk straight in to the desk, give me your identification and walk back out. Got it?"

"Yes," Tom said, ducking under the tape and grabbing a pair of paper booties. He approached the desk slowly, looking all around the office, hoping to see something useful. But Tom had not been in Alex's office in over a year and could not remember what it looked like before. He did not see any evidence of disruption, however, and concluded that the office had not been ransacked.

. Tom intended to look over the desktop items when he could see them all, but those clever intentions vanished seconds later; when he got that close the only thing he could stare at was the grotesque figure twisted on the floor with his head severely bashed and the blood and brain matter strewed around the body. Tom swallowed deeply and turned to Rocky, "I can't really see his face."

Rocky signaled to the officer kneeling at the body, and she gently turned the head toward Tom.

Tom nodded and turned away. "Yes. That's Alex. Alexander Abbate." He said quietly to Rocky. Then, after pausing a few seconds to gather himself, Tom walked back to the doorway and shed the booties. Rocky followed him to the door and began to question him about the victim. "He got any enemies? Does anybody want him dead?"

Tom shook his head. "No. Not that I know of."

"Who does he work with here at New City?"

"He is a cancer doctor and works particularly with the Chemotherapy Infusion Unit. But he consults throughout the hospital."

"You got a list of the names of the people in this Infusion Unit?" Rocky asked, making an entry in a small notebook.

"Yes. I can have that for you fairly quickly."

"Thanks, doc." Rocky was far more polite than before, so Tom thought perhaps the moment was right for a strange request.

"Uh, Rocky," he said appealingly, "You said you know Ron."

"Yeah, I know him."

"Perhaps you also know that he and I have worked together on a couple of cases here at the hospital before."

"Yeah, I've heard about that, too."

"So, I was just wondering, maybe Ron could take this case, and we could, you know, build on our previous success."

Rocky stiffened slightly and braced his shoulders. "You want me to step aside and give this case to Walker?"

"Well, I don't know about that." Tom and Rocky locked steady stares. But, perhaps that's exactly what I'm asking."

"Listen, doc. I don't know how you doctors and surgeons handle cases. But I bet you don't just hand 'em off because somebody asks you to. We certainly don't do that in Homicide. This case is mine, and I'm gonna keep it. You can deal with me just like you deal with Walker. Capische?"

"All right, detective. I wasn't meaning to insult you. I just thought because Ron and I had ..."

"That don't count for nothing, doc. Water under the bridge, as they say. This case is mine, and I'll appreciate your assistance and cooperation. When can you get that list for me? And when can my partner and I come and interview you?"

Tom nodded and took a step backward. "I'll have my assistant pull the list as soon as she arrives this morning. It will be available from my secretary by eight-thirty."

"And the interview?"

Tom thought for a moment. "Anytime after nine. I'll keep the calendar open for you. Here's my card, it's got my number."

"Thanks, doc. See you at nine or so." Rocky turned abruptly and walked away, the conversation over.

CHAPTER 3

Tom returned to his office, tossed his go-bag on a chair and headed into the small toilet area in the corner of his office. He splashed some cold water on his face to complete the routine of starting the day and then examined what he saw in the mirror. Tom saw a face that was affected by more smile lines than worry lines but a face surrounded by his gray hair. Once again, Tom thought he was happy he had not decided to grow a mustache. It, too, would be gray and that would age his face - and him - more than he cared to admit. He turned the water to warm and re-wet his face in preparation for a morning shave. He found a tie in his closet, pulled socks and a clean shirt out of the go-bag and finished dressing for the day. As Tom mechanically and automatically prepared for the workday, his thoughts were all about Alex. Whatever could Alex have done to deserve such a fierce attack? Who could have perpetrated it? For what purpose? What could Tom say trying to explain to the director and others at the morning meeting? Tom also worried about Katherine, Alex's wife. Tom felt acutely the residual of his years of command, remembering the far too often he had to deliver the news of a death of a service member under his command. Those were never comfortable events but Tom firmly believed he should be the one who presented Catherine the news of her husband's death.

He fiddled with some papers on his desk, mostly rearranging them and wishing he could call Ron to get an update. He checked his watch several times, urging the hands to move to six o'clock when

Nick opened the Green Bean kiosk, and he could get his morning coffee. At one point he considered starting a list of people who he thought might have a grudge against Alex. This thought dissipated soon, however, because he couldn't realistically identify a single person. As Tom sat there, desktop awash in the light of the desk lamp and the remainder of the room dark, Tom felt himself relaxing; he realized he would soon be asleep if he didn't change what he was doing. He got up from behind his desk and went to the bound journals in the large bookcase at the end of the room. With minimal searching he found a journal edition discussing various types of skull wounds and deformations resulting from blast injuries. Tom took the volume and sat in the nearby overstuffed chair and began reading. Shortly before six, he became aware that his office was lightening and the building was slowly awakening as early workers arrived. Tom walked out into the lobby to greet some of them and to wave at Nick.

Nick was curious about the early appearance of the chief of staff but he restricted his inquiry to raised eyebrows. Tom responded, "Just the usual, please, Nick." Tom's usual was a 'Red-eye', a cup of strong coffee with an added shot of espresso. The barista turned to his machines and produced the requested drink within a minute. He waved Tom off about paying for it since the cashier was not yet at her station. Tom saluted the young man with his cup and started back to his office.

When his mobile phone rang, Tom was surprised. No one knew he was here at the hospital. The caller identification number listed was unfamiliar and he briefly considered not answering.

"Dr. Bolling." He finally answered, somewhat frostily.

"Yeah, doc, this is Rocky. Are you still around?"

"Yes, I am. Why?"

"Well, I could use a little of that help now. Can you make your way back over here?"

"Yes, of course, I can. I'll be right over." Tom hung up and signaled Nick for another cup of coffee.

Back in the Railway Building a few minutes later, he handed a cup of black coffee to Rocky, who mumbled thanks, said, "Follow me," and escorted Tom to the security closet on the first floor. Hector was standing there, as well. He looked more than a little uncomfortable. Rocky pointed at the screen and asked, "Do you know how this system works, doc?"

Tom nodded, "I understand the basics."

"Well, then, you know that every time a card user opens a door to come in, one of these lights turns on. So, Security can see how many people are in the building."

"Actually, I didn't know that. I know the system tracks who's in and when they leave."

"That's almost right, doc. This system doesn't track specific cards or people, just numbers."

"I see." Tom was puzzled how this information of was assistance.

"But your man Richmond here, did know who was in the building, right, Richmond?"

Hector looked at Tom and sheepishly nodded.

"Who was it, Hector?" Tom asked.

Rocky answered, "Richmond says when he came on at seven last night, there was only one light on. A little after that he saw the dead guy working in his office. Then, just before eight, Richmond says he ran into the guy from the Dialysis place coming in from the stairs wearing a scrub suit and heading to his office. Two lights. Later, only one light and that's the dead guy."

Tom immediately saw where this conversation was going.

"Now wait a minute, if you are suggesting …"

"I ain't suggesting nothing, doc. I'm saying the Dialysis guy was the only other person in this building when the doc up there got killed."

"I think it is highly unlikely …"

"I appreciate the coffee an' all, doc, but I don't want your speculation. I want to know this Dialysis guy's name and where I can find him. That's all."

The hospital director at New City was Sam Mastone. Mastone looked as if he were playing a role in an Italian movie. He was not tall and was built somewhat bulky with dark, slicked-down hair and a complexion of pale olive color. Sam Mastone held a morning meeting to be aware of significant happenings in the past 24 hours in 'his' hospital. Commonly, there were few matters of sufficient significance to spend much time discussing. As a consequence, Sam often tried to lead the conversation toward addressing items that he deemed important. Unfortunately, the key players responsible for those items were not present. Attendees at the Morning Meeting were key executives: Tom and his executive assistant, Beverly Hancock, the chief nurse, Roslyn Burke, and her executive assistant, Alena Preston, RN, Ph.D., and the assistant hospital director, Allen Defarge.

All the players arrived just before 0800. Roslyn arrived proudly carrying her cup emblazoned with the slogan 'World's Best Nurse' and sat across from Tom at the head of the table. Tom, and others who had disagreements with Roslyn, harbored a secret belief that she had bought the cup for herself. Roslyn was in her mid-fifties, five foot ten inches tall, White and well-filled out. She provided a striking comparison to her executive assistant, Alena, gray-haired, Black, and very thin. Both wore nurses' white uniforms with Nursing Association pins on their collars like soldiers' campaign ribbons. Tom had spent much of his first several years battling issues with the nursing executives, winning most but losing some.

The seating arrangement for the morning meeting with Tom and his executive officer on one side and the nursing members on the opposite created a sense of conflict from the beginning. Tom had made some attempts in his early days to allay the feel of divergent goals by changing the seating arrangement. Wherever he sat, however, Roslyn managed to sit facing him and maintaining an image that they were not on the same side. This was a reality Tom did not care for but that he came to believe was a goal of the nursing executives. Sam Mastone entered the conference directly from his office, carrying a coffee cup from the lobby kiosk. He had shed his suit coat for the more relaxed look of office work, but the tightly tied and noosed tie against the bright white of his shirt said anything but 'informal'. As he always did, Sam entered carrying the printout results of the hospital activities for the past twenty-four hours: bed occupancy rates on various services, admissions, and discharges, number of visits to the Emergency Department, and volume of clinic visits in all the specialties. Tom and Roslyn were given the same printouts at 0745 each morning; Tom asked that Beverly review them and warn him if he were going to get static from any side in the morning meeting. This morning she had indicated there were no problems.

Sam dismissively tossed his pile of reports on the table in front of his seat at the head of the long conference table, and said, "Tom, what's going on with the business in the Railway Building?" Tom had spoken with Sam when the director first arrived that morning, and Tom recognized the question was an offer to give everyone in the room an update.

He said, "Well, the short story is that sometime last night Alex Abbate was killed in his office in Railway. Hector found him around midnight and I've been here with the police since then."

"Does that mean your buddy from the Air Force?" asked Sam.

"No, sir. The detective in charge is someone else. Rocky Knudson."

"Does he have a suspect?" asked Roslyn.

"He thinks it may be Jim Donaldson. It seems that Jim was the only other person in the building at the time."

Everyone was quiet for a moment, and then Roslyn said, "You know Dr. Donaldson has been very unsettling in discussions about the staffing of the unit."

Tom said, "No. I don't know anything about that. I do know Jim is a fine man, a very good physician, and I have my doubts about him having done anything like this."

"Well, the police are usually right about these things …," Roslyn left her implication dangling in the air.

"Whatever," Sam jumped in to interrupt any incipient argument, "I want to be kept up to date on all this." He was looking at Tom as he spoke and Tom immediately followed up with, "Certainly, Sam. Probably not as frequently as Ron would have kept us apprised, but I'll certainly stay on top of it."

"And, keep us out of the newspaper, too," Sam commanded.

Tom stared back at the director and said in a flat tone, "I think that train has left the station."

"Well then, keep it muted," Sam said. Then, he turned to the Associate Director, Allen Defarge, and asked, "What's this about the excessive overtime for engineers?"

CHAPTER 4

Rocky and Mac were in Rocky's car. They finished their review of the murder scene at Railway before Rocky asked Tom Bolling to identify the "Dialysis guy". Once they had Donaldson's address, the two detectives went to the parking area and got in Rocky's car.

"Whatcha bet this guy has already split?" Mac asked as they pulled out of the parking area.

"I don't know. Doctors think they're smarter than you an me. He might think nobody knows he was there." Rocky replied after a thought.

"Really?" Mac asked. "You think he doesn't remember he was seen in the building by this Richmond guy?"

"I don't know. I just know doctors think they're so much smarter than the rest of us. But I will bet that he denies it. Never seen one of them crump the first time they get accused."

"We'll see," Mac sat back in the seat and chewed on his toothpick.

They pulled in to the Donaldson's drive a few minutes before seven that Friday morning. The other discussion in the car on the drive from Railway to the Donaldson's focused on the decision whether to question him at the house or to take him to the station. Both detectives believed that questioning a suspect in their home allowed the friendly environment to lower the person's anxiety. On the other hand they agreed that questioning at the station signified deeper concern by the police and heightened defensiveness on the part of the suspect. Mac's argument won the day and they agreed to start the questioning at the suspect's house; Rocky agreed, but said he would be doing so while applying a low bar to the decision when to change the venue.

Jim Donaldson answered the door. He was a good-looking man, 47 years old, clean-shaven, his blond hair showing some gray at the temples. Donaldson was casually dressed in flannel slacks, a white long-sleeved shirt, and loafers without socks.

"Hello," he said to the two men. "Can I help you?"

"Dr. James Donaldson?"

"Yes, that's me."

"My name is Rocky Knudson. I'm a detective with the Cincinnati police. This is my partner, Detective Harry Macnamee." Both men flashed their credentials.

"Okay. How can I help you?" Donaldson seemed puzzled by the presence of two policemen on his porch before breakfast.

"We'd like to ask you a few questions. May we come in?"

"Uh, yes, certainly. We were just starting on breakfast. Would you like a cup of coffee?'

Both men indicated they would not and waited inside the door while Donaldson told his wife he would be 'just a few minutes' and then led them into the living room.

The detectives waited for Donaldson to take a seat and then arranged themselves on either side of him. Rocky started the questioning.

"Were you at the New City Railway Building last evening?" he asked opening his notebook.

"Yes, I was."

"What time were you there?"

"I think I got there a little after six." The detectives looked at each other.

"And what time did you leave?" asked Mac. Donaldson turned to face his questioner.

"About eight-fifteen, I think."

"What were you doing there, sir?" Rocky inquired, causing Donaldson to turn to face him.

"I was checking on the patients in the dialysis unit. What's this all about?"

"Did you see anyone there, sir?" Rocky went on, ignoring Donaldson's question.

"Of course. I saw the seven patients in the unit and all of the nurses there."

"And did you see anyone in the north end of the building?"

"All I did in the north end was change into some scrubs for rounds."

"Did you see anyone there?"

"I don't think … wait, yes, I did. I saw the night watchman, Hector, when I returned from the unit." He raised his eyebrows and looked questioningly at each of the detectives. They did not acknowledge him or his answer.

"What time was that?" Rocky wanted to know.

" I don't know. Just a few minutes before I left, I guess. Why?"

"Did you see anyone else while you were there, sir?"

"I already said I did not. No. Are you going to tell me what this is all about?"

"Did you see Dr. Alexander Abbate while you were in the building?"

"Alex? No. I did not."

"Can you account for your time in the north building, sir?"

"Yes. I'm pretty sure I can. But I'm not going to do so until you tell me what this is all about."

"Sir, are you saying you don't want to cooperate with our investigation?" Rocky asked coldly, closing his notebook with more effort than necessary.

"I'm saying I want to know what your investigation is all about?"

Rocky paused and stared at Donaldson. Mac took a deep breath and said, "Dr. Abbate was killed in the Railway Building last night."

Donaldson responded, "Oh, that's terrible. I didn't know." His voice had become louder than usual just before this exchange and his wife, Winnie had come to the doorway. When she heard of the death of Alex Abbate, she made a noise of sympathy and both detectives turned to her.

"Do you know anything about that, Mrs. Donaldson?" Rocky asked.

"No. No, of course not," she replied entering the room and sitting next to her husband.

"What time did your husband arrive home last night, Mrs. Donaldson?"

"I'm not exactly sure ...," she began before Donaldson interrupted her, saying, "Wait a minute. Are you suspecting me of killing Alex?"

Again, the detectives stopped questioning and stared at him. Then Rocky said, "You were the only other person in the building when he was killed, Dr. Donaldson. And yes, I do suspect you killed him. There really isn't any other option."

The Donaldsons were stunned by this revelation. They instinctively reached out and held hands.

Donaldson spoke without a tremor in his voice, "I did not do any such thing."

"That's right," Winnie said, nodding vigorously.

"Please stand up, sir," Mac said, rising himself and pulling out his handcuffs.

"I did not kill anybody," Donaldson said, slowly standing.

Mac pulled Donaldson's arms behind his back and handcuffed the wrists together.

Rocky said, "Dr. James Donaldson, I am arresting you for the murder of Dr. Alex Abbate. You have the right to remain silent. Anything you say can and will be used against you at trial. You have the right to an attorney. If you cannot afford one, one will be provided to you by the court. Do you understand what I said?"

"I didn't kill anybody. This is ridiculous!" Donaldson said loudly.

"I heard you the first time. Did you hear and understand what I said?"

"Yes. I heard you and I understand it. But this is all wrong."

"Yeah," Mac said as he pushed Donaldson toward the front door. "We've heard that, too. Many, many times."

Donaldson seemed totally at sea with these events. Just before they pushed him down the porch steps toward the car, he turned to Winnie standing in the doorway and said, "Call Tom."

CHAPTER 5

Gwyneth Donaldson did call Tom Bolling. She began dialing the hospital number before the car carrying her husband left the driveway in front of her house. Gwyneth had the physical characteristics common to her Welsh background and breeding. She was almost five foot ten inches and only 125 pounds, but she always appeared larger in person, especially when arguing a point. Her hair was below shoulder length, full and rich, black and framing her face in a way that highlighted her light blue eyes. Her face carried the genetic feature common in the Welsh, being nearly perfectly symmetrical and gave her the look both of an ancient goddess and a current beauty queen. Those who knew her personally, however, said her most striking feature was the fire of competition her forebears carried into battle and that she exhibited in every part of her life. She was a fan of rugby, played table tennis for keeps, and was so feared at the bridge table she could not keep a partner for long.

She identified herself to Mary Brighthouse, Tom Bolling's secretary, and asked to speak with the chief of staff. Winnie intended to conceal her anger until she could speak with Tom about the scene at the Donaldson's. She was not successful in making Mary Brighthouse consider the call of passsing importance.

Mary said, "Yes, Mrs. Donaldson. I think he's in, and I'll get him right away."

Ten seconds later, Tom was on the phone. He opened by saying, "Listen, Winnie, …"

She interrupted, "No, you listen, Tom. They've already been here this morning. Barged right in before breakfast. And they arrested him! Right there in our living room! They said he killed Alex Abbate!"

Tom tried to get into the conversation, "Winnie, listen to me."

"I am listening, Tom. But I don't hear you saying you can get him out of jail. What's going to happen next, eh? And whose silly idea is this that Jimmy would kill someone. Me, I agree it's possible. But not Jimmy. You know that, Tom."

"Winnie, I do know that. And I will do everything I can to stop this charade soon. But you need to slow down and understand some facts."

"Facts? I know facts. I know my husband came home last night and took me out to dinner, and we talked about silly little things. He did not act like a man who had just killed a man. That's a fact, Tom."

"And that's a good one, Winnie. Their entire case happens to be based on opportunity, and I think we can do something about that."

"And are you going to do this 'something' right now or not, Tom?"

"Winnie, this is now a major legal case. I don't know exactly what will be the next step right now, but I'm going to find …"

"I want something done right now! Jimmy should not be in jail. I want him out!"

"Look, stop yelling at me, Winnie. I didn't cause this problem, but I promise I will be doing something about it right now. Do you want me to keep you informed?"

"Of course, I do! What do you think …"

"Then calm down and let us go to work on things. Unless you want to put on your rugby shirt and go down to police headquarters to break Jim out of jail!"

"Oh. Well, right. Okay. No more yelling. Just get him out, Tom."

"I'll be back in touch soon. I've got an idea."

That afternoon, Tom drove downtown to the city jail. He signed in, indicated he wanted to visit a prisoner, and waited for more than a half-hour before he was able to visit Donaldson in his cell. Donaldson was clearly shaken by the events of the morning; he appeared disheveled, worried, and almost furtive. Tom sat beside him on the narrow iron bed and tried to lighten the mood, "That orange jumpsuit is not a good look for you, Jim."

He was somewhat relieved when Donaldson's response was, "Yeah, the guards told me they only have two sizes. Too Big and Way Too Big."

"At least you don't look like you need to lose weight."

"Tom, I'm kinda scared, here. These guys have some kind of case against me, and I didn't do anything."

"Do you have a lawyer?"

"Sorta. Well, not really. Winnie and I have a neighbor who is a lawyer, and he has drawn up our wills and things like that. She called him, and he said he would try to find us a good criminal lawyer, but I haven't seen anyone yet."

"You know enough not to be talking to them without a lawyer, right?"

"Oh, sure. But these guys pointed out they could always talk to me. And they did. This big detective, Rocky something, he told me the whole case against me."

"Really? Did he lay everything out? What do they have?"

"First, he said they have proof that the only people in Railway at the time Alex was killed were me and him."

Tom nodded briefly, "Yeah, Rocky told me that earlier."

"You've met this guy?"

"Yes. I went to Railway when Alex's body was found early this morning and identified him. I talked twice with Mr. Rocky. He acts like he's got his mind made up."

"Absolutely. He said the key card system shows that I was the only guy in the building at the time of death. That can't be true since I didn't do this. I did not kill Alex, Tom. You gotta believe me."

"Listen, Jim, I do believe you. That key system has to be wrong."

"And he thinks he's got a motive."

"Wait, what? Surely not that silly complaint about his mother?"

"Oh, yes it is. Somebody told Rocky about Alex's rant, and the possibility of an ethics charge so all that dirt is gonna get dug up again."

Tom put his hand on Donaldson's shoulder and said, "Look, you and Alex worked that all out in my office. I have a full record of everything. We discussed it completely with the lawyers, and Alex agreed he was emotional. I can't believe the police would consider that a serious motive."

"Well, Rocky is. He said an ethics charge would close down my practice, and he considers that a strong motive for murder."

"Listen, Jim. I'll get the records on our discussion and get the hospital lawyer to come down here. He can argue that 'motive' business away."

"But that's not all, Tom. Rocky said he found Alex's blood on my shoe?'

"On your shoe? They found that at your home? When did they search your house?"

"No, they found it in my office."

"On your shoe?"

"Yes. I always change clothes before going to the Dialysis Unit. Just a habit from the old days, I guess. I slip into scrubs, and I wear some old white bucks."

"I didn't know that."

"Yeah, well, I do. Apparently, Rocky found some of Alex's blood on the shoe I had been wearing."

"What? How'd that happen, Jim?"

"Don't ask me. I have no idea. Wait a minute. Why're you looking at me like that? I told you I didn't do it!"

"Look, Jim, we have to get you some good help."

"I know that, Tom. But, I want you to believe me. I didn't kill Alex Abbate! And I want a lawyer that believes that, too."

"I'm thinking you need something else, including a savvy lawyer. You're telling me that Rocky thinks he's got everything he needs to pin it all on you. He believes the ethics charge is a sufficient motive, and I guess he's convinced that the key card system provides him with an understanding of your opportunity to kill Alex. Last, with this blood on your shoe, he probably thinks he's got the proof of you being there when the deed was done."

"You make it all sound bad, Tom."

"Trust me, Jim. It is all bad, When the cops can pile up the Means, the Motive, and the Opportunity, they think it's light out! So, when This Rocky character has something that puts you in the room as well, then . . .yeah, this is bad. That's why I'm gonna go get you the one thing you need more than anything else."

"A good lawyer?"

"Nope. I'm gonna get you a better detective."

CHAPTER 6

Tom Bolling stood in front of the Lobby Directory in police headquarters looking for Ron Looney's name. He had only visited Ron at Headquarters one time and had an escort at that time. He remembered an elevator ride, a short walk to the office of Ron's boss, Captain Arne Thorason, and being treated to some barely tolerable coffee. He scanned the board twice before realizing only Captains and above were listed by name. He started over, looking for Captain Thorason. He found the listing; Fourth floor, a corner office. Tom started for the elevator but stopped when addressed by a policewoman behind a thick glass window.

"Sir. Excuse me, sir."

Tom turned to the window. "Yes?"

"Where are you going, sir?"

"Uh, fourth floor. To see Detective Looney."

"Is he expecting you, sir?"

After three 'sirs', Tom caught on to the idea that he was in territory requiring accompaniment. He said apologetically, "I'm afraid not. I just happened to be in the area." He held his phone up and went on, "I can call him now if you wish."

"That's all right, sir. I'll make contact." She picked up the phone on the desk in front of her and checked a numerical listing on the wall before dialing. Her communication with someone on the other end was short and muffled through the glass window.

The officer hung up the phone and said, "He'll be right down, sir."

Tom wondered how the administrative people at New City would react if he wanted to install a security check like the one at Cincinnati police headquarters? The thought of their reaction cheered him somewhat until Ron arrived.

"Hey, General. You get lost?" Looney said, stepping off the elevator.

"Nope. I still have my sense of direction. This is where I intended to be."

"Oh-oh. When a General goes on his own mission, somebody is not gonna like it. Glenda, better get SWAT up here pronto!" Looney was smiling at the officer behind the window.

She responded without a smile, "Tasers?"

"Oh yeah, definitely Tasers. This guy is High Brass and Full Metal Jacket." As he said this, Looney stepped to the window and said, "Officer Grayson, let me introduce a very good friend, Dr. Tom Bolling. He is the chief of staff at New City Hospital and a retired Air Force General. And he's also from Arkansas. He's good people."

"Nice to meet you, sir."

"You certainly did a fine job of keeping me in my place, Officer. I'd promote you on the spot if it were up to me."

Ron jumped back into the conversation saying, "Well, our standards are higher than those of the officer corps, General. Officer Grayson has a few more months to go before promotion."

Tom continued to engage Officer Grayson. "You remind me of a sentry in World War II," he said. She cocked her head, interested. Ron said, "Oh, no."

Tom continued, "One night, in Belgium, a General and his driver approached a guard gate and the sentry challenged them for the password of the day. The password changed at sundown, and the general didn't know the new one. He instructed his driver to 'just drive on.' The sentry, a lowly private, then said, "I'm new at this, sir. Who do I shoot, you or the driver?"

Both police officers laughed, and Officer Grayson said, "I'll remember you when you come next time."

Ron escorted Tom to the elevators. Ron had been nearing the end of his successful military career when he and the young Major Bolling met at Sheppard AFB. Ron had enlisted in the Air Force right out of high school, telling everyone, "I'm likely to get sea-sick if I went in the Navy." By that point in his life, Looney had not been out of the county of his hometown in Squashton, Arkansas. After Basic Training, Looney joined the Security Police, Law Enforcement Branch and rose through the ranks. He took a distance-learning course from Arizona State University and went on to get a degree in Criminal Justice. When he retired, Ron Looney moved to his wife's hometown of Cincinnati and joined the police force. On patrol, he preferred walking. He gained the trust of citizens in his area and earned the nickname 'Walker'. After taking some refresher courses, he was recruited into Homicide and had been a happy and successful detective for ten years.

Since Tom's arrival in Cincinnati, the two men had been involved in murder cases at New City, with Ron Looney as the lead detective. Their friendship also included attending each other's holiday parties, Christmas at the Bollings' and Fourth of July at the Looneys'.

On the fourth floor, Ron led the way to his desk and asked, "Do you want a cup of coffee?"

"Unless you have hired a barista since the last time I was here, I'll take a pass," Tom said. He waved at Gene Novalchek who responded, "Doctor." Ron pulled up a spare chair and Tom sat down at Looney's desk.

Gene asked, "Is this a business chat or should I make a coffee run?" Both Tom and Ron nodded to the suggestion about coffee, and Gene grabbed his coat and headed for the back stairs. Ron took his seat in his chair and turned to Tom, "I bet I know why you're here."

"It's about the murder in the Railway building."

"And, lookee there. I would be right. I should be betting the ponies today."

"I don't like the way things are going."

Ron nodded sympathetically. "It just happened last night. And you know that's an ongoing investigation, Tom. Plus, it's not my case. I can't really tell you anything."

"Well, I can tell you some things about the case. And none of them are good. This Rocky fellow is just running roughshod over everyone. He only spoke to me at the scene because he needed to identify the body. He found a couple of strands and arrested the least likely person at New City to murder someone. That's what's going on."

"It's still not my case," Ron said cocking his head and pursing his lips into a crooked smile.

"That's why I'm here," Tom almost shouted. "I would like for you to take over the case."

"Whoa. That's not gonna happen, Tom. You're way out of your lane, there."

"Look, I know the guy that's been arrested. I'm sure he didn't do it. In fact, he possibly is being framed. But this Rocky guy is falling for it."

"Tom, hold on. Let me remind you that you knew some of those other guys that turned out to have killed somebody. You didn't suspect them, either."

"That's not a fair assessment. And this is completely different."

"Well," Ron said, leaning back in his chair, "The big difference I see is that we had to figure out who was doing things in those other cases. This one is not so opaque."

"What do you mean?"

"Tom, I know what Rocky found, and I think he did the right thing. This guy he arrested was the only other guy in the building, right?"

"I'm not so sure."

"Well, Rocky is. He's got the record of the ins and outs and he has an eye witness who saw your guy coming off the staircase, excited and breathless right about the time of the murder."

This information was new to Tom and he stopped talking with his mouth open and stared at Looney.

Ron continued, "And, Rocky says he's got Motive, too. Put that with Means and Opportunity, and he was able to close the case quickly. He did things right, Tom. Everything by the book. He'd be laughed off the floor if he hadn't arrested your guy."

Tom regained his composure and argued, "The man claims he's innocent. Does Rocky know he took his wife out for dinner and small talk right after? That doesn't sound like a killer to me."

"Psychopaths are like that, Tom"

"I've known this guy for years. He is no psychopath. You gotta take over this case. Rocky is missing something."

"Calm down, Tom. I'm not taking over the case. It's Rocky's case. I don't know what you medical guys do about changing horses in midstream but …"

"I've done it several times. Whenever I feel I'm over my head or in too deep I don't hesitate to ask for help."

"I don't think you're listening to me, Tom. Rocky doesn't think he's missing anything. And he doesn't think he needs some help to get the right guy. He believes he has the right guy. He is not asking for help."

"Well, he oughta be." Tom was beginning to sound somewhat deflated.

"But he is not asking for a second opinion. And the captain would never agree to change the lead investigator at this point in one of our cases."

Tom slumped in his chair and sat quietly for several moments. He made little recognition of Gene's presence when he returned with the coffee until Gene put a cup in front of him. Then, Tom sat up and took a long draw on the contents of the cup before saying, "Would you at least promise me that you'll go talk with this man, Donaldson?"

Gene quietly took his seat, his eyes swiveling between the two men on the other side of the desk. He had missed the entire conversation. Nonetheless, he knew this was not the time to interrupt and ask for a recap.

Ron picked up the cup in front of him and took a swallow. He looked at Gene, who shrugged, and then back at Tom. "Okay," he said with a touch of resignation in his voice, "I agree to talk with him. But that is absolutely all."

Tom smiled and stood. He nodded at Gene and said to Ron, "At least the effort won't take you out of your way. The guy is right here in the building, downstairs in a cell."

CHAPTER 7

Ron sat quietly at his desk. He watched Tom walk away, thinking that the General had gotten what he wanted from the conversation. Nonetheless, a promise made being a debt unpaid, Ron decided to honor his promise right away. But first he slowly swung his gaze away from the exit and looked at his partner. Gene sat quietly for a minute or so but finally said, "Tell me you're not thinking about doing this."

"Define 'this'."

"Taking a case away from Rocky."

"Of course not."

This blatant statement was followed by another moment of silence, but with Gene's eyebrows uplifted. Then Gene spoke again, "If not, what is it that you're thinking about doing? I can see those little wheels in your head turning around, you know."

"Got on my transparent skull cap, have I?" Ron said, dodging the question.

Gene nodded, finished his coffee, and threw the cup in the trashcan beside his desk. He stared at Looney and pointedly raised his eyebrows, asking his partner to share his thoughts, one of the many unspoken signals they used to communicate.

Gene Novalchek favored his Nordic mother's side. He was six feet tall and 195 pounds with a boyish face that always seemed to be smiling. His medium-cut blond hair topped a narrow face with a high forehead, prominent eyebrows, short nose, and that ever-smiling mouth. The smile was not out of character for Gene as he acceded the informal title of department optimist. He and Ron had been partners for more than eight years, and Ron knew he had won the lottery for the best partner.

Every detective in the department was competent and good at their job. However, Ron knew he would not have been happy if tied daily to any of the others and their peculiar quirks. The partners, Jim-Bob, spent far too much time talking about extraneous things. Both men were from Alabama, one was named James, and the other was Robert. Few people knew which was which, and both answered to the 'dual' name. There was no one wanting to have half of that for a partner. Then there was Rocky, who was always expecting that the world was going to end without everyone recognizing his accomplishments. Rocky had once wanted to arrest everyone in a bar where a man had died from a blow to the head. According to his partner, Macnamee, Rocky's reasoning was based on a comment by a former NFL All-Star defensive end who said his secret to success was to "grab everybody in the back field and throw them out one at a time 'til I find the one with the ball." Mac was the silent one in the department, largely overshadowed in a group by overshadowed by Rocky's bluster. Individually, however, Ron thought Mac was a smart detective. Then there was Nance who complained about everything. Nance's partner, Allison, was the only woman in the department. Ron thought she was competent but also noted that she was a little prickly and always seemed defensive when asked a question. Ron was convinced he would have fared far less well in Homicide had he been paired with any of the others. He and Gene had a smooth working relationship, mutually responsible and honest.

For all these reasons, Ron believed he owed Gene a full explanation of his thinking, especially when Gene, as he was at that moment, directly asked him about his plans. He nodded at Gene, finished his cup, and said, "I'm thinking I need to honor that promise I made to Tom."

"To talk to the guy Rocky has arrested for murder."

"Right."

"With exactly what intent?"

"Uh huh. How about I save you some time? I can tell you his story."

"C'mon, Gene."

"Seriously, what's he gonna say? 'It wasn't me. I didn't do anything. It was some other dude who did it.' That's it, isn't it? If he had a better story, we would've heard about it by now."

"That's a little simplistic, Gene."

"Is it? He's sitting in a jail cell and charged with murder. He's got two options - confess or deny. We already know he's denying the murder. So, what are his other options - tell who did it or blame it on some other dude. You know that, Walker. I fear you are going to not only waste time but give yourself an incurable headache with your old buddy."

Ron thought again of his partner's strengths at seeing the truth and the lies in a defendant's story from the outset. He also knew that he was planning to do something underhanded by going to talk with Rocky's arrest suspect behind Rocky's back. A thought quickly flicked through his head about how he would feel if one of the other detectives did that with his suspect. But, as he also quickly reminded himself, he had promised Tom Bolling that he would talk to the man. Therefore, he had to talk to the man.

But, even the short discussion with Gene made Looney more uncertain about his decision, and he thought about parsing the situation. He and Gene carried the theoretical questions and answers further. After thinking about possibilities, both detectives agreed with the assessment that they should not request to assume the lead investigation responsibility. The discussion established that such action would be the terminal step of a decision-making process and that they were quite a way away from that point. Before that decision point was reached, Ron Looney would have to possess strong, detailed information suggesting that justice was not being done. It was not sufficient that Tom Bolling felt his man was innocent. It was necessary that he, Ron Looney, could only obtain that kind of information directly from the accused; Rocky's case would not contain that material of he would not have arrived at the conclusion he did. Thinking through the circumstances in this manner, Looney looked at Gene and indicated his readiness to move on, saying, "You don't have to go."

To Gene's credit, he understood the reasoning of his partner and accepted the decision with no further ado. He looked around his desktop and saw no work needing his attention, and noted it was time for him to go home. Ron nodded, but added, "I'm going to go see this Donaldson guy now. Get this over with."

"Right," Gene said, saluting him and heading for the door.

Looney had no trouble getting into the cell area. The guard let him into Donaldson's cell and re-locked the door behind him. The prisoner was sitting on the edge of the bunk and he watched Looney's entrance without speaking. Looney watched the man until the guard was out of hearing before speaking.

"Dr. Donaldson, I'm Detective Ron Looney."

"Are you the better detective that Tom Bolling said he would get for me?"

"Well, sir, Tom did ask me to talk with you but ..."

"Great! I need someone who will actually listen to me to hear my story and believe me."

Ron remained standing with arms crossed. "I'm sure that Detective Knudson has carefully analyzed your story and ..."

"Carefully analyzed? Carefully? Analyzed? He did not."

"I'm not certain I know what you are saying, Doctor."

"For starters, I'm saying Detective Knudson has never asked me to tell my 'story', as you put it. He doesn't know anything about where

I was or at what time I was there because he didn't ask me. He asked me a couple of questions, and when I asked if he was thinking of me as the murderer, he arrested me and said there was no one else there to do it. He didn't listen to me at all. So I say he did not carefully analyze anything! In medicine we would say he approached this case with a strong tendency to early closure."

Looney was impressed with the fervor Dr. Donaldson exhibited; he tried to assess whether he was being played. "Did you kill that other doctor?" Ron asked, closely observing how Donaldson reacted.

"I did not, sir!" was the immediate and forthright answer, delivered with eyes staring directly into Ron's face. At that moment, Ron felt that justice was not rolling down like waters. This realization caused him to blink several times and then take a backward step followed by a deep breath. He looked again at Donaldson, sitting on the edge of his bunk, and took in the whole picture of the man.

The man in front of him appeared to be about five foot ten inches tall and to weigh less than 180 pounds. He wore the orange jumpsuit surprisingly well, despite the garment's inappropriately large size. Donaldson was handsome with an open face, strong chin and pale blue eyes. His generous curly blond hair added to an impression of youth. His posture on the bunk was upright and alert without aggression, and his eyes were clear and carefully watching Looney.

After a moment of assessment, Ron made a decision. "May I sit down?" he asked, indicating the other end of the bunk. Donaldson let out a breath of air and indicated that Ron should sit. Both men took the gesture for what it was: an indication of offering an unbiased ear.

Looney looked at Donaldson and said, "This doesn't mean anything, right now. I'm just doing what Tom Bolling asked me to do; listen to your story. That's all." Looney felt a strong need to not mislead the jailed man.

"Okay. Where should I start?" Donaldson asked, nodding his understanding of the limitations of the encounter.

"As they say in the movies, let's start in the beginning."

"Which is …?"

"Why were you in the Railway building last night? And what you did there."

Donaldson got up from the bed, crossed his arms, and rubbed his upper arms while he paced around the area at the end of the bed. He told the story as he paced, his eyes went from watching his feet to a quick look at Looney or darting to look at the door whenever a sound occurred outside.

"Tom may have told you some of this already. I am the chief of the nephrology service at New City. I have two associates, and the three of us cover consults in the hospital or clinics, the dialysis unit, and the care of our transplant patients." As he mentioned transplant, he noted Looney cocking his head. "Yes, we have transplant patients. We don't do the actual surgery, that's done at the University, but we follow our patients afterward."

"How many?" Ron asked, curious but hesitant to distract from the main story line.

"Only twelve right now. We have had as many as fourteen. One died, and the other is back on dialysis." Ron nodded, and indicated he should go on.

"One of my associates covers the dialysis unit. We have ten chairs for chronic dialysis, and we run two shifts a day, six days a week to care for the current number of 34 patients. My associate sees every patient every dialysis day, so sometimes the other physician and I will cover a weekend for him to have a break. That's what I was doing last night."

"Wait, you were covering for someone else?"

"Yes, is that important?"

"I don't know. Who would have known about the coverage change?"

Donaldson paused and thought before answering. "Well, we made the decision for the cross cover more than a week ago so Pete could make plans. It was really just an agreement between him and me. I mean, we didn't publish a schedule on the main bulletin board."

"Still, were there others who knew about it?"

"Of course, our families for one."

"I mean others in the hospital, people with keycards to the Railway Building."

"Oh, right. Uh, not that I can think of. There was more than a week for someone to say something but I can't recall."

"Okay. Go on." Looney made a mental note to follow up on this possibility if an opportunity came up.

"Okay. When I cover for Pete, I see the first shift of patients in the late morning. Then I come back after finishing things in the hospital and see the second shift close to seven that evening."

"Got it."

"So, I came over a little after six and went to my office …"

"Your office in South Railway?"

"Yes."

"Why? The dialysis unit is in the North End of Railway."

"Oh. I always change into some greens before making rounds."

"Greens?"

"Scrubs."

"And you do that in your office?"

"Yes."

"Why?"

"Uh, habit, I guess. I keep a couple of sets of scrubs in my office."

Ron grinned tightly at Donaldson and said, "Okay. Go on."

"So, I changed into the scrubs and went down the stairs to the Unit."

"Wait. Hold on a second," Ron said, holding up his hand. Where's your office?"

"Fourth floor."

"South Railway?"

"Yes."

"And the Dialysis Unit is where?"

"First floor, North Railway."

"So, you went down the stairs in South Railway and left the controlled area where? On the first floor?"

"Yes, that's right."

"What time was that?" Ron wanted to know.

"I don't know. I was only in my office long enough to change clothes and shoes, so it wasn't long - maybe ten or twelve minutes."

Ron held up his hand. "Wait. Back up, there. Did you change your shoes, too?"

Donaldson stood up and ran his fingers through his hair, and walked a small circle showing a little frustration. He calmed down quickly and said, "Right. You asked me to tell you what I did, and I haven't been completely accurate."

"Okay. I want to know exactly what you did. Just take it slow and be complete this time."

Donaldson took a deep breath and leaned against the wall. "I changed shoes, too. I have an old pair of white bucks that I wear when

I'm in the Unit," he said, and then stopped speaking. Eyes closed, he bowed his head. Thirty seconds later, he straightened up, looked Looney in the eye, and said, "Okay. Then, I left my office and walked to the west staircase, and went down to the first floor where there's an exit from South Railway into the lobby area. I walked across the lobby and entered the door to the Dialysis Unit. I went into the Nurses' Station and said hello to the nurses there and asked about problems. They said there were none, and I then went into the Unit and talked briefly with each patient."

"How many patients were there?"

"Thursday evening we have seven. I spoke to each of them for a few minutes. Do you want their names?"

"Not right now. I can always get them if it's important."

"I don't think I was in the Unit a whole hour. I looked at my watch as I left and thought there was time for me to get Winnie for a late dinner out."

"Wait a minute. Who is Winnie?"

" Gwyneth. My wife. Everybody calls her Winnie."

"I see. Okay, what time was it?"

"About seven-twenty. I know that because I calculated I could get home and make it to the restaurant by eight-thirty."

"Go on."

Donaldson sat down on the bed again, put his hands on his knees, and went on, "I called Winnie and asked her about going out. She was reluctant, and I stopped in the stairwell to talk with her."

"Where?"

"I'm not sure. Around the second floor, I think."

"What did you do?"

"I sat on the stairs and tried to convince her we could make an eight-thirty reservation. She finally agreed and …"

"How long did you talk on the stairs?"

"Oh, uh, I'm not sure. Maybe three minutes." Donaldson appeared ready to chase that rabbit for a distance, so Looney interrupted his thoughts, asking, "And then?"

"I hurried up the stairs, went to my office, and changed clothes …"

"Did you see anyone?"

"What? Oh, yeah, I said hello to Hector, the night watchman. Say, right. He can vouch for me."

"He has." Looney allowed.

"Okay. So, I changed clothes, called the restaurant, and left for home."

"What time?"

"Quarter to eight or so."

"Did you go to the restaurant?"

"Oh yes. We got there at eight-thirty on the nose. Seated right away. I had flounder, and Winnie had veal cutlet. Shared a chocolate pie slice for dessert. Left about ten after ten. Then home and to bed."

"Anything else?"

"No. Got up this morning and had breakfast interrupted by Detective Knudson."

Looney waited for a minute, but Donaldson made no other offer of explanation. Looney stood and walked to the cell door. He indicated to the guard that he had finished his visit. "Anything else?" he asked Donaldson.

Donaldson shook his head as he met Ron's eyes. As Ron left the cell, Donaldson said quietly, "Thanks for listening."

Ron left the cell area and took the stairs up to the fourth floor where the Dick Pen was, He used that exercise to measure the time it took, checking on Donaldson's story, and to reflect on what he had heard. Minutes later, sitting at his desk and making a few notes on his conversation, Ron realized he believed the man's story. And he knew that Rocky did not know this story. And he realized he was starting to have a slight headache, one that threatened to become much larger. He considered the possibilities concerning Donaldson and his story of innocence.

The first possibility, and one that Rocky would no doubt endorse, would be that

Donaldson did kill Abbate and was an exceptionally good liar. Looney thought about this possibility for a few minutes and decided he had never encountered a good enough liar to make him believe his story like Donaldson. But Looney's main reason for thinking Donaldson was innocent was the history Looney shared with other suspects who were good liars. Every one of those individuals had also carefully planned their crimes and carried them out in a manner that pointed the finger at various other people. Even the best liars would not have committed murder with a keycard system showing them as the only possible suspect.

That decision moved Looney's thoughts to the two possibilities if Donaldson was innocent. Either he was a victim of cruel circumstances or he was actively being framed.

Those possibilities, by nature, imposed very different requirements on an investigation team. Clearing the name of the victim of circumstances would require finding sustainable proof of Donaldson's innocence; not the easiest issue to address in a justice system that purportedly treats a suspect as innocent until proved guilty. Nonetheless, with good alibis that clearance can be obtained.

On the other hand, if Donaldson was being framed for the murder, his clearance might depend entirely upon finding the actual murderer, perhaps even getting a confession. Looney realized that a Perry Mason lawyer might be able to prove Donaldson's innocence directly or use the Some Other Dude Did It defense but he was stuck in the mental maze of how to start an investigation with no suspects. Looney didn't favor either of the two possibilities involving Donaldson's innocence. Either one meant tedious work to provide an ironclad alibi for the time of the murder or digging into a very complicated medical research issue and interviewing medical personnel about their work and whereabouts. To make that commitment he needed to know his partner had his back. That meant he would have to spend some time talking to Gene about the case, and then he'd have to go to the Captain. And he knew he couldn't go there without first sitting down with Rocky. And that insight made his headache even worse.

CHAPTER 8

Ron pushed his desert plate toward the center of the table but did not attempt to stand. Meg looked at him steadily over the rim of her coffee cup.

"Want to talk about it?" she asked quietly.

"Not really. Well, yes. But only a little."

"Can you do that?"

"What?"

"Talk about it only a little? You've been brooding about it all evening. My memory is that something like that takes a lot of talking, not just a little."

"I don't know. It's really just a little thing, but it's so big it's given me a headache."

"And that also makes all the sense in the world. You make this sound like a country and western song title."

Ron cocked his head and frowned at his wife. "What in the devil are you talking about?"

"It's so little, and it's so big."

"Oh. Yeah. Well, it is."

"Now my curiosity won't allow me to sleep until I get the whole story. C'mon, cowboy. Tell the girl what's eating at you."

Ron grinned at her and said, "All right. But it's gonna take more coffee."

A half-hour later, they sat on the living room sofa, both pondering the story. Ron sat at one end, facing straight ahead; he had tried to express the facts in an unemotional voice, but he knew he had wavered. One of the attributes he loved about Meg was her ability to listen to his accounts of murder and mutilation without aversion and then ask the most insightful questions.

Meg, already dressed for bed, sat cross-legged at the other end of the sofa with her head in her hands, looking at Ron and catching every word and nuance of his presentation. When he stopped talking, she said, "You believe him, don't you?"

"I suppose so."

"No supposing there, I can hear it in your voice. You think somebody's done him wrong."

He grinned at her and said, "Talk about a country song title."

"Well, you do, don't you?"

"Yeah, I do. I watched Donaldson tell his story, and I believe him. So, one way or another, by accident or on purpose, he's being accused wrongly."

"But that's not what's bothering you, is it?"

"How do you know so much about me?"

"Just been paying attention for all these years. It's Rocky, isn't it?"

"Yeah. Well, Rocky and Thor. And maybe even Gene."

"You know that Gene will support you."

"I know I'd really like that, but I do not think I can count on it in this instance." As he said this, Looney sat upright, arched his back, and then rubbed his face with both hands.

Meg swung her feet to the floor, stood, and extended a hand. "Come on," she said, "you need a good back rub and a good night's sleep. Then you'll go in tomorrow and do the right thing."

"I wish it were that simple," he said, taking her hand.

The next morning, Gene arrived at his desk to find a fresh cup of coffee from the small shop down the block sitting on his desk. He noted that Ron held a similar cup, and as he hung his jacket on a hanger by his desk, he asked, "Long night?"

Ron indicated that Gene should pay attention to his cup and said, "Not long, but hard."

Gene sat and sipped at this cup. "And I'm guessing this is because you found something in the doctor's story that bothers you, right?"

Looney looked steadily at his partner and slowly nodded, "Yep, something alright."

"Big something or little something?"

"Depends."

"Oh, wait a minute. You let this guy convince you he didn't do it! He's got you chasing the Some Other Dude, right?"

"Keep your voice down. Yes, I came away convinced he was set up."

"By who? And why?"

"Well, those are the right questions, aren't they?"

"Aw, come on. Tell me what you think you heard. No, on second thought, don't tell me what you think you heard. Tell me you're not going to stick your nose - our noses - into this, are you?"

"Can we at least talk about it, Gene?"

"I know we have all but wrapped up these two cases here and don't have anything sitting on our desks right now, but ..."

"Our caseload doesn't have anything to do with this, Gene. I think this guy is getting set up."

"Why do you think that? And, by the by, thanks for the coffee."

"Sure and you're welcome. Let me tell you what I heard. It was not just one thing. I mean, Donaldson tells a very provable story. Lots of chances for corroboration. And he says that Rocky hasn't tried to hear his story. Rocky jumped on the business about the keycard system indicating the doctor was the only other guy in the building."

"And you believed him. The doctor, I mean. And on that one point."

"I did, and I do. But that doesn't mean I know what to do about it."

Gene sat his cup down and stared at Looney. "Oh, so now I'm being called in for a consultation? Okay, here's my recommendation and final answer: I say you should share your concern with Rocky and call it quits."

"Really? You think he's going to like that?"

"Who said anything about liking it? He's not gonna like anything about you having stuck your nose in his case. But that's the cheapest way to get this off your chest and avoid a Rocky-Top blowout."

"I thought about that, Gene. What if Rocky ignores what I tell him?"

"I don't know. Maybe you could provide your thoughts to the defense counsel."

"Even if I did do something like that, my suspicions are only about the fact that Donaldson may have an alibi - and it's right under Rocky's nose. If we wait until counsel can get the DA to listen to Donaldson's story, he may be in jail for months. And, that won't get anybody looking for the real murderer."

"Oh, now it's more than 'we gotta show that this guy didn't do it'. You are fixing to go whole hog on this aren't you?"

"That's what Razorbacks do," Looney said trying to introduce some levity into the conversation.

"And underneath it all you are preparing to get us mired in to a case of 'we gotta find the Other Dude', isn't that it?"

"Well, Gene, look at it this way: the only evidence that exists right now says this doctor Donaldson was the only person in the building who could have killed the man. And right there on the face of it, that's wrong."

"Wait, wait, wait. I don't know much about this case but that one point has been made by everyone. There's some kind of electronic tracking system and even an eye witness that proves this Donaldson guy was the only other person in the building. What do you mean, that's wrong?"

"Think about it, Gene. The night watchman, the important eye witness, was in there, too, wasn't he?"

"Well, yeah, but …"

"Yeah. But, what? Then Donaldson was not the only other one in the building. That's a false fact being circulated."

Gene was silent for a moment and then said, "Look, partner, you know I trust your instincts. But I don't want to be poking Rocky even with a long stick."

"I understand. But if I'm going to go talk to Rocky about my concerns, I got to know you are behind me."

After a pause, Gene looked at Ron and said, "Okay. I'm behind you. Just let me be way behind, like perhaps out of town, you when you talk to Rocky."

"That's a deal, partner. I won't expect you to go talk to Rocky with me. But you have to stay in town to help me with the investigation. Why don't you sit here at your desk and do some research about keycard systems and how to trick them."

CHAPTER 9

Rocky looked at Ron suspiciously, turned halfway in his chair to face him, and asked, "What for?"

"I just want to talk with you, and I thought a cup of coffee would be a good way to do it."

"What do you want, Walker?" Rocky crossed his arms and remained seated, not indicating any interest in Looney's suggestion.

"Coffee?" Ron asked, motioning with his head toward the doorway.

"We can do it right here," Rocky reached to the side of his desk and shoved a chair in Looney's direction as he said this. Ron looked at it and considered accepting. He wanted to meet with Rocky outside of the office environment. Rocky was more likely to 'play to the audience' in headquarters and Ron wanted a more serious discussion. He tried one more time. "When's the last time I offered to buy you a drink?"

Rocky paused to think about that and Ron pressed his advantage. "Do you want this to be the last time? And you turned it down?"

"I know you want something, Walker."

"I don't deny that. But I also want to buy you some coffee."

"I think I'll have a pastry, too."

"Good idea," Ron said as he turned and moved toward the stairwell. Rocky made a big show of straightening the papers on his desk and breathing a loud sigh before following. Rocky continued to complain about the interruption to his day as the two men made their way down the stairs and then down the block to the small coffee shop frequented by the officers in headquarters.

Since it was barely mid-morning when they arrived at the nearby coffee shop, the line was short and moving rather quickly. Rocky ordered a fancy drink with four or five words in its name to go along with a sticky bun. Ron asked for his usual mid-sized Red Eye, and they found a table near the door. Rocky grinned at Looney as he unwrapped his bun and began to smear it with butter. "Okay," he said having his fancy drink and well-festooned bun ready to eat. But, before taking the first bite, He harshly asked, "Out with it. What do you want?"

"It's pretty simple, actually," Looney said, sipping his coffee. "I just want to talk to you about the Railway murder."

Immediately suspicious, Rocky stopped before taking a bite of the bun. His chin dropped, and he stared at Ron for a long time before asking, "That chief doctor at the hospital put you up to this?"

"What? Oh, you mean Tom Bolling."

"Yeah. You know Bolling showed up at the building that morning and asked for you."

"Yes, I know. And yes, Tom and I have talked about this." Ron's reply was flat and unemotional, hoping he could elicit a similar response from Rocky.

"And I suppose you want to know all the ins and outs of the case so you can report to him about it." Rocky's response was, on the other hand, snarky.

"C'mon, Rocky. You know we don't talk to civilians about ongoing cases."

Rocky took a big bite of the bun and mumbled around it, "So, if you aren't looking for the gossip, what are you interested in?" Rocky had been certain that Looney's interest was entirely driven by curiosity and a desire to pass interesting tidbits on to that 'chief doctor'.

"I need to tell you something." Looney said, taking a swallow of coffee and setting the cup down on the table.

"What?" Rocky's tone became frosty and his eyebrows threatened to become intertwined.

"I went down in the keep yesterday and talked to your suspect. Donaldson." Again, Looney tried to keep his voice flat, unemotional and even.

Rocky's head moved closer to Ron's, his eyes narrowed, and he spoke menacingly, "What for?"

"I wanted to hear his story."

"Why?" Rocky was starting to talk through clenched teeth.

"Why not, Rocky?"

Taken aback by Looney's question, Rocky took a deep draw on his coffee and then said, "You could just read the folder. All that's in there. No reason to tamper with my suspect."

"C'mon, Rocky. I did no tampering. But what I did find out is that you arrested Donaldson without hearing his story. I might have learned that from your Murder Book but maybe only if you made a written statement that you didn't get his story about how he spent his time in the building."

"What are you talking about? I got his story. He says he didn't do nothing! Just went to that Dialysis Unit, came back and changed clothes, and went home. That's it."

"Really? He told me about his movements with much greater detail than that. The story I got was he spent some time in the stairwell talking to his wife. He gave me a story that has all kinds of time checks in it."

"Yeah? So what?" Rocky posited, shrugging off any idea he had been less than thorough. He put a large bite of bun in his mouth, looked at Looney, and raised his eyebrows.

"So, this story of his can be checked. Extensively." Looney made this last point with some emphasis.

"Yeah? So what? And what do you mean 'extensively'?"

"I mean it is possible to time when he left the Unit by an entry in the electronic medical record, when he called his wife and how long they talked by checking with the phone company, what time he opened the keycard door to go change clothes and what time he left the building for good. Those are all hard data points, Rocky. And I think they will show that he could not have had the time to kill that other guy."

Suddenly Rocky understood. "What're you saying, Walker? Do you believe this Donaldson is innocent? You're way off base here, my friend. He was the only other person in the building when that guy was killed!" Rocky's voice was starting to get loud enough to attract attention. Both men realized it, and they turned their undivided attention to their cups for the net minute. Then, Ron said in a muted voice, "You're wrong about that, Rocky, and I can prove that to you without getting up from the table."

"Listen, Walker, I don't want some theory about fake keycards or …"

"No theory, Rocky. Hard fact. There was somebody else in that building."

"How do you know?"

"You wrote it in your report."

"The hell I did. Gimme a break, Walker. I would have remembered something like that."

"Right. I'm sure you do remember. You interviewed this person, in fact. It's the night watchman, Rocky. He was there, in the building, all night long."

Rocky almost choked on the last bite of the bun. "What are you saying? You think the night watchman killed that doctor?"

"No. I'm only saying that your statement about Donaldson being the only other person in the building is wrong." He paused and then went on, "And that we need to have a broader look for suspects."

"We? Wait a minute, here buddy. Who is 'We', Walker?"

"That's the other thing I wanted to talk to you about. I'd like your permission to pursue the case."

"What? Pursue the case? My case? You want me to rent a billboard to announce that I don't know what I'm doing and I need your help on my case?" His voice again became steadily louder during this tirade.

Looney held up a hand to indicate they should lower their voices again. Rocky said, "Don't shush me. You're the one that should shut up!"

Looney leaned back and made no response. He stared at Rocky until the other man calmed somewhat. But, when Rocky did not lean back in his chair, Looney worried tha he was about to stand and walk away. Looney said, "Look, I'm speaking to a brother officer, here. All I'm saying is, I have a gut feeling that you have charged the wrong man. I'm giving you the benefit of the doubt. But there's still that gut feeling."

"I know about your gut feelings," Rocky said, in an oddly quiet voice.

"So, all I'm saying is, if my gut is right, then it's likely that somebody, somewhere, is going to raise those same doubts. Maybe Donaldson gets a smart defense attorney and hires a good private detective. Somebody will look into the whole, 'no one else in the building' theory and blow it up. Then where will Rocky Knudson be?"

Rocky stared at Looney and took a deep breath, "But I could still be right, couldn't I?"

Ron nodded as he answered, "Surely that's possible, Rocky. Here's the way I spread the odds. I think there are three possibilities. One is he did it. Two is he didn't and was accidentally there at the time. And the third is, he didn't do it but looks really guilty because someone set him up for it. That's a 33% chance that you're right. Want to ride that bet very far, Rocky?"

Rocky sat quietly for several moments, staring past Looney. Ron allowed him his thoughts and also sat quietly, finishing his coffee. When Rocky started shifting his weight in his chair, Ron asked, "Thought about it long enough, Rocky? Ready to take my offer?"

"What offer? I haven't heard any offer. Just you, yammering about how I screwed up."

Looney sat up straight and leaned across the table, "Here's my offer, then. You remain the face of the case, and Donaldson remains in jail, fully charged. That's to cover the one in three chance that you are right. But, at the same time, Gene and I will look around Railway and get into the lives of Donaldson and the dead guy, what's his name?"

"Abbate."

"Right. Abbate. We will see if there's a plausible Other Dude, and we will try to discover how this Other Dude could do it without a trace."

"And then you talk to the newspaper, and I end up with egg all over my face," Rocky was stirring up his anger again. Ron quickly intervened, saying, "No. I've got a stipulation about that."

CHAPTER 10

Captain Arne Thorason was in his office when Ron knocked on the door. The Captain, often referred to as 'Thor' but only when he was out of hearing range, was a 23-year veteran of the Cincinnati police department, and predominantly known for running a tight and effective department. Since Thorason had become chief, the Homicide Division consistently closed 60% or more of their cases with an arrest, and the bulk of those ended in conviction. The Captain had a couple of quirks in his behavior, at least one of which likely was generated by his college experience as middle linebacker on the football team. Thor still carried his height and heft like he could plug holes in a defensive line. He stood five foot eleven and a half inches and his 265 pounds was distributed more in his shoulders and thighs than the waistline. A squarish head topped Thor's bulk, balding in the front but carrying bushy eyebrows over intensely dark eyes separated by a crooked nose. The eyes were the most significant feature. If someone failed to meet the departmental standard - meaning Thor's standard - that individual was likely to be confronted with 'The Look'. Known, and feared, throughout the department, The Look was a steady stare of assessment from those intense eyes coupled with squared shoulders and a tucked chin. The package was sufficient to make anyone feel like a freshman running back about to hit the ground hard.

The Look accounted for no small part of the success and work ethic in the homicide division. None of the detectives wanted to fail to meet

Thor's standard, which was plainly and simply comprised of 'Don't ask me how to do your job', 'Do your job quickly and right', and 'Stay in your lane'. Curiously, in spite of a standard that seemed standoffish, the Captain was always available for a consultation and often showed up beside a detective's desk to get a brief update on a case.

A second notable peculiarity of Thor's was his tendency to minimal involvement on his part of a conversation highlighted by repeated use of one word in response to almost everything. That word was 'huh', delivered in what casual observers deemed a neutral and unchanging voice, and usually without inflection. Detectives in the division, however, held differing opinions about what inflection they heard. Various camps believed Thor's 'huh' expressed dismissal, others were certain it meant surprise. The largest segment of the force believed Thor simply signaled, "I'm listening".

Ron Looney had found that his own style of working meshed very well with Thor's leadership style. Over the years Ron had few instances where he had been the recipient of the 'The Look' from Thor. Ron rather enjoyed working for Thor. He remembered when he had been offered a leadership role in the Air Force and found that he was most uncomfortable telling others how to do their job. Or, as it sometimes was, just to do their job. Thor's methods of leadership involved a good deal of personal respect for the detectives even when they exhibited highly variable work habits and approaches. As long as the necessary boxes were checked, and offenders were apprehended, Thor was not interested in how that came about. Ron Looney could not have designed a better place in which to work.

The Captain looked up at Looney's knock. "Huh," he said.

Ron stepped into the office and answered, "Just a quick consultation. I want to get your thoughts on a proposal."

When Thor did not respond, Ron continued, "As you know, Rocky picked up that case up at New City the other day." He noted the quick nod of Thor's head. "He's already arrested someone and gotten them charged."

Another nod.

"And, I know you are aware of the connection between Tom Bolling at New City and me, right?"

Slow nod.

"So, I had a little chat with this guy that Rocky arrested, and Captain, I have to say, I think the guy is innocent."

"Huh." This was accompanied by a slight narrowing of the space between the bushy eyebrows.

"So, just being sure that we are all working on the same page, I had a coffee with Rocky this morning and told him about my suspicions. You know, sharing thoughts and like that."

"Huh." This time the eyebrows separated.

"Well, Rocky was surprised and all that but he listened to me and after all was said and done, he and I thought maybe it would be best if I took over the case and ..."

"No." Chief Thorason accompanied this explanation with a brief nod before returning his gaze to the paperwork in front of him.

"Sir, if you would just let me explain." Looney inched closer to the front of Thor's desk.

"You strong armed him into agreeing, didn't you?" The Captain's head did not move and his eyes remained on his paperwork.

Looney took a partial step backward and said, "That's a rather negative way to frame our discussion."

"It's his case. He thinks he's got a slam dunk." Thor continued to face the top of his desk.

"Not any longer."

"Huh." The Captain's head came up and his eyes met Looney's. The eyebrows were definitely closer together.

"Yes, sir. The entire case seems built around the circumstance that the man he arrested and the man who was killed were the only people in the building at the time."

"Huh." This was accompanied by an emphatic, but short, nod.

"Well, right. I pointed out to him that the night watchman was also in the building."

"Huh." The Captain, struck by this obvious point, leaned back in his chair.

"Then, the more we talked, the more he thought it best if I were to take over the case and …"

"No." The Captain's intent was clear but the forcefulness of his rejection suggested he was less opposed than before.

"Sir, you seem to be disinterested in our reasoning."

"Huh."

"Rocky and I have come to an agreement." Looney was aware that Thor was about to give another negative answer and he hurried on with an explanation, saying, "We agreed to leave the man he arrested in jail and not announce anything about a change in lead for the investigation."

"Huh."

"That's right. No one outside the department will be aware and Gene and I will keep things on the down low."

"Walker, if I have to give you an answer again, 'no' will have two words."

"Sir, Rocky thinks this is a good idea."

"What?" The Captain's eyes widened in disbelief. Ron was slightly taken aback as well, by Thor's use of a different word.

"Yes, sir. Perhaps if I told you that Rocky agreed with a stipulation that I think is perfect for such a situation, would you reconsider?"

There was a brief pause on the Captain's part. Then he asked "What kind of a stipulation?"

Looney took the opportunity to sit in one of the chairs in front of Thor's desk to explain what he and Rocky had agreed. Five minutes later, the Captain made a small nod to Looney, who promptly stood up.

"You'll need division resources, right?" The Captain asked.

"Some. A little, maybe."

"Huh."

When Looney left Thor's office, he beamed at Gene across the Dick Pen, and made a 'thumbs up' sign. Gene grinned wryly at his partner's audacity and success. Then he turned back to his computer search and began to prepare his mind for the next stage: solving the 'locked building' murder.

CHAPTER 11

Rocky agreed to brief Ron and Gene on his paperwork and the information he had that led to his arrest of Dr. Donaldson. Initially , he told Ron that everything was in the evidence box but Ron convinced him that hearing about the evidence and information from the collector would be invaluable. Everything should be included in the Murder Book, a notebook containing the detective's findings at the scene with photographs of key areas, typed transcripts of their formal interviews, and descriptions of particular aspects of the crime. Ron persuaded Rocky to brief he and Gene to provide them a more 'personal' insight. Rocky said he preferred to do the brief at Ron's desk rather than using his own; his partner was not pleased with the deal Rocky had struck with Ron. When Rocky arrived he was carrying the cardboard box containing all the relevant items, evidence, and transcripts collected at the scene or later. The key item, of course, was the Murder Book.

Rocky sat the cardboard box down on Ron's desk a little more emphatically than necessary and said, looking down somewhat wistfully into the box and not looking directly at either Ron or Gene, "This is the lot, then."

"Take a chair," Ron said pleasantly, sitting down. "You can begin wherever you like."

"I'd mostly like to take my box and go back to my own desk, thank you very much."

"C'mon, Rocky. We have a deal," Ron said, trying to be accommodating.

"Yeah, yeah. And a stipulation, right?"

"Right," Ron said and then quickly went on, "Why don't we try something unusual and start from the beginning."

Rocky sat down in the provided chair, glanced at Gene, and took the lid off the box. "It started with us getting the call that Friday morning about one in the A.M."

Rocky told how he and his partner, Harry Macnamee had met at the station and taken Rocky's car to the scene. He said they arrived at the scene in the Railway Building shortly before two o'clock that morning and found the victim, Dr. Alex Abbate, lying on the floor of his office behind his desk bludgeoned to death. Also present at that time were three security officers from the hospital, one of whom was the Railway building guard and the man who had discovered the body. Rocky briefly read from his notes about the setting and the findings he and his partner had found and their initial actions, including notifying the Medical Examiner, Dr. Darringer. Mac had interviewed the security guard, and Rocky shared his notes. He handed Ron the ME's report, commenting, "There's a lot of big words in there." Then, Rocky seemed to have a secret laugh when he mentioned that Tom Bolling had shown up at the scene and had asked for Ron.

Ron showed no emotion when Rocky went into detail about how he explained to the chief of staff that he, Rocky Knudson, had everything under control. When Rocky finished his brief recitation, he brushed his hands and sat back in the chair.

"You got pictures?" Gene asked.

"Yeah. Of course. Help yourself." Rocky reached into the box and retrieved a manila envelope that he shoved across the desktop at

Gene, who politely replied, "Thank you." Gene hefted the envelope momentarily, then pulled the glossy photographs from the envelope and handed half to Ron.

The two of them looked briefly at the pictures of the body, and the room, and the desk. Rocky fidgeted, no longer the center of attention before Ron asked, "Weapon?"

Rocky nodded, "Pretty obvious. This little statue thing." He initially pointed to an object in one of the pictures and then reached into the box and extracted a plastic bag containing a 10-inch high metal figure of an abstract fist and forearm. The lower portion was enlarged and flattened to provide a standing surface and this area was heavily coated with dried blood and other material, including a few hairs.

Ron took the offered instrument and raised it above his head, assessing its value as a murder weapon. " How much does this thing weigh?"

"Right at four and a half pounds. Big enough and heavy enough to do the job."

"Was this his?" Gene asked, meaning the dead man.

"Yep," Rocky nodded. "Some kind of award he got a couple of years back. Kept it right there on his desk, everybody says."

"How did you and Mac picture the murder happening?" Ron asked and sat back to sip his coffee and get a mental picture of the scene.

Rocky became a little more energized about his presentation with this question. "We think this guy, Donaldson, walked in while the good doctor was working at his computer. Since they knew each other, the doctor probably didn't think anything about it. Donaldson then grabbed this statue thing and bashed him on the head."

"How many times?"

"What?"

"How many times was he hit?"

"Uh, twice, why?"

"I think, even with that heavy statue thing, it would take a strong blow to crush the skull, like in that picture. I thought it might be three or four hits, that's all."

"Nope. M.E. said two. But the skull was crushed. She also said the first blow probably incapacitated the doctor and the second knocked him out of the chair."

"Huh."

"Now you're sounding like Thor. What's that mean, anyway?"

"Just a little surprised, that's all. So, there were no defensive wounds, then?" Ron asked.

Rocky stared at Ron for a second before answering. "No. None. Darringer thinks he was out with the first blow and maybe didn't see it coming."

"Two blows and the skull is crumpled. Sounds like a lot of anger."

Gene nodded his agreement. Ron went on, "Did you identify the motive?"

Rocky braced his shoulders and said proudly, "Oh yes. Got that early on. Seems Donaldson was treating the dead guy's mother on dialysis and she died. Abbate said it was unethical treatment and was going to bring Donaldson up on charges."

"Really? That would certainly make a fella mad. Did Donaldson seem like an angry man when you questioned him?"

"Well, he got upset when we arrested him." Rocky grinned at the memory.

"I mean before that. Did he look and act like a guy with suppressed rage?"

"I don't know, Walker. I'm no psychologist."

"Alright, Rocky, I just wondered. Can we talk some more about the actual murder?"

"Yeah, sure. What do you want to know?"

"The killer would have been standing on the right side of the victim?"

"Yeah."

"And Darringer thinks the second blow knocked him backward and onto the floor?"

"That's right." Rocky was on firmer ground and he crossed his arms.

"Gene, let me see that picture of the desk."

Gene handed the packet of pictures to his partner. Ron opened the packet, and took out the pictures. He laid them on the desk in front of him and began shuffling through them. Several minutes passed quietly as he arranged the pictures.

Rocky huffed, "You want me to come back when you're ready to talk?"

Ron didn't look up when he said, "No, Rocky. Please wait right here."

Rocky looked surprised at the pleading request but sat back in his chair and waited. Gene watched his partner scan through the pictures quickly before he handed them back and turned to Rocky.

Appropriating some objects on his desk, Ron asked Rocky, "So, if I'm seeing those pictures correctly, the door to this guy's office was here," he put a stubby pencil in place, "and the desk was here," indicated by the stapler placed parallel to the pencil and about four inches away.

Rocky nodded, "Yeah, that's about right."

"And the dead guy was sitting here," a small bottle of White Out was placed near the center of the stapler, "facing this way, right?"

"Yeah, yeah, yeah. The desk was facing the wall where the door was. What're you trying to prove, Walker?"

"Not proving anything. Yet. Just trying to get the lay of the land. So, that means the killer would have approached him on his right side. I'm just a little surprised that he didn't see the blow coming."

"Well, he didn't. At least, according to Darringer." Rocky was, in spite of himself, a little curious about Looney's thinking.

Ron nodded sagely before saying, "And that's why no defensive wounds, right?"

"Yeah, right." Rocky agreed and felt better.

Ron leaned back and asked, "Did I understand that the murder weapon was sitting right there? On his desk?"

"It was really on that low piece of furniture at the side of the desk."

"The credenza?"

"Whatever. It was on the floor when we found it but everybody said the victim kept it on that denza-thing."

All three men were quiet for a moment, and then Gene asked, "Tell me again why you settled so quickly on this other doctor, Donaldson?"

"He was the only other person in the building at that time. Pretty straightforward. Even for a pair of dunces like Mac and me." This last sentence was aimed at Ron, who simply raised his eyebrows at Rocky.

Gene went on, "How did you know that? I mean, who was taking attendance?"

"Well see, they got this fancy electronic system with keycards. Everybody has to use a card to get in and to get out. The system tracks how many people are in at any particular time. The security guard knew there were only two people in the building a the time of the murder - and the other one was Donaldson."

"That does sound pretty air-tight," Gene agreed and leaned back in his chair, and looked at Ron.

Rom made a slight grimace and shrugged his shoulders. "Remind me how you knew the time of death?" he asked Rocky.

"Again, simple and straightforward so even the dunces could figger it out. The guy's watch was smashed in the attack and stopped at 7:34. Both the guard and the electronic system show only the dead guy and this Donaldson were in the building between seven and quarter to eight PM; Donaldson clocked out just before eight."

Ron leaned back and said, "Huh."

"There you go again, sounding just like Thor. What's bugging you about what I said?" Rocky asked, sounding a little on edge.

"It's just some funny little things, that's all Rocky. I'm sure there's an explanation."

"For what, Walker?"

"Well, for why the watch was smashed, for one. According to the report, he was right-handed …"

"What's that got to do with anything?" Rocky blurted. Gene sat forward in his chair to more closely watch the interplay as he had an inkling of what his partner was asking.

"Well, let's think about it, Rocky. Look, if you were over here," Ron turned so that Rocky was on his right, "and you raised your hand to strike me," and he indicated that Rocky should do so, "then my natural response would be to raise my right arm to block you. Like this." Ron raised his arm and countered the possible blow from Rocky.

"Yeah, so?"

Gene filled in the blank quickly at that point. "So how did the watch on the left wrist, which is where right-handed people wear their watch, get busted? Especially if there were only two blows and they went to the head."

Ron nodded and winked at his partner.

Rocky stopped and put his hands on his hips. "I don't know. Probably when he hit the floor."

"I don't think so, Rocky," Ron said. "That's an expensive watch, and the office is carpeted. Not likely."

Rocky shrugged and said, "Okay, and so what?"

"So," came Ron's clear answer, "I think the watch was purposefully smashed. It was not broken accidentally."

This idea was completely new to Rocky and it gave him pause. But after a few seconds of consideration he went on, "Okay, maybe that's true, but I still wanna know, so what?"

"Because somebody wanted to fix the time of the murder at a time when there was only one other person in the building."

"Wait a minute. Are you saying the murder happened at some other time?"

"I'm saying I sincerely doubt that 7:34 PM that evening was the actual time of the murder, and that makes me very suspicious that Donaldson is being set up."

Rocky stared at Ron and said, "Huh."

Chapter 12

The café was not crowded, but Ron and Gene waited until their favorite booth became available. They had come to this café daily at lunch for years, only partly because of the good American food selection. Mostly they kept returning so Gene could continue his mid-day contact with Sandy, the shapely, red-haired waitress. Their early visits to the café occasioned Sandy referring to Gene as 'honey', and Ron made a running set of comments about that until Gene finally asked Sandy on a date. Now, years later, the two were a couple and had recently vacationed together in Kauai. Sandy winked at them in the waiting line and promptly seated them when their booth emptied.

They had made this booth their favorite from their first visit to the café. The seating allowed one of them to sit facing the entrance with capability to see whoever came in. Important as that was, the main reason they favored this particular booth was because it allowed both of them the vista of watching Sandy walk from their table all the way to the back of the café. Ron had given Gene a hard time about his intensity of 'watching', but he was just as involved. It was, after all, satisfying to watch. Sandy seemed aware of this practice and seemed to move more slowly and deliberately away from their table.

"The usual, guys?" She asked as they slid into their seats.

"Sure thing."

"Right."

"Back in a jiff, then," she said, turning and beginning her walk to the rear of the café to put in their order.

Both men dutifully observed her stroll without comment.

Ron asked, "Have you started a list of Knowns for the Donaldson case?"

"Of course," Gene said, not facing his partner until Sandy had disappeared.

"Well, let's go, then," Ron was rubbing his hands in eagerness.

"All right. It seems to me the big one is Abbate got killed in a locked room mystery."

"Well, locked building to be more accurate."

"With only one other person present."

"Again, to be completely accurate, only two other persons were known to be present. I think there was a third."

"Is this case going to include a list of things we imagine?"

"Okay, point taken. Let's stick to the knowns."

"Oh, yeah," Gene stopped for a moment and cocked his head before asking, "Are we gonna list all the stuff like 'killed by blunt force' and 'may have known his killer'?

"You know, we list the major things that help us move toward a solution. Those things usually are included."

"Right. I just wondered if it was the same when we get a case that's already investigated, like this one. It's a lot easier to remember all those things when we were the ones standing at the scene and uncovering the facts."

"I agree, partner. But our list is our list."

"Okay. Starting over, we have a man killed in the locked building alone," he winked at Ron as he said this. Ron nodded, and Gene went on, "Killed by blunt force trauma, probably by a known assailant." He stopped and raised his eyebrows.

"Yep," Ron said, moving out of Sandy's way as she placed their drinks in front of them. "I agree, that's about all we can say for sure right now."

"I'll be back with your sandwiches in just a minute, honey."

"Thank you, Sandy," Gene smiled at her, and again their discussion was momentarily interrupted by her amble to the back of the café.

"Not a lot to go on, partner," Gene said, giving Ron a quizzical look. "Under other circumstances, it might make one partner wonder if his other partner knew something else. You know, something to make him want to take this case."

"I told you. I believe Donaldson. He said he didn't do it, and I believe him."

"And now, we simply have to get the rest of the information and fill in the rest of the story before we go to court."

"Exactly. That's why I like working with you, Novalchek. You're so quick on picking up on what's needed."

"Maybe what we need then is a list of Unknowns, or rather Things we Need to Know."

"How about a 'Do List'? Ron asked, smiling.

"So old-fashioned," Gene said, smiling back. "Okay, then. I'd start that list with a couple of obvious things that need to be re-done by us. Number one is interview Donaldson, his wife, and that guard."

"Alright, except that sounds like three items."

"And I want to see this locked building."

"As do I. I've already talked with Tom about that. He's going to give us a tour and set us up with keycards of our own."

"Good."

"Next?"

"What?" Gene asked, distracted by watching Sandy walking toward them carrying their orders.

"Never mind, we have more important issues right now."

Sandy put their plates in front of them, checked their drinks, and left, creating the inevitable hiatus in their discussion to watch her walk away.

"This looks really good today," Gene said, looking at his patty melt.

"Don't let that stop you from adding to our list," Ron said, lifting the rye bread on his pastrami sandwich and adding some mustard.

"In a minute,' Gene commented and turned his attention to eating.

Several minutes later, sandwiches reduced to their final bite or two and their drink glasses almost empty of tea, Sandy reappeared and filled their glasses.

She said, "You have not been talking very much in the last few minutes, have you?"

"Nope," Ron said, speaking through a mouthful of pastrami and pickle. "But only because the food is so good."

"That's what we like to hear, honey."

Gene managed a gesture of 'thumbs up' with his mouth full, as well. Sandy smiled at him and said, "I also like those clean plates." They watched her walk away.

Ron finished his food and made a dent in his drink, then said. "I'd like to spend some mental energy on the topic of Motive."

"I guess you're not impressed with what Rocky told us. That ethics charge."

"No, I'm not impressed. I talked with Tom briefly about that, too. Something Rocky didn't uncover is a meeting between Abbate and Donaldson with the New City hospital lawyer and Tom. They discussed the issue, and Abbate learned he had no ethical charge; his mother decided to stop her dialysis by herself. Donaldson simply allowed her to put her decision in effect. He continued to be her physician."

"So, that's what Rocky thought Abbate did to anger Donaldson?"

"Yes, he thought Donaldson talked his mother into thinking her life on dialysis was too big a burden for her and the family."

"Was there anything to it?" Gene asked as he mopped up the last of any crumbs on his plate with the last piece of bread from his sandwich.

"According to Tom, Abbate's mother brought the subject up with the nurses, and then she had a long talk with Donaldson. He presented both sides and let her make her own decision. Tom says Donaldson did not try to talk her out of the decision to stop dialysis."

"So Abbate accused him of unethical behavior."

"Right. Tom said he got pretty heated about it and threatened to go to the State Board. That's when Tom set up the meeting with the lawyer, and they talked Abbate out of it. Tom said Abbate was apologetic to Donaldson at the end of that meeting."

"So, we have no motive, then?"

Looney tipped his glass of tea to his partner and commented, "Right, something else Rocky slid past in his hurry."

"So, what else could be a motive for Donaldson?"

"Tom didn't suggest anything. That should go on a list. Ask Tom about other motives."

Gene nodded, "Okay, got it. But maybe there's something else we should consider. Maybe Abbate is not the primary target. Maybe somebody is trying to get Donaldson out of the picture, so they set him up for a murder; any murder might do. While we are out there fishing for motives, I suggest we keep our ears open for motives to frame Donaldson."

"You are a very devious person, Gene Novalchek."

"Funny. Sandy said that to me just last weekend."

Chapter 13

ooney opened the door to the cell and said, "Doctor Donaldson, this is my partner, Gene Novalchek."

Donaldson stood, stuck out his hand to Gene, and replied, "Jim Donaldson."

Ron went on, "Gene would like to hear your story, as you told me. He is going to ask the questions rather than me. Please bear with us on this. Gene needs to hear you explain yourself in your own words. Okay?"

Donaldson made a tight grin, nodded, and sat back down on his bunk. Ron leaned up against the bars behind Gene, who had brought a metal folding chair in with him. Gene opened the chair and sat down, facing Donaldson.

"If you don't mind," Gene said, "Could you just tell me about your visit to the Railway Building on the night in question?"

"Certainly," Donaldson replied. "Bear in mind that after talking with Detective Looney, I have been rethinking that time and rehearsing what happened. I think I can give a more thorough account than I did previously." He looked at Ron and smiled.

Gene said, "Take your time. I just want to hear you say it."

Donaldson nodded and began, "I went to the Railway Building to round on the patients in our dialysis unit. I had already been there earlier in the day to see the patients on the first shift. I went back in the evening to see patients on the second shift. The rounding activity is routine for us; one of our staff makes quick rounds during each shift to check on the patients, and I was covering for the physician who usually made those rounds."

Gene held up his hand and asked, "Why?"

"Why was I covering for him? Well, Pete is the director of the dialysis unit and has that responsibility every day of every week, and sometimes he needs a break. He wanted a four-day weekend away with his wife, and I agreed to cover his responsibilities on Thursday and Friday. Our other staff nephrologist was going to cover on Saturday. I guess he ended up covering Friday, as well."

"How long had this plan for swapping days been in place?" Gene inquired.

Donaldson shook his head and made a slight grin in Looney's direction. "I'm not really certain but at least a week or maybe ten days."

"And who else knew about these plans?" Gene probed.

Donaldson shook his head slowly, "I don't know. It wasn't a secret but we didn't announce it to everyone."

"Okay," Gene said, making a quick note in his notebook. "Go on."

"That's funny," Donaldson said, nodding toward Ron standing against the wall. "Your partner asked the same question."

"Yeah," Gene smiled, "sometimes it scares us when we think alike."

"Anyway, I finished up seeing our consult patients in the hospital and went over to Railway a little after six that evening. I went to my office in South Railway and changed clothes."

"Why do you do that?"

"Like I told Detective Looney, I always change into scrubs to make rounds. It's more like a habit, I guess. When I was in training, I wore scrubs in the unit because I often had to draw blood or change a line, and I didn't want to get blood or anything on my clothes. That isn't much of a risk now, but I feel better rounding in scrubs. Funny, I know. Habits."

"Okay," Gene indicated his understanding.

"So, I guess it takes me less than 15 minutes to change clothes and shoes and head for the unit."

"Shoes, too, huh?"

"Yes. I explained to Detective Looney that I have a pair of old white bucks with rubber soles that I wear to the unit."

"Habit, again?"

"Actually, yes. Those are the very shoes I wore during my training. I kept them because they are comfortable. I dug them out years ago when I started covering for Pete."

"Got it," Gene made another note.

"And I guess I left the South End about six-thirty and went to the Dialysis Unit .."

"Could you just tell me how you got there?"

"Oh, yeah, sorry. I left my office on the third floor, south, and took the west stairs to the first floor. I used my keycard to leave the South end and enter the lobby on first. I walked directly across the lobby to enter the Dialysis Unit."

"Okay, got it. And what did you do in the unit?"

"I did what I always do, first. I stuck my head in the nurses' station to let them know I was there and to ask if there had been any problems. Janey, the head nurse, came with me to make rounds. We walked the unit and talked to every patient."

Gene asked, "How long with each patient?"

"I'm not sure, but not long. I was doing mostly Howdy Rounds. There were no problems, no requests for a new prescription. No issues, so I guess we took about an hour, certainly no more."

"And then you left."

"Yes."

"What time was that?"

"It was about seven twenty."

"And then …?"

"Well, as I explained earlier, I decided to take my wife out for a late dinner, so I called her and asked her to be ready when I got home."

"Did you call from the lobby or after you got back to your office?"

"I called her while walking across the lobby. She answered as I was keying open the door to the stairs. We continued talking as I started up the stairs. Winnie didn't want to go out at first, so I sat down on the stairs and talked her into it."

Gene was genuinely puzzled by this and asked, "You sat on the stairs?"

"Yes. I know that sounds strange, but I was intent on our discussion and sat down. I told Winnie we hadn't been out in a while, and I felt guilty covering for Pete and not taking my wife out. I said she could pick the place and …"

"And she agreed?"

"Finally. When Winnie said she would get ready, I ran up the stairs to change clothes. Detective Looney reminded me that I saw Hector, the night watchman, when I got to the third floor, so he can probably help with what time that was. Anyway, I hurried into the office, changed clothes, and was back out of there by quarter to eight."

"What do you mean 'out of there'?"

"Oh, right. I mean, I went to the east stairs, down to the first floor and keyed out through that door at quarter to eight."

"Where did you sit on the stairs?" Gene asked casually.

"I think it was at the start of the second floor. Why? Detective Looney also wanted to know where?"

"Gene nodded and made a wry grin, "I can't tell you why he asked, but I wanted to check your details in your story."

"Why? Don't you believe me?"

Gene allowed Donaldson to gather himself before proceeding, "Make it to the restaurant?"

"Yes. I forgot to mention that I called ahead for a reservation while I was changing clothes. We got there on time and had a lovely meal, and got home a little after ten. Straight to bed. That's the whole story."

"Uh-huh. Did you know that Dr. Abbate was in the building?"

"Not exactly."

"Explain what you mean by that, please."

"Well, everybody knows Alex spends Thursday night in his office, updating all his charts. But if you are asking whether I saw him or not, the answer is no, I did not."

"Did you see anyone else in the building?"

"Only Hector."

"Did you kill Dr. Abbate?"

"What? No, I did not!"

"Do you know who did kill him?"

"No. I have no idea."

"Do you know of anyone who would want him dead?"

"No." Donaldson was becoming stiff and quick with these answers and Gene sensed a resentment growing.

"Look, doc," he said, "I got to ask these things. I'm not accusing you of anything."

"Okay," came a slightly less stiff answer.

"What do you know about Detective Knudson's case against you?"

"He came by here earlier and said I didn't need to talk or say anything, but he would do the talking. He said he had an airtight case. He believes he has a strong motive, and he thinks I had the opportunity as the only person in the building."

"Is that all?"

"No. Knudson said he had a witness."

"Who?"

"Hector. He said Hector told him I was out of breath when he saw me coming out of the stairwell."

"Huh."

"I just ran up two flights. I may have been breathing fast, but I wasn't out of breath."

"Okay," Gene said, making another note. Then he looked at Donaldson and asked, "Is there anything you'd like to know from us?"

"Yes. When can I go home?"

"Probably not anytime soon. We will work on getting that done as soon as we can."

The men shook their hands, and the detectives called for the guard to re-lock the cell as they left.

On the stairs back up, Ron stopped Gene and looked him in the face, and cocked his head in question.

"Oh yeah," Gene said. "I agree with you. He sounds innocent, and I don't think he did it. But now I have a new concern."

"What's that?" Looney asked as they trudged back up the stairs.

Gene said, "I wonder why Rocky didn't tell us about the night watchman."

CHAPTER 14

The next morning, Ron and Gene made short work of their appearance in the office and left their desks shortly after eight. They decided to not do their usual of getting a travel cup of coffee from the small shop down the block since they were on the way to New City and wanted to take advantage of the barista in the lobby.

Rather than discussing the case or even voicing anticipation for Nick's fresh coffee, Gene's first question as Ron pulled out of the city parking garage was, "Have you done something with this glove compartment?"

"Of course not. Why?"

"I think it's several inches closer to the seat than the last time I was in your car."

Ron was accustomed to this semi-serious grousing from his partner and played along with the game. "That glove compartment hasn't moved a millimeter."

"NO, really, it's closer. Look, my knees are almost touching."

"I'm not looking, Gene. Straighten your legs and your knees won't be anywhere near that glove compartment."

"You know I can't straighten my legs all the way in this seat. I've told you that before." Gene's 'complaining' was losing a little steam by this time.

"You can always ride in the back seat, if you wish."

"That wouldn't be right. I've gotta be where I can see where you're going and like that. Remember that one time you took a wrong turn?"

"Scoot the seat back."

"It doesn't move. I've told you that, too. Your car is damaged and uncomfortable. We need to take a department car. You should ask if we could use the Lincoln Town Car the Chief uses when he goes downtown."

"And I've told you many times there are no unmarked vehicles available. If you want to take a black and white, drive yourself."

"C'mon, partner." Gene was almost out of complaints.

"Or I can let you ride like a hood ornament."

"Hmmm. I think I'll pass on that." Gene nodded at his own comment.

"You can also pass on the critique of my car." With that, the common and customary griping Gene did about Looney's car faded away.

Conversation ceased for a few blocks until Gene asked, "Do you think Nick remembers us?"

"I do. Remember he knew who we were after that first case at New City."

"Yeah, well I'm looking forward to having one of those 'regular' drinks he makes for us."

"You mean a 'usual', don't you?"

"I do. A regular 'usual', that's exactly what I mean."

Ron shook his head and almost laughed out loud. "I certainly hope your memory for details of the case is better than your recall of the name of your favorite coffee drink."

"I want a 'usual'. That's all and then I'll be my 'usual' self."

Ron pulled into the visitors parking area in front of the main entrance to the hospital, next to a small physician parking lot. Gene got out of the car and stood staring at the collection of expensive sedans and roadsters in the other lot. "Who gets to park in there?" he asked.

Ron said, "Tom limits space in there to senior executive physicians, professors and the like. Everybody wants to park there because their offices are so close off the lobby."

"Lot of money in that lot," Gene said without moving. "Which one is Tom's?"

"Tom doesn't park there. He uses a designated space near the walkway from the parking deck."

"That's very egalitarian of him."

Ron started to nod and then said, "That sounded rather wise of you, but I'm pretty sure he does it because his truck is so big it would take up two slots. But he'll appreciate your thinking of him as egalitarian."

The line at the Green Bean coffee kiosk was short but Nick, the barista, was not too busy to check the doorway. When he saw the detectives come through, he waved and as they approached he called out, "The usual, fellas?"

Both men nodded and got in the line to pay at the cashier. Moments later, Nick personally brought their drinks and commented, "Terrible stuff again, eh?"

Gene took his cup and answered, "We're just here for you to tell us what's going on. You're the bartender here, right?"

"Barista, but pretty much the same. I do hear the gossip."

"Who did the deed, then?" Ron asked before taking an approving sip of his drink. "Maybe you can help us cut right to the chase on this one, okay?"

Nick shook his head and leaned over the counter. Speaking conspiratorially, he said, "Scuttlebutt has it there's only one possibility. But I don't like him for it. Too nice a guy."

"I think that makes three of us," Ron said.

Nick went on, "Hey, if you clear him your next coffee is on me."

"Now I'm really psyched up," Gene said. "Let's go catch somebody."

They saluted Nick with their cups and moved around the kiosk toward Tom's office in the Executive Suite.

Mary Brighthouse looked up as they approached. "Good morning, detectives," she said starting to rise from her seat.

"Keep your seat, Mrs. Brighthouse," Ron said, "We're not visitors anymore. Is the boss in?"

"He's waiting for you," she said, indicating the door to Tom's office.

Ron stepped to the door and knocked.

"Come," said a voice from within.

Ron opened the door and he and Gene entered to find Tom Bolling at his desk with his sleeves rolled up, wearing half-glasses and staring at a pile of papers in front of him.

"Hey, Razorback, is this a good time?" Ron asked.

Bolling looked up at the detectives, peering over the top of the half-glasses and commented dryly, "That's like what the old man in the nursing home said when asked whether he wore boxers or briefs."

Ron waited as he had heard this before. Gene eagerly asked, "What'd he say?"

"Depends."

Gene almost choked on his coffee and Tom handed him a tissue from the box on his desk. "Sorry about that," Tom said, "I thought you had heard that one before."

Ron recovered from his partner's discomfort and asked, "Depends on what?"

"This pile of administrivia on my desk. I'm reviewing the quality reports from the radiology department. I can see I'm going to have to give them the talk on data presentation."

Ron nodded knowingly, "Yeah, time to hit 'em with Tufte."

Gene looked puzzled and Ron added, "Later, partner."

Tom said, "But I promised you some time this morning and we'll do it right now. He took off the glasses, placed them in a case and put the case in the top right hand drawer of the desk. He picked up a packet from the desktop and handed it to Ron saying, "Here's a keycard to Railway for each of you. We're going to go over there in a minute and take a brief tour. You can see the scene and Donaldson's office and all that. Also, I arranged for Hector Richmond to come in early today so you can question him."

"That's good stuff, Tom. Thanks," Ron said, moving toward the door.

Tom looked at them and replied, "Let's get out of here before my conscience grabs me. I need another Red Eye from Nick." He got up from his desk and the three men pushed out of the office and back into the lobby.

With drinks in hand, Tom led the detectives to the rear of the lobby and through the 1950's annex to an outside door where the annex was connected to the Railway building via a sidewalk. Tom led them to the left hand access door and showed them how to engage the keycard to trigger the opening of the door from either side. Then he took them to the cross hallway and displayed the master panel for the keycard system. Gene looked at the lights and watched the slow subtraction and addition of lit bulbs in the display before asking, "Is one of these lights me?"

Tom said, "Technically, yes, Gene. But I would have to be standing here at the control panel to see which bulb lit up when you used your key. That bulb lights up almost at random, really next bulb not used, when anyone comes through the keycard doorway. It stays lit until they leave but even if they come right back, its more than likely that a different bulb will indicate their presence."

"What's the value of that?" Asked Ron, immediately concerned that he sytem would not account for individuals.

"Well, this system is one of the earliest keycard record systems produced. It was installed before I got here. It provides simply a check on how many people can enter Railway, since the card is required to open the door in both directions. The light panel seems like a complete after-thought. Probably a sales gimmick. It can tell how many people there are in the building. But it doesn't track who they are."

"Ron looked at Tom and asked, "Let me ask my question a different way. What's the value of that?"

Tom grinned at Looney and replied, "Not much. But it was an early system and it would take more than $150,000 to upgrade it to a tracking system. For all intents and purposes, we haven't needed a tracking system until now."

Huh," said Ron, looking at the board.

Gene nodded at Tom and said, "Don't mind him. He's channeling Thor. He thinks that helps him think."

Over the next hour, Tom Bolling walked the detectives around the Railway Building's South end. He showed them every entrance and walked each hallway from the elevator bank in the middle to the south end of the building. To enter the building, he showed them the doors from the main lobby into the east-west hallway that formed the elevator lobby. Elevators in the main lobby opened there but South elevators opened only into the south end of the building. There was also a controlled exit on the third floor that entered an elevated walkway from Railway into the old 1950s building. From the elevator lobby in the south half of Railway, a central hallway ran north to south. All physician offices opened into this hallway on each of the five floors. At the extreme south end on the first floor were three doors, one at the end and one on each side.

Tom explained that the side doors were supply cabinets for the office needs and the double door at the end opened onto the loading dock.

Looney noted there was no keycard mechanism for the loading dock door. Tom said that door was always locked unless there was a supervised delivery. The detectives examined the loading dock and were convinced they couldn't open the door from outside even with their keycards. Tom then took them back upstairs to the third floor to show them the crime scene. The room been cleaned but was not occupied. Gene brought out the photographs of the scene from the file Rocky had given them. They compared every photograph with the position of the camera and commented on position of the body and other objects. Ron asked about the probable location of the murder weapon on the low bookcase to the right of the desk but Tom was not certain. They all agreed, however, it would have been between the doorway and the man sitting at the computer.

Finally, Tom took them to Donaldson's office on the fourth floor. They looked around and noted a set of drawers under a bookshelf. The top drawer contained three sets of green scrubs, pants and top, carefully folded and clean. No shoes were evident, so Ron looked further, under the desk and in the small bathroom. Finally Ton asked, "What in the devil are you looking for. Ron?"

"His shoes," cam a terse reply. "He told us that he kept a pair of old white bucks for rounding in the Dialysis Unit. They aren't here."

Tom nodded without apparent concern, "I would suppose that the police have them."

Both detectives' heads snapped in Tom's direction and they simultaneously asked, "Why?" Tom turned to Ron and said, "I'm sure it's for evidence in the trial. It's really going to be hard to get over Abbate's blood on Jim's shoe, right?"

Both detectives became transfixed and simply stared silently at Tom; he instantly recognized they had not been aware of this fact.

"It's true," he said holding up his hands as if to ward off blows. "Jim told me that Detective Knudson said he had found Abbate's blood on Jim's shoes." The silence persisted and became uncomfortable. Tom checked his watch and said, "Not a good way to leave, but I got to go finish that paperwork." He left the office for the elevators.

The door closed behind and the detectives turned to look at each other.

"Crap," Gene said, 'this just keeps getting better and better."

CHAPTER 15

Ron wanted the interview with Hector Richmond to occur in the Railway Building, involving all relevant scenes. The detectives met him in the cafeteria first and asked him to show them around. Neither mentioned that they had already seen the crime scene and the interior of the building with Tom Bolling

Ron asked Hector, "Can you just walk us around and show us the key aspects of your testimony? We'd like to see things from your perspective."

Hector agreed, and so they entered Railway via the east access on the first floor where Hector had entered the building after parking in the parking deck the night of the murder. He walked the detectives to the intersection of the elevator passage and the hallway running the length of the south end of the building.

"This here is where I start each shift," Hector said. He used one of several keys he had on a ring fastened to his belt to open the cabinet housing the keycard display.

He went on, "I get the time key from the drawer there, and I check to see how many people are in the building."

"And you can tell that from looking at the lights on that display," Ron asked.

"Yep. Each light means somebody has come in using their keycard, and they're still in here."

"How many are usually here when you sign in?" Gene wanted to know.

"Not a lot at all. I'd say maybe five or six at most."

"And, on the night of the murder, how many people were in the building when you checked in?"

"Oh, that night, there was only the one light that was on. That was Dr. Abbate."

Ron asked, "How did you know that was Dr. Abbate's light?"

"Well, I seen him in his office."

"Hector, let's back up here a minute. You were telling us that you were standing here," he indicated in front of the display, "and you saw only one light, and you knew right then that the light was because Dr. Abbate was in the building. Is that right?"

Hector bent his head for a moment and then said, "Uh, not exactly."

"Well, how was it then?"

"Uh, well, I seen the one light, and then I went up to five to start my rounds, and I saw Dr. Abbate in his office. So, that's when I knew it was his light that was on." He smiled at Ron, satisfied that he had explained himself.

Ron nodded and asked, "Does each person have a particular light in the display?"

"Hector frowned at this question and said, "I don't rightly know. It don't seem that way, though."

Gene then asked, "Do you always start your rounds on the fifth floor?"

Much more comfortable with this line of questioning, Hector answered. "Yessir. I ride up to the top and then walk down the stairs."

"Could you show us that, please?"

"Sure," Hector said. He carefully closed and locked the door to the display and moved the group to the elevators. Their visit was occurring during regular working hours, and other individuals were also using the elevators. They were able to catch one in less than a minute. Hector grinned and noted, "The elevators is a lot quicker at night."

Only one other person rode to the fifth floor with them and scurried off quickly when the door opened. Hector showed the detectives that each office door had a clear glass top that allowed light to spill into the hallway. He explained how that allowed him to stand at the intersection and see whether any offices were occupied.

"That's when I knew that light I had seen belonged to Dr. Abbate. His office was the only one lit up," Hector beamed his explanation, and both detectives nodded. Hector went on, "So, see my rounds are to walk down each hall and put my time key in the box at the end of the hall. That shows I really was here." They continued down the hallway to the south end and retraced their steps to the elevators. The 'tour' on the fourth floor was nearly identical. When they got off the elevator on the third floor, however, Hector's intensity increased. He showed the detectives the small break room where he had eaten his midnight lunch and then walked down the hallway, and pointed into Abbate's office. "When I went past here, I seen him sitting at his desk there, working on his computer." Hector's voice was almost apologetic.

"Did he see you?" Gene asked.

"Ah, no. He was busy, and I didn't stop or nothing."

Ron pushed on, "And what did you do then?"

"I went on with my rounds."

"Please show us."

"Yessir. After I went all the way down the hall, I went back to the elevator bank, and I took the stairs here down to two." They had returned to the elevator hall, and Hector indicated that he used the west stairs to go down to the second floor. All three men followed his path and did the same. On each floor, Hector repeated his routine; he went down the longitudinal hall, turned his time key in the mechanism mounted on the wall, and returned to the elevator passage. He noted that all the doors were locked at night, and his responsibility was to ensure they remained locked. Then he turned to the east stairwell to descend to the next floor.

They repeated this drill again, down the hall, engage the time clock, check all doors and return to the elevator hall. At one point, when Hector turned toward the west staircase, Ron interrupted him with, "Do you always alternate the stairs you take going down?"

"Yessir. That way I can tell if someone is hiding in the staircase."

"Very clever, Hector," Gene said and clapped him on the back.

As they approached the stairwell on the fourth floor, Ron stopped Hector and said, "I understand that you met someone right about here on that night."

"Uh, well, yes, yes I did."

"Could you tell us about that?"

"Sure, I guess. I was heading this way, and Dr. Donaldson come busting out of the stairwell and headed for his office."

"How did he appear?"

"Whatcha mean?"

"Could you describe his appearance or his manner?"

"I think he was in a hurry."

"Did he speak to you?"

"Oh, yeah, he said, 'Hi Hector', or something like that."

"Did he stop to chat?'

Hector cocked his head and looked at Gene, who had asked this question. "No," he said. "He was in a hurry. He was breathing kinda fast and didn't look like he had time to stop and chat."

"I see. Then what happened?"

"Well, he headed down the long hall toward his office, an' I went down the stairs to three for my rounds."

"What time was that?"

"It was right after seven-thirty."

"You looked at your watch?"

"Yessir. I usually does that whenever I see someone in the building."

"Did you see him again?"

"Dr. Donaldson? No. He went out the other way, I guess."

The trio went down the west stairs and performed the ritual steps of Hector's rounds on each of the floors. Repeating his habit, Hector. Alternated whether he used the east or west stairs back down to the first floor. Back at the display console, he pointed out that a dark glass door fronted the display. Through the door, however, it was possible to see the many lit bulbs indicating people in the building. Hector pointed out the lights and said, "So, when I got back here, I could see only Dr. Abbate's light. So I knew that Dr. Donaldson had left."

Ron asked about the frequency of the rounds that Hector made and learned that Hector often sat there between rounds and went there to eat his 'lunch'. Hector's schedule called for him to make a complete round of the five floors every hour. He said the trip usually took no more than twenty-five or thirty minutes and he would otherwise sit in the break room and read.

"What are you reading," Gene asked.

" I'm reading a lot of books by Zane Grey right now. That guy can really tell a story."

"Can you tell us about finding Dr. Abbate?" Ron asked.

"Well, yeah. I was sitting here in the break room when I get a call from Jack about him."

"Jack?"

"He was the guard in the hospital that night. He calls and says Abbate's wife called and said he should be home and something has happened."

"What did you say?"

"I told Jack that the light in Abbate's office was on ever time I went by there."

"Did you see Dr. Abbate on your rounds?"

"Uh, well, not really."

"Hector, what do you mean 'not really'?"

"Well, I mean the light were on but he wasn't sitting at the desk. I looked through the door but I didn't see him."

"When was the last time you saw him?"

"You think he was dead all that time?"

"Hector, when did you last see Dr. Abbate alive."

Hector thought for a moment and then said, "I guess it was that first time I was making rounds. I don't think I saw him after that."

"What did you do when Jack called you?"

"I went to Dr. Abbate's office to check on him."

"And, what did you find?"

"The door was locked, you know and I used my master key. I went in and called his name but there was no answer. I went over to the desk and found him, you know, lying there on the floor. I called Jack and said we needed to call the police."

"Did you touch anything in the office?"

"No. I got out of there real quick."

"Where did you go?"

"I stayed right there in the hall until other people came and took care of things."

The detectives asked him a few more questions and reviewed his story about his rounds that evening. Then, they thanked him and headed for Ron's car. Sitting in their seats a few minutes later, Ron asked Gene, "Did you notice anything about Hector?"

"Such as?"

"Anything that might suggest he left something out."

"What are you talking about?" Gene was used to these conversations with Looney.

"Anything?"

"No. What? I don't want to play twenty questions."

"Okay, then. Never mind," Ron said and turned to start the car.

"Wait a minute, partner. You can't start a conversation like that and then let it die," Gene said.

"Oh yes, I can. Watch me," Ron noted and shifted into gear.

CHAPTER 16

Back in the office, Looney grabbed the box of evidence given to them by Rocky and hefted it back on his desk. "We can't have any more of this evidence popping up unexpectedly," he said, removing the top and grabbing the Murder Book.

Gene sat at his desk across from Ron and pondered why Rocky hadn't told them all the evidence he had against Donaldson. "Maybe he forgot about the blood," he said.

"What? Oh no, he didn't forget. He didn't like the idea of us looking into the case, and he wanted us to get jarred when that piece showed up. I wonder if he thought we would overlook it."

"Well, we kinda did, the first time around," Gene said, grabbing the box and starting to look through it.

Ron said, "Alright, I just looked at every sheet in the Murder Book. There's nothing about either Hector saying Donaldson was out of breath when he saw him or anything about the blood on the shoe."

Gene said, "I have the request to the lab about the blood. No results, though."

"Let me see."

Gene handed the paper to Ron and kept pawing through the materials in the box. Before Ron had finished reading the request, Gene pulled a packet of additional pictures from the bottom of the box. "Look at this!"

The packet was labeled, "Donaldson Office", dated and initialed by Rocky. Inside were pictures of scrubs hanging on a hook and a pair of white bucks. Close-up pictures of the shoes showed a single drop of blood on the right shoe. The blood was on the outside, where the top and the sole meet slightly ahead of the saddle.

They each sat in their chairs and looked at each other.

"Just to be clear about this, we now have two pieces of information highly suggesting that Donaldson ran up the stairs after leaving the dialysis Unit, killed Abbate, and ran back down to change clothes. He was seen by Hector and left blood on his shoe," Ron said in a monotone voice.

Gene nodded and said, "Rocky wasn't just jumping on the 'only other person in the building' then, was he?"

"Doesn't look like it. But where is the interview with Hector? An eyewitness seems like an important piece of the picture, doesn't it?'

"We need to ask Rocky."

"First thing in the morning."

When Looney got home that evening, Meg immediately noted his frown and asked for an explanation. Ron noted, not for the first time, that his wife was exceptionally astute to his moods. Since supper was not quite ready, he grabbed a beer from the refrigerator and sat on the couch with Meg.

"It's Rocky," stated simply.

"Could I have a little more detail," Meg asked, cocking her head.

"Sure. You know Gene and I got this case after Rocky did the first day's work."

"And arrested a friend of Tom's that you believe is not the killer."

"Yeah, right. Well, Rocky gave us his Murder Book and the box with all the items from the scene, but he didn't tell us two important pieces of information. He let us get out there and run into these facts and look like dopes."

"Wait a minute, are you certain he was withholding?" Meg asked after checking on food on the stove.

"Yeah. I am. Well, I think so. Both items were facts he mentioned to others but not to us. When those other people mentioned them the whole case looks different."

"How?"

"Gene and I were pretty convinced that Rocky arrested this Donaldson guy because of one fact: He was supposedly the only one in the building other than the dead guy. Now we find out that the night watchman saw Donaldson come out of the staircase breathing hard and Rocky found blood on Donaldson's shoe."

"Donaldson's blood?"

"That's what he said. But Donaldson just came from the Dialysis Unit. Maybe it is somebody else's blood. Huh."

Meg stood and indicated it was time to go to the supper table. "I think it's good for you to consider that Rocky was not blindsiding you. Maybe you'll be less aggressive when you and Gene talk to him tomorrow."

For his part, Rocky was just as puzzled as they were about the missing information. He explained that the lab had called him about the blood report but that happened after he gave the evidence box to Looney and Novalchek. He admitted lying to Donaldson about knowing whose blood it was, hoping to get a quick admission of guilt. The report on the interview with Hector and his eyewitness account of a hurried and out-of-breath Donaldson coming from the stairwell was also not a complete mystery. He had dictated it and the unit secretary typed it up and put it in his box for signature; that also happened after the evidence box was transferred. Rocky put his hands in the air and swore that he told people to route those things and all future information on the case to Looney.

"Still, you made no comment on either of those issues when you briefed us. You were hiding something from us, weren't you?" Gene tried to sound inquisitive rather than angry; he succeeded to some degree and Rocky answered, "Yeah, a little. I mean, I thought those two items were in the box. I hadn't looked in there since Thor told me he agreed with Walker about the second look."

Looney stared at him, "So, you thought we would either go run to New City and find out about these things and get all embarrassed or maybe find them in the box and shut down this whole second look thing before it got started?"

Rocky looked at his shoes and mumbled, "Something like that. I just didn't want you messing around with my case, that's all."

Looney went on, "We had an agreement and a stipulation. We're playing on the same team, here, Detective Knudson."

"Alright. I get it. You're pissed because you spent some time on a case that is a slam-dunk, okay? But now here we are. You got nothing new, and I still have a case with incriminating evidence and an eyewitness!"

"What's your point, Rocky?"

"Give it up, Walker. Walk away. This Donaldson guy did it, and I've got the proof." Rocky was raising his voice more than necessary.

Looney stared at Knudson for a long minute, waiting until he saw the man swallow, then he said, "We are not walking away. I have an agreement with Thor to examine this case, and Gene and I intend to do just that. For the moment, you better keep your head down, or I will tell Thor about your evidence-hiding trick." That threat caused Rocky to swallow twice more. But he bit his lip and did not speak. He stared at Looney and then made a quick nod and turned to look at the materials on his desk.

Ron and Gene headed back to their desks. When they had returned their paperwork to the evidence box, Gene looked at Ron, raised his eyebrows, and made a gesture like drinking from a cup.

Ron grinned a little and said, "Absolutely. I think I'd rather have a beer right now, but it's too early for that."

They did not even sit down but headed directly for the stairwell in the back corner and on to the small coffee shop down the street.

With their coffee and seated at their favorite table in the rear of the shop, Ron began to relax slightly. Gene was sipping his drink when Ron looked up and said, "Next steps, partner?"

Gene scratched his left eyebrow and slowly responded, "Let's consider both of these items as new evidence."

Ron nodded.

Gene went on, "If we consider them as something we would have found on our own, we should try to evaluate each item in depth for its accuracy, value, and meaning."

"I'm agreeing with you, Gene. Now, unpack what you just said."

"Okay. First is the so-called eyewitness. I believe we have already assessed Hector's story to the right degree. Importantly, he did not see the murder itself, he only saw Donaldson hurrying back to his office."

"Away from the crime scene," Looney added.

"Well, yes. But only to the extent that the crime scene was two floors away and Donaldson was coming from the staircase."

Looney nodded again and set his cup down. "Further, Donaldson already told us about his reason for hurrying a couple of flights on those steps."

Gene tapped his right forefinger on the tabletop and said, "And Hector didn't say anything about Donaldson looking shamefaced or trying to avoid being seen. When we gave him the chance to describe Donaldson, Hector did not say he looked guilty."

"So, after all that, your point about this eyewitness report is …?"

"I think we have already done what we usually do. We examined the story and the evidence it brought to the investigation."

"And concluded …?"

"Well, we haven't talked about it yet, have we? But I'm not convinced Hector was describing a murderer fleeing the scene."

"Me either. Plus, I think we have a way further to undermine such a concept."

"What's that?"

Ron smiled smugly, "Let's get the timing of the phone call Donaldson made to his wife. If his story is correct, he would have to have been on the phone with her when he committed the murder."

Gene slapped his hands together, "Great idea."

They saluted each other with their cups and drank deeply.

Ron then said, "Then there's this business with the blood on Donaldson's shoe."

Gene nodded, and his smile faded. "How are we going to approach that?'

"Like any new evidence. First, does it fit? My answer to that is no, it does not. At least, it won't fit if our information on the phone call turns out the way we think."

Gene perked up, "Oh, I see. If the phone data is correct, then he wasn't at the crime scene and …"

"And, the blood on his shoe is a red herring, probably planted by the killer."

They looked at each other and Gene said, "That still leaves the question of how did a murderer get in and out of that building without leaving some evidence in the keycard system."

Chapter 17

They walked back to the office, still bouncing ideas and potential explanations off each other. Gene stopped by the toilet, and Ron sat at his desk and called the phone company. He was still on the line, giving the supervisor Donaldson's phone number and the times he wanted covered in a report. His good luck had connected him with a supervisor who had done this sort of work for the police before; his request was being aptly handled.

Gene pulled the evidence box and started going through it again. When he located the packet of photographs, he began laying them out on his desktop. Ron came around to Gene's side of the two-desk arrangement, and the two of them began sorting and positioning the pictures in a rough geometric fashion. The pictures from Dr. Donaldson's office were in a separate envelope. When they were both satisfied with the layout of the images from Abbate's office, they stood, side-by-side, arms folded, and studied the pictures.

When Gene broke the formation and moved to look at the Donaldson set, Ron picked up one of the original groupings and studied it carefully.

Gene said, "This blood drop looks funny to me." He held out a photograph to Ron that showed the blood on Donaldson's white buck shoe.

Ron made a small noise of assent and handed Gene the photograph he had been studying.

Gene accepted the photograph, looked briefly at Ron, who shrugged, and then studied the picture intently. Finally, he said, "I think you agree with me, right?"

"Well, it would almost have to be funny-looking, wouldn't it?"

"Again, I presume you are noting that this credenza is strikingly free of blood spatter."

"That I am, partner. That I am. If we accept the rest of the scenario, the killer stood beside this credenza and leaned over to strike Abbate in the head."

"Twice."

"Okay. I'll even grant that the killer hit him twice, so we have a backstroke that might have caused some splatter of blood from the first blow. But, even granting that, how likely is it that such a drop would be not only the only drop to get on the outside of the credenza but that it would take a curveball trajectory to get on the killer's shoe?" Ron smiled grimly at Gene.

"I get you, partner. The blood drop looks like it was a plant. And a plant screams 'set up' to me."

"And to me. I bet this will agree with the phone call information and the rigged time of death."

Gene said, "I think we should tell Rocky and Thor. We've got good evidence to keep digging."

"Thor isn't going to stop us right now, Gene. We'll tell him whenever he asks for progress."

Gene frowned a bit at this comment but nodded and said, "Okay. Waiting will give us time to get more information anyway."

"Right. We should hear about the phone call any time now. But we want a little more than the length of the call, right."

"Uh, yes. Sure we do." Gene said with all the lack of confidence in his voice and body language that Looney immediately said, "If Donaldson killed someone while talking on the phone, it just might have been noticed, don't you think?"

"Right," Gene said. "So we need to talk to the Mrs."

Ron went back to his side of the desk pair and sat down. He took out his little notebook, looked up a number, and dialed his phone. Gene took a seat on his side and listened.

"Hello, Mrs. Donaldson, this is detective Ron Looney." He paused, then said, "Yes, ma'am." After another short pause, Ron asked, "Would this be a good time for my partner and me to come by to ask you a few questions?" Another pause, then, "Thank you. We will see you soon." Looney hung up the phone and gave Gene a 'thumbs up' sign.

In Ron's car heading north toward the Donaldson's home, Gene mused, "There's another thing bothering me about this killer in the building."

"What's that?"

"How is he getting into the offices? I mean, they're locked aren't they?"

"I don't know, Gene. Another question for Tom. I'd bet that Donaldson locked his office after leaving, but maybe Abbate's door was unlocked since he was in there."

"Still. We are walking ourselves into making a case for a guy that escapes tracking by the keycard system who can get through locked doors. I'm having a funny feeling that we are chasing a ghost."

"Ghosts don't kill people, Gene. Homicide 101."

"Anyway, it's a puzzle."

"I agree with that," Ron said, making a sweeping right turn.

"Here's another puzzle, partner," Gene said, brushing the car seat between his legs. "It appears that you have allowed a troop of Girl Scouts to eat several boxes of cookies in this seat."

"There's no eating in my car."

"Well then, where'd all these crumbs come from? Mighty uncomfortable."

"'I would guess those crumbs will turn out to be from that pastry you gobbled down at the coffee shop. That's why there's no eating in my car."

"You think I brought these crumbs in? That can't be true, I eat very carefully and try to get all the crumbs the first time."

"Well, you didn't, and now I'll have to vacuum the car when I get home tonight. In the meantime, don't grind them into the seat cushion or the floor mat."

"What? First, you want to make this problem something you can blame me for, and now, second, you want me to levitate for the rest of the trip, so I don't spoil your carpet?"

"That's right. Is this the house?"

Ron pulled to the curb and indicated that Gene should brush the seat when he got out. He waited at the end of the sidewalk to see that Gene did appropriate brushing before they walked up to the door.

Winnie Donaldson opened the front door as they started up the porch steps. She was wearing a white shift dress but was barefooted. Her black hair hung down over her shoulders, and she fixed the detectives with a steady gaze from light blue eyes. Her smile was small and somewhat uncertain. She indicated they should come into the house.

They sat in the living room, Ron and Gene together on a small sofa and Winnie across a small coffee table in a wingback chair. She asked, "Which of you is the 'best detective' that Tom said he would get for James?"

They looked at each other and pointed to the other. Winnie smiled and said, "Okay then, what do you need to know to get my husband out of jail?"

Ron spoke first, "We would like to know your version of the events on the evening that Dr. Abbate was killed."

Winnie looked at him and said, "That other detective didn't seem interested. He said there was no other way for Alex to be killed than by James."

Ron went on, "We are not of that opinion, Mrs. Donaldson."

"Winnie," she said, smiling again.

Ron looked uncertain, and Winnie continued, "My name is Gwyneth. It's Welsh. But today using that name seems like I'm either trying to be like an 18th-century warrior heroine or a pale imitation of a successful actress. Everyone calls me Winnie."

"Gene said, "Winnie."

"Yes," Winnie said, looking at him. "You know, like the Pooh Bear."

"Yes, of course," Ron said, taking hold of the conversation again. "As I said, we do not believe that the only explanation for Dr. Abbate's death involves your husband."

"Well, that is good news. How can I help you?"

"Dr. Donaldson told us that he made a phone call to you that evening."

"He did, that's right."

"Can you tell us about that call?"

"Well, asked me to get dressed and go out to dinner."

"Is that all?" Ron asked, scribbling in his notebook.

"Yes. That was really all it was."

Gene and Ron looked at each other and raised their eyebrows. Winnie's information was punching a large hole in her husband's story.

Winnie observed the detective's reaction and said, "Of course, he went on and on about it."

"How long?" Ron inquired.

"I don't know," Winnie said." I didn't want to get all dressed up, and he was insistent that we hadn't been out for some time, and he had finished in record time, and I don't know how long he went on."

"You did decide to go out, though, didn't you?" Gene asked.

"Oh, yes. I mean, the man kept after me." She smiled at the memory.

"And how long did the two of you talk on the phone?" Ron persisted.

"Goodness, I don't know. I thought he was nuts to think about going out that late, but he said it was time for the second seating. Then he went on about this particular place he wanted to visit."

"How long was the conversation," Ron asked again.

"He just went on and on until I said I would go get dressed. Maybe fifteen minutes. It seemed like a long phone call."

Gene leaned forward and asked, "What did you talk about at dinner?"

"My goodness, you two are quite interested in our conversations, aren't you?"

"Just topics."

"Well, we talked about choices for our next vacation for one."

"Uh-huh. What were the choices?"

"The usual. Beach or the mountains."

"And did you decide?"

"No, we were going to continue to discuss and get some options before making a decision."

"I see. Was there another topic?"

"Yes. James had such a good time he wanted us to set a date night and go out to dinner more often."

"Did you agree?"

She smiled and nodded. "Yes, I agreed. It had been a good time."

They asked her about any anger between Donaldson and Abbate and she gave them the story of Abbate's mother needing dialysis and being treated by Donaldson. When she decided to stop dialysis, Abbate had made charges against Donaldson for unethical behavior and practice.

Gene said, "Huh. She wanted to stop her dialysis? Really?"

Winnie cocked her head and looked at him before answering, "Of course. People can choose not to get chemotherapy or have necessary surgery, so why not stop dialysis? James said she was miserable."

"What about these ethical charges?"

"Well, first of all, they weren't true. It was all her idea. James had nothing to do with the decision. He just allowed it to happen and continued to care for her."

"Charges like that could seriously hurt his practice, I imagine," Ron said.

"Oh yes," Winnie replied. "That's when Tom Bolling stepped in. He got the hospital lawyer together with James and Alex and together they convinced Alex there was no ethical issue. The lawyer drew up a statement, and all parties signed it. Tom kept a copy, I'm sure."

"So, it's all over, then. No charges or legal action?"

"Nothing. It was all settled."

Moments later, as they walked to the door and were in the process of saying goodbyes, Ron turned to Winnie and said, "Just one more thing. What did James have for dinner that night? At the restaurant?"

Winnie drew herself up, stared at Ron, and asked, "What's this, some Columbo trick? He had the flounder. It made him tell me some joke about hospitals serving only pancakes or flounder for every meal to HIV patients in the early days of the epidemic."

Gene cocked his head and, as Ron said "Thank you " and went out the door, asked, "Why did they serve flounder for every meal?"

"James said it was because they could slide it under the door."

CHAPTER 18

The following morning, Ron drove them back to New City.

"There's got to be a better motive than a resolved concern about ethics," he said.

"I agree," Gene said, for once not complaining about the seating in Ron's car. "But remember, if we are working on this case with the idea that Donaldson is not the killer, then we're looking for a motive for someone else."

"Gene, you are the master of the B.O."

"C'mon, man. Why insult me?"

"It's what my kids say, Gene. You have just laid out the Blatantly Obvious."

"Oh, that old B.O."

"Yes. We are looking for a needle in a haystack. At least I think we have the right haystack."

"You mean New City."

"I do. And since we both agree that the case against Donaldson doesn't hold together, it means we are now starting over from scratch."

"What does that mean, anyway?"

"It means we have to talk to a lot of folks and stir up …"

"I know that! I want to know the meaning of 'starting from scratch'. I've heard that all my life, and I don't know where that comes from. I sure don't want to start scratching."

"And you're asking me about this because?"

"Because you always seem to know all these country sayings. Plus, you usually have a funny story to go with an explanation. And I'm ready for something funny in this case."

Ron made a hard turn and grinned at Gene. "Well, to my understanding, it doesn't mean you develop itching problems. It probably has a secondary meaning of suggesting chickens in the yard, scratching in the dirt to find a single kernel of corn."

"That's gonna be us, then, right? Scratching in the dirt."

"Well, yes. I think that's what we'll end up doing. But that's not what the saying is all about."

"Well, keep talking. And don't forget the funny story."

"My understanding is the figure of speech refers to scratching a line in the dirt as the starting point for a race. Anybody cheats, then you would have to start over … from scratch."

"Huh. Only people who spend a lot of their time in the dirt would come up with a saying like that."

"That would be me and my folks, Gene. Farmers. People of the land. We know and do things you guys who think the world should all have sidewalks will never understand."

"Yeah. Okay. Where's the funny story?"

"Don't have one. But now we're here, anyway." He pulled into the circle in front of the main building and a parking spot reserved for guests.

"Why is that spot always open when we come here?" Gene asked.

"You know how on television cop shows, there's always a parking place right out front for the hero? That's me, partner."

"Nah."

"Really. Of course, it helps that I call Tom and tell him we're coming, and he clears a place for me to park."

"I knew there was a trick to it!"

As planned, they waved at Nick as they approached the Green Bean kiosk. He waved back, grinned, and asked, "The usual?"

Ron answered, "Yes, for us both but with a side of conversation." Nick looked at Ron and raised his eyebrows. "With me?" he asked.

"Yes, sir," Gene said, smiling at Nick.

Nick turned to the other barista and said something, the girl nodded, and Nick turned to the machine. Moments later, he stepped out from behind the counter and carried the drinks to Ron and Gene, seated in lobby chairs.

"What's this about," Nick asked.

"Relax, man," Ron said, "We are at an impasse in the Abbate case and we decided we needed a real chat with you and not pleasantries at the cashier's desk."

"Oh, okay. I thought you were after me."

Gene looked at Nick and asked, "Why, what did you do?"

"Well," he said, "I forgot to put the Irish whiskey in that last drink I made for you."

"Yeah, we noticed."

Ron said, "We want to know whether you have any further information or thoughts about any comments made around the coffee bar about this case."

"Ah, the undercover barista, eh?"

"Whatever."

"Look, I'd love to help. Old Doc Abbate was a quiet guy but not a bad one. Donaldson is a really good guy and friendly. I haven't heard any scuttlebutt from anybody, though. Most people are asking what I've heard, not telling new stuff."

"Huh. That's disappointing. You will keep listening for us, right?"

"Sure. I'll tell Doctor Bolling if I hear anything."

"Good plan," Ron said, rising from his seat.

Everyone shook hands and headed back to the kiosk. Ron went to the cashier to pay for their drinks, and Nick said, "Hey. I said the next ones would be on me."

Ron waved him off, saying, "We haven't met your criteria yet." He paid for the drinks, and he and Gene headed for Tom's office.

Mary Brighthouse was expecting them and indicated they should go and knock on Tom's door. They were now such accustomed visitors she no longer needed to introduce them.

Tom said, "Come," and indicated they should sit. Gene took the upholstered chair to the left of the desk, usually reserved for important guests. Ron sat in the straight-back chair to the right of the desk.

"What's up?" Tom asked to start the discussion.

"We have reached a lull in the information flow," Ron said and took a sip of coffee.

"You mean you've got nothing new, right?"

"See, Gene, I told you he could make a good cop."

"Yeah, you're right. Knowing the lingo is half the game."

Tom asked, "So, why are you here?"

"We need some new place to start."

"Where do you see things right now?"

Ron took and released a deep breath before saying, "We both agree the motive for Donaldson is very weak. We also have developed serious concerns about the usefulness of that single drop of blood on his shoe and of Rocky's interpretation of Donaldson's appearance coming out of the stairwell."

"So, you're looking for another suspect?"

"Yes, I guess that's a fair way to put it. I was going to ask if there were any other 'little clashes' that Abbate had with others."

"You know, there are little clashes between professionals all the time, right?"

Ron looked at Gene and winked, "I think we're about to hear some of the dirty laundry of New City."

Tom spoke tiredly, "No, you're not. Because there isn't anything else I can think of."

Ron looked sharply at him and said, "Except …"

Tom shrugged and shook his head. "I've talked this all over with Sandra. She reminded me of an event. Two years ago, at our Christmas party, Alex had too much wine and made a clumsy pass at someone's wife. It ended quickly, there were mumbled 'sorrys', and the Abbates left. And that's the only thing I could come up with."

"Whose wife," Gene asked after an uncomfortable pause.

"Donaldson's."

CHAPTER 19

"Well, that's a big disappointment," Gene said.

"I do not have any other suggestions," Tom added, leaning back in his chair.

Ron looked at his old friend and said, "You know, at this point in a murder investigation, cops like us would take a deep breath and bore in on the victim. But you and everybody else we talk to about him suggest he was just a nice quiet guy. Except, as we now learn, when he's in his cups."

Tom nodded in agreement, "Yes, he led a life that was pretty unnewsworthy."

Ron went on, "And I promise that we will continue to examine him in our way."

"But ..." Tom smiled at him.

"But, there's got to be a part of what he does, like cancer treatment, that cops are not going to understand, right? We need some help in deciding if there's anything funny going on in his practice. Would you go back over his activities in the last several months and see if he ran into anything out of the ordinary? Maybe somebody died, and a family member created a fuss. Anything."

Tom didn't hesitate. "Of course," he said, "I'll get a little help and we'll go over his recent work in the unit and his consults."

Ron held up a hand. "Help?"

"Yes. I'll need some help just with the volume, let alone the intricacies of chemotherapy. Remember, I'm just a carpenter here."

"Don't play that 'dumb surgeon' card on me, Razordoc. Can you find somebody, and maybe just one person, that will be completely out of the realm of suspicion?"

"You're still thinking it was someone here at the hospital, aren't you?"

"Yes, I am. Someone who knew Donaldson would be available as a patsy, someone who understood Abbate's work habits. Someone who knew the Railway Building."

Tom sat quietly for a moment before asking, "How do you feel about Monique? She's knowledgeable about toxicity and cancer and like that."

"That little lady would be great. But, please, keep it to just the two of you. And let me know of anything you find, okay?"

"Yes, sir, Master Sargent," Tom said, abruptly while throwing a mock salute at Ron.

Ron grinned widely and said, "At ease, General. We'll be in touch."

They headed directly for the café and lunch. Sandy saw them as they came in the door, and she changed the direction in which she was walking to intercept a couple heading for the booth favored by Ron and Gene. Gene grinned at Ron as Sandy took the man's arm and gently steered the couple further into the café to a smaller booth. She fussed over the man after seeing them seated and promised she would be right back. Then she scurried over to get some menus and indicated that Ron and Gene should seat themselves in their usual and preferred booth. Gene's grin grew more pronounced during this scenario, and Ron was chuckling to himself when they had taken their seats in the best booth in the café.

The café was a half-block in length, kitchen on one end, and entryway on the other. The booth in question was at the front of the café, close to the entrance. The detectives fancied this particular booth for watching Sandy; Ron had teased Gene about watching Sandy walk to the kitchen and now Sandy was setting him up for that duty. These two were turning out to be a matching set.

Sandy appeared at their table and asked, "the usual, fellas?" Gene was quick to agree. Ron, planning to take Meg out for fried fish that evening, decided to have only soup and salad for lunch. Gene became interested in the discussion about choices of soup; he preferred the clam chowder.

"I don't want that heavy a meal," Ron said.

"Our chicken noodle is very good," Sandy added.

"What's the other soup of the day?" Ron pushed back.

"Vegetable mushroom."

"I'll have that," Ron decided. Sandy headed back to the kitchen with their orders and they halted any conversation to take in the view.

When she disappeared into the kitchen, Gene said, without moving his head or gaze, "How well do you think we have discussed the possibility that this whole set-up intends to take Donaldson out of the picture somehow?"

Ron fiddled with the salt seller and asked, "What do you mean?"

"You know what I mean. Here we are running down possible motives for killing Abbate, but if the real target here was to get Donaldson hung for murder, we might be missing the picture."

"Gene, that doesn't make sense to me. I admit that clever crooks sometimes set things up to implicate an innocent individual. But that almost always involves a major crime on the other end. It doesn't track for me to think that someone wanted to get Donaldson out of the way for an unspecified reason ..."

Gene interrupted, "Wait a minute, partner. You saw his wife. That's not an unspecified reason."

Ron paused before saying, "We have no credible information indicating that the Donaldsons have an unhappy marriage or ..."

Interrupting again, Gene said, "Doesn't have to be her, does it? I mean, there could be someone else who wants the husband out of the picture so he could make a move. We haven't looked into that."

Ron leaned back and said, "No, we have not. And I don't think that's where we should be putting effort right now."

"We don't have any other leads right now, do we?"

"Not at the moment, no."

"Then why isn't my idea good enough to float to the top and have us spend a little time looking into the Donaldson's marriage and whether Winnie has an unknown player interested in her."

The discussion continued during the meal. As his soup was set down in front of him, Ron picked up the peppershaker and made some moves over his soup; little pepper fell out.

Ron made a wry grin at Gene and took the top off the shaker. "Look here, partner. This is one of the all-time silly things that go on in restaurants today."

"What? I don't want any criticism of Sandy's place."

"Look right here," Ron held the shaker out toward him. "See how this shaker is completely full, up to the top?"

"Yeah? So what?"

"Well, when's it's that full, nothing comes out when you shake it." Ron made this point, then tipped the topless shaker to put a small mound of pepper in his hand.. He recapped the shaker and put it back in its rack and proceeded to add sprinkles of the pepper in his hand to the soup. "See, this is the way chef's work anyway."

Gene changed the subject but felt he was making a little headway with his arguments to consider the target of the murder being Donaldson until Ron pushed his soup bowl to the side and said, "Tell you what, I agree we should re-interview Donaldson. We did not push him very hard for suspects who might be framing him. Let's set that up for tomorrow."

Gene agreed and, for a moment, it seemed the case and next steps were now determined. Then Gene shook his head, "I know that we've come to view the circumstantial evidence against Donaldson as suggesting the killer was someone else. But I can't get over the fact that Donaldson was the only one still in the building. You gotta admit, that's a pretty hard fact to overlook."

Ron nodded soberly and said, "I think that's the way it was set up to be."

"You're thinking it's not Donaldson when you say that, right?"

"That's right."

"How can you keep saying that? There was no one else in the building."

"Not true, Gene. We all know that Hector was in the building."

"And nobody really thinks Hector is the killer."

"I agree."

"Then that only leaves Donaldson."

"And the killer."

"C'mon, partner. Make some sense. Who is this mysterious killer?"

"I don't know that, yet, Gene. We're planning on starting a new avenue to search for that person tomorrow, remember?"

"Yeah, I know, and I'm glad we're going to do that. But in the back of my mind, I'm having these thoughts that Donaldson is a bright guy and might have set things up to throw a lot of suspicion on the circumstantial evidence."

"What are you thinking, Gene?"

"Well, he could have put the blood spot on his shoe, and he would have chosen a spot where it was unlikely to have occurred naturally."

"Can't disagree. What about the long telephone call with Winnie that overlaps the time of the murder? How'd he do that?"

"I don't know, maybe he played with the mute button or something."

Ron looked skeptically at him and went on, "And the encounter with Hector while out of breath?"

Gene started tapping the table with his index finger, "I think he had Hector's schedule and could have arranged that. Especially if he thought his trick with the phone had worked."

Ron nodded and granted his partner had made some positive points. "But I'm positive that someone else could have been in that building."

"On what basis? We have no idea how a person could have done that."

"Again, you're using the royal 'we' a little too loosely."

"I thought I was using the 'we' as in 'us'." Gene made a circle with his hand, indicating the inclusion of himself and Looney.

"Actually, Gene, I think I know how someone else could have been in that building. I don't know who, but I think I know how."

"And when did you come up with this idea?"

"When we got that tour of the building and the explanation of how the system works."

"Well, I didn't see it. What did you discover?"

"Tell you what, Gene. Why don't I show you how it could be done? You and Tom can be witnesses."

"When?"

"Tomorrow night."

CHAPTER 20

Ron and Gene met with Tom at New City shortly after six the following evening. Ron had talked with Tom and explained the challenge. Part of the 'game', however, involved having everyone believe this was a usual evening. Ron was concerned that his idea might not work if folks thought they were part of a David Copperfield disappearing act.

As part of the plan, the three men walked over to the Railway Building from New City and used their keycards to access the eastern door into the south elevator lobby. They moved to the display at the hallway intersection. According to the lights on the board, more than a dozen people were in the building.

They stood and watched the board for another thirty minutes and saw the number of lights slowly turn off until there were only four left on. Ron checked his watch and asked, "Doesn't Hector start his watch at seven?"

Tom nodded, "Yes, I did as you asked and made sure he would be on the watch tonight.

Gene said, "I still don't see what you're going to prove about this with us all here in the building."

Ron replied, "In just a minute, Gene."

A few minutes later, one of the lights winked out as someone left the building on the third-floor walkway. Ron pointed to the board that showed three lights remaining and held up his card. Tom and Gene held up theirs, and everyone agreed they were the final ones in the building.

Ron said, "Okay, guys. This is where we part. Use your keys and leave the building. You know I'm here, and there should be one light on when Hector checks things in less than a half-hour. If I leave, Hector will see no lights, right? You go on down to Don's Diner just across the tracks, and I will meet you there at midnight to show you how it was done."

"The only thing I like about this plan of yours is that it involves a diner," Gene said as he turned to leave.

Ron watched them walk to the doorway and check out. He noted that the light on the board confirmed only one person was in the building. Since it was close to seven o'clock and Hector's arrival, Ron moved quickly once his friends were out of sight. He went to the western door that opened into the main lobby of Railway on the opposite side from where Tom and Gene had left. Looney used his card to open the door. But he did not leave, standing still beside the door until it swung shut again. He walked back to the keycard display, confirmed that it indicated no one was in the building, and then he returned to the west stairwell and went up to the third floor.

Once there, he easily found Abbate's office and used his credit card to force open the Qwikset lock allowing him to enter the office. Ron had observed the door locks of the various offices on his earlier tour and had noted that none of them involved a deadbolt. He also noticed all doors opened into the office spaces rather than into the hallway. This arrangement meant that the cylinder bevel of the knob lock faced toward the hall. Every room in the building was susceptible to being broken into with a credit card.

Ron closed the door and confirmed it was locked. Then he went over to Abbate's desk and did a little work. Afterward, he sat on the floor near the door and waited.

He heard the elevator open and then perceived Hector's keychain rattling as he walked down the hall, checking each door. Ron scooted closer to the wall when the knob to Abbate's office rattled. Hector walked on to the end of the hall, checking the doors, then moved back to the elevators. Ron relaxed and looked at his watch.

When he judged the moment to be right, Ron got up, took care of some business at the desk, and went into the hallway. He closed the door behind himself, assuring that it was locked behind him, and walked as quietly as he could to the elevator bank and then to the eastern stairwell. Ron opened the door a crack and listened intently. When he was certain Hector was not using the stairs, Ron slipped into the stairwell and crept quietly up to the fourth floor.

Again, he listened intently through a small door opening. Hearing no rattling of keys, he again slipped out and into the longitudinal hallway. He found Donaldson's office and was inside in less than a minute, using the credit card. As he had done before, he went to the doctor's desk and took a few minutes to complete some business.

Ron knew from his interview with Hector that the night watchman ate his lunch in the third-floor break room at eleven o'clock. Ron needed to be away from that area before Hector took that break; he had plenty of time. The concern was being seen by Hector. Ron had planned his moves to include using the stairs that Hector didn't use between floors; realizing that Hector used the elevator on his first set of rounds changed that dynamic. Ron remembered that Hector had said he used the stairs between floors but also noted that the night watchman moved slowly both up and down stairs when he was with them. He decided Hector had misled them about his use of the stairs, so he left Donaldson's office, locking the door behind, and moved quickly to the elevator bank. There, he became still and listened. Five minutes later, he heard the elevator motor start. Ron listened as one of the cars went from below him to the fifth floor. That would be Hector, starting his second watch round.

Confident that he had time for his next move, Ron took the stairs to the first floor and walked to the loading dock door area. Directly across from the door to the loading dock was a storage room door. This door also opened easily with Ron's credit card. He entered and found a place to sit and wait. He was glad he had brought his phone and ear buds to pass the time.

Sure enough, at eleven-thirty-five, Ron heard the door to the loading dock open, and he sprang into action. He opened the storage room door, slipped across the hall, and grabbed the loading dock door as it started to close. He could hear Hector's cigarette lighter clicking just a few feet away. Ron held a small cork in his right hand, and, holding the door partially open with his left, he pushed the cork into the aperture on the doorframe where the latch fit. Ron then allowed the door to close, making its usual sounds of heavy metal against metal.

Ron returned to the storage room and sat quietly on the floor. After seven minutes or so, he heard Hector return from outside, listened as the door make its metal closing sound, and caught the sound of Hector's keys rattling as he went back to start another round of his watch. Five minutes later, Ron slipped out and opened the loading dock door. It had not locked on closure because of the cork. He extracted the cork and slowly closed the door, hearing an assuring click as the latch found its usual home in the frame.

After checking his watch again, Ron walked around the building to where he had left his car and, grinning broadly, drove to Don's Diner.

CHAPTER 21

Tom and Gene had secured a corner booth. At twelve-ten, Tom still appeared awake and interested in the surroundings. Gene, on the other hand, looked like he had missed his bedtime hours before. Nonetheless, both men perked up at Looney's appearance. Gene scooted to his right to make room for Ron in the booth.

Tom spoke first, "You told me and Gene you wanted to meet us here to show some major discovery about Railway. We left you there more than four hours ago. What is going on?"

Looney nodded and signaled to the solitary waitress. "Easy, General. I do have something important to show you. But first, I must have a piece of pie and a cup of coffee."

The waitress pulled out her pad as she approached, and Ron repeated, "Piece of apple pie and a cup of coffee, please."

Gene said, "Coffee at this time, huh? It's gonna keep you awake all night."

"Good observation, Gene. You should try it. You look like you're out on your feet." Looney grinned at his partner.

"I'll wake up enough if you actually have something to show us."

"Oh, I do. I should tell you that I wasn't certain it would turn out when I asked you to come." Looney's grin got larger and that brought Gene's eyebrows together.

Gene scowled at his partner, "You mean getting us down here in the middle of the night was chancy? You must think we trust you a lot."

"I was hoping that you trusted me enough. And that the whole thing would work out."

Tom asked, "Well, what is it, then? We're here and you're here and we want to know what's the new finding."

The waitress slipped his pie and coffee in front of Ron, and he indicated with his fork that conversation would have to wait for a bit. He took the pie in five bites and finished the coffee in two long pulls. In between the second and third bites, Ron said, "We have to go back to the hospital."

Gene made a face and commented, "Not only is this a midnight revelation, but it also requires us to go on an excursion, too."

Tom timed his move to Ron's second swallow of coffee. He stood and said, "We're going in my truck." He threw a $10 bill on the table and walked toward the door. Ron and Gene scrambled after him.

As they walked toward the parked vehicle, Ron whispered to Gene, "I've never been in his truck before."

He told Tom they needed to get back into Railway and talk to Hector, so Tom parked in the Railway parking lot and used his card to enter the building from the west. He called Hector from the keycard display area, and the watchman showed up riding an elevator two minutes later.

"What's up, Doc?" he asked, exiting his ride and looking at the three men.

Tom said, "Detective Looney here would like to ask a few questions, Hector."

"Okay."

Ron asked first, "Hector, when you came on duty tonight, how many people were in the building?"

"You mean right then?"

"Yes. When you signed in and started your watch. How many people were in the building?"

"None."

"None?"

"None. There was no lights on."

"Are you aware of anyone entering the building during the night?"

"No, sir, I am not. Never saw any light on at all." Tom and Gene exchanged a sideways glance and then stared at Looney.

Ron nodded and asked everyone to get in the elevator and ride to the fifth floor. They rode in silence, although Ron could tell that Gene had questions. When they arrived on the fifth floor, Ron asked Hector to check Dr. Abbate's office. They all stood at the door as Hector noted the door was locked and used his key to enter.

Ron asked Tom to examine the top of Abbate's desk while he, Ron, stayed near the doorway. Gene went with Tom, and they found an envelope on Abbate's desk addressed to 'Tom Bolling & CPD, Homicide Division'.

Tom held up the envelope and asked Ron, "This it?"

Ron answered, "That's it. Open it and read it aloud, please."

Looking skeptical, Tom opened the envelope and read the note on the piece of paper inside. He shared it with Gene, and they both stared at Ron. Tom, a fan of the Cincinnati Reds, pulled out his phone and opened an app.

Hector looked at Ron and said, "What's in that letter?"

Ron replied, "I was in this office last night, Hector. I snuck in here during your watch and wrote down the score of the baseball game around the same time that Dr. Abbate was killed on that other night."

Tom cleared his throat and, holding the letter carefully in front of him, read, "*I was in this room unseen from 1905 hours to 1935 hours. During that time, the Reds started their game with the Cubs. Cubs got one hit and a walk in the top of the first but no runs. Reds' first batter in the bottom of the first struck out, second batter grounded out to short. That was when I had to leave. Signed Det. R. Looney.* "

Hector wailed, "Why did you do that, sir? That's going to make me look bad. I could lose my job."

"No, Hector, you won't. I'm simply showing how a single night watchman can't cover this building. You'll be fine."

Tom said, "Okay. I get your message. And I checked it against the box score. The game started at seven-oh-five, and you got the events right. So, you were here and hidden from Hector. What's your point?"

Ron turned toward the doorway saying, "My first point is that Hector had no idea I was here. And I was here at the time of the murder."

Out in the hallway, they watched Hector relock the door and then, at Ron's instruction, used the elevator to go down to Dr. Donaldson's office.

They again encountered a locked door, which Hector unlocked, and Tom and Gene found another envelope addressed to them on Donaldson's desk. This letter read:

'I got in here at 1952. I hid on the east stairs after leaving Abbate's office and waited until the time Donaldson left at 1945. Then I came in his office and listened to the game on my phone. I left here at 2130 hours when the game was tied at one, seven and a third innings. Reds new bullpen pitcher was coming in (can't spell his name, starts with an A) with two on and one out. Signed Det. R. Looney.'

After reading this message, Tom and Gene stared at Ron, looking for an explanation. Ron said, "That gave me sufficient time to come in Donaldson's office and put a blood drop on his shoe."

"Okay. But why stick around?" Gene asked.

Ron nodded at Hector and said, "Remember, Hector has no idea I'm here. I can't just go out a door, even if I have a keycard. That would alert Hector and indicate that someone was in the building other than Donaldson."

Tom nodded. "I get that. But where did you go, and how did you get out?"

Ron explained, "I'm going to show you how I got out. But first, I had to get in position and off the third floor before Hector took his lunch down the hall in the break room." Ron looked at Hector, who nodded dispiritedly and said, "Always, about eleven o'clock."

"So, where did you go to get out?" Gene wanted to know.

"Come on. I'll show you." Ron led them to the stairs and down to the first floor, where he headed for the loading dock.

Tom said, "You better not have jimmied the loading dock door. I had that checked after Abbate was killed. No one got out that way."

Ron replied. "Nope. Didn't do that." He stopped in the area, however, and turned to the locked storage door. When Hector started to open it with the Master key, Ron stopped him and said, "Even though you have not asked, somebody has to be wondering how I got in those locked offices, right?" Gene nodded.

Ron took out his credit card and quickly opened the storage room door to everyone's astonishment. Tom said, "This is supposed to be a highly secure place."

Ron said, "Probably was, when it was built. But having the bevel on the cylinder facing out is not secure anymore. But you'll have to turn the doors around to fix it."

Hector said, "I never know this."

Ron indicated that Tom should find the envelope he had left in the storage room. Tom opened the envelope and read, *'I got here just before 2200. Left at 2345. Signed, Det. R. Looney.'*

Gene wanted to know, "So, where were you when you weren't in one of these rooms?"

"On a staircase. I knew Hector's schedule, start at the top and work his way down. I stayed behind him as much as I could."

Hector nodded at Tom, "I didn't know, Doctor Bolling."

Tom made soothing moves with his hands and asked, "How come you're not still stuck in the storage closet, then?"

"This will embarrass Hector, but he let me out."

"I did not!" Hector claimed.

"After Hector eats his lunch, he goes out on the loading dock to have a cigarette," Ron said quietly. Tom and Gene turned to look at the watchman. Hector took a step back and looked at the floor. After a brief moment, Ron said, "Please, Hector. Go do it."

Hector looked at Tom who stared at him and nodded. Hector took a step forward and opened the door to step outside. Before the door closed, Ron grabbed it and stuffed the cork into the opening on the doorframe. He then allowed the door to shut. Almost immediately, Hector used his key to re-enter. The door closed, and Ron said, "Then he goes back to his rounds." He indicated that Hector should move away from the door.

When the area was clear, Ron moved to the door, pushed it open, pulled out the cork, and allowed the door to shut. "Easy to get out after Hector is far away," he said, pocketing the cork.

Tom shook his head, "Damn, I thought we had a secure facility here."

"Oh, it is," Ron replied, "unless someone is intent on using that belief to commit murder and pin it on someone else."

CHAPTER 22

The detectives bypassed the office by agreement and met at the coffee shop near the station the following morning. They agreed extra coffee would be needed that day because of the long night previously. Ron bought Gene's coffee and morning roll, feeling a little guilty for not including his partner in the secrets of how to get in and out of a theoretically locked building.

"You okay?" he asked as they took seats at their favorite table in the back corner.

"Will be after this," Gene said, indicating the morning roll.

They were quiet for a few minutes, each consuming a pastry. Then Gene said, "When did you figure that all out?"

"It came in pieces, mostly," Ron replied. "First thing I noted was the doors into the offices all opened inward. That would put the angle on the cylinder to the outside to hit the striker plate correctly. That's a lock that is never really locked."

"Yeah, I know that. I didn't notice the angle on the cylinder, however. And the rest of it?"

"I watched some of the people leaving the building when we were there with Tom. If a group went through, it would be possible for one person to exit without using their card since the door stayed open for so long. Of course, if they did that the light from their entry would keep burning all night."

"Let me guess. So you figured that if that were true, then someone, by themselves, could likely use their card to open the door as if leaving, but never go through the doorway."

"Exactly. Thus, with a little planning, someone could trick the keycard system to record they had left. Hector would not 'see' that person in the building and all like that."

Gene let his eyebrows go together, "Still, how did you think that Hector would let you out?"

Ron smiled, "Remember I asked you if you noticed anything about him?"

"Yeah, and I didn't."

"I noticed he had a tobacco smell. He is a smoker."

"Okay. Still, so what?"

"There's no smoking in the building, right? So, if he's sticking to the rules, he was going to go outside to smoke at some time in the night. Where he did that was not certain, but I reasoned he wouldn't use one of the keycard entrances. First, that would leave a pattern of 'out then in' on the system, and someone might ask about that. Second, it ran a risk, small but real, that he might be seen by someone coming to the building."

"And that's why you guessed the loading dock."

"Exactly. And then, Tom and Hector just gave me all the reasons in the world to stick with that guess."

"Such as?"

"That door is not keycard controlled. It opens on the rear loading dock where no one is ever around at night, and it has no alarm. Plus it worked on a simple panic bar that I knew I could block."

"You are one tricky detective, Walker Looney."

"And now we know how someone else can get in the building without Hector's knowledge, go to the office and kill Abbate and then get out of the building undetected."

Gene smiled at Ron and said, "Well, yes, we do know all that now. And maybe that can narrow down the possible suspects to everyone who has a keycard."

"Yes, there is that slight downside to the new knowledge. But our initial goal was to see if it was possible that Donaldson was not the killer. I think I just did that."

Gene nodded and added, "I think you may have done more than that, partner."

"What?"

"Well, maybe now someone could begin to think that maybe Abbate was not the primary target. Maybe the real goal was to get Donaldson framed and out of the picture."

Ron stared at Gene, "Are you going back to that idea that someone is interested in Winnie?"

"It is not impossible."

"I'm going to grant you that. She is a fine-looking woman. But Tom tells me she made a huge fuss about his arrest, and it wasn't a fake. You and I have talked with her, and there's no indication she's anything other than the faithful wife. So, where are you getting this idea?"

"I'm not sold on the whole thing being her idea, Ron. I'm saying someone else could be cutting the husband out of the picture with plans to move in later. That's all I'm saying."

"My Grandma, what a devious mind you have!" Looney grinned at Gene.

"Are you certain that I'm wrong?"

"No. But on the percentages, I'm betting against it. However, you do open a Pandora's Box."

"Huh? Do you mean Panera's box?"

"Are you already thinking about food, there's still crumbs from your pastry on your napkin. I guess we do have to consider whether Donaldson was a target or not. Having a clear idea and method for something bad to happen in the Railway Building when there's a single person inside to blame means Donaldson might be the target and Abbate is collateral damage."

"Even though it's my idea, I think it must be a pretty severe situation where murder is collateral damage."

"Agreed. But now you have put it in play."

Food and coffee finished, they started back to the office. They took the back stairs and dodged around Thor's open office door. Once again seated at their desks, Gene said, "One little thing, partner."

"Yeah?"

"Did Donaldson suggest any of these steps or methods about how to circumvent the keycard system to you?"

A moment's pause was followed by, "Nope. Pretty sure not. Why?"

"Just thinking about who your disclosure helps. Donaldson is the only one we can see right now. You have shown that anyone with a keycard could get in the building, appear to leave but actually vanish into the woodwork. That person could come out later, do a dastardly deed and escape without anyone suspecting. What a great lead in to the Some Other Dude Did It defense. But, if he had suggested the manner of deception to you then …"

"Then we might have to consider he was bringing it up to remove suspicion altogether or to get facts into the record for a trial where he could be acquitted if the case went to trial." Ron put a mock frown on for Gene. "You know, if that was his plan, an acquittal in an early trial would keep him from being tried later because of the double-jeopardy thing."

"I'm just saying, Ron."

"Yeah, I know. That's good, Gene. I don't remember him steering me, but I'll think about it.

"Okay. I'd hate to think that we've come all this way, and we're back to the original suspect."

"No siree," Looney said, "as you pointed out earlier, we have more likely gone from a single suspect to eighty."

CHAPTER 23

After more conversation discussing the next steps, they walked back toward the precinct but before they arrived they agreed that a reasonable approach would be a second interview with the accused. They were puzzled by the late revelation of the blood on Donaldson's shoe and now they wondered whether he had enemies with sufficient ardor to make him the real center of attention. As they approached the building, Gene checked his watch and did mental calculations before agreeing to interview Donaldson right then. Ron finally had to say, "C'mon, partner. Sandy will still be there if we get a late lunch. You just had a pastry."

"I know that. But we can't be certain to get our booth if we wait too long."

"If the booth is occupied when we arrive, we will wait for it to be available. Let's go talk to Donaldson."

Once again, as they descended the stairs to the cells, Looney felt the dispiriting air of the place. Puke-colored tile walls, gray concrete floors, and black iron bars did not make an uplifting ambiance. Similarly, half the fluorescent bulbs taken out of the overhead lighting for economic reasons added to the almost medieval atmosphere. It was no wonder prisoners became depressed.

The guard let them in Donaldson's cell. The prisoner heard them coming and talking with the guard and was standing when they entered. "Any good news?" he asked, hopefully.

"That depends," Ron said, indicating for Donaldson to sit on his bunk.

"What do you know about the keycard system at Railway?"

"Uh, not much. I have a card. It allows me to get in whenever I want. I mean there's no time restriction on use."

"What about getting out?" Ron followed up, casually.

"Oh, yeah, the card opens the door for exiting as well."

"Do the cards track individuals?" Ron was still trying to be casual.

"What do you mean?"

"Can we access the system to see who has used their card and what time it was used?" The detail of this question helped Donaldson understand these were not minor issues and questions.

Donaldson looked puzzled at this question, so he slowly said, "I don't know. I think you can put my card in a reader and see when I used it."

"What about any record kept within the system itself?" Ron pushed.

"I don't know anything about that." Donaldson's answer was terse.

"Has anyone ever explained to you how the system works?"

"I don't remember any such explanation. When Security gave me a keycard, they said to keep it away from magnetic cards and that it would cost me $35 to replace it if I lost it." Donaldson decided to keep his answers to a minimum.

Gene asked, "Have you ever left the building without using your card?"

Donaldson frowned and said, "Yeah, once. Several of us were going to a conference in the Main Building, and we all left at the same time. I didn't think anything about it until I tried to get back in."

"What happened then?"

"The door wouldn't open. Security took my card and checked it and said the card indicated that I was still in the building and hadn't left."

Gene looked at Ron and raised his eyebrows. Ron nodded slightly and asked, "Are you aware of anyone trying to trick the system?"

Donaldson suddenly became more excited and eagerly asked, "No, why would we? Does this mean you have found something wrong in the system?"

Ron looked at Gene, who shrugged. Ron turned to Donaldson and said, "I believe we have proved that someone else could have been in the Railway Building that night and not shown up on the keycard system."

"All right! That's good, right? I mean, that's good for me, isn't it? Will that mean I can go home?"

"No. It doesn't mean that. At least, not yet. Remember I said we only showed that something like that could have happened - not that it did. What it does is open up a whole mess of new issues and questions."

"Such as? Doesn't that mean I didn't do it?"

"Look, doctor. The fact that someone else could have been there does not constitute proof that there was another person. Plus, even if they were there, such knowledge does not prove your innocence. Remember the blood drop on your shoe. You will not be going home until we can clear up several things, including some new questions. Have you given any thought to how that blood drop could have gotten on your shoe""

Donaldson slumped onto his bunk, shook his head and then didn't move for a moment. Then, he looked up and asked, "What new questions?"

Gene answered, "Well, if we want to push the idea that someone else was in the building we have to ask, why did they murder Abbate while you were there? Was that an accident or were they specifically timing the murder to frame you? And if we go down that path we have to ask who would want to hurt you in such a fashion? That's one of the new questions."

"Oh, I see." Donaldson's face belied the statement; he did not understand what Gene had implied

Ron pressed, "Can you think of anyone who might want to hurt you that way?"

"You mean enough to kill someone else just to get at me? No, I can't think of anyone." For a moment, Looney thought the doctor was going to laugh at the idea.

"You answered way too fast, there, doc. Take a minute. Try to ignore the murder piece and ask yourself who have you quarreled with who might want to frame you for something big?"

"I can't think of ..." Donaldson stopped in mid-sentence. "No, that's crazy."

"What are you thinking, doc?"

"You've got me thinking crazy, that's what. He wouldn't do anything like that. At least, I don't think he would."

"Who are we talking about, doc?" Gene pushed. "C'mon, man. We're trying to help you here."

"I know, detective. I just ... I don't want to make crazy accusations."

"Right. Just because someone did it to you, no sense in making this all about yourself. Does that make sense to you?" The sarcasm in Gene's voice was clear.

"You're saying fight fire with fire, eh?"

"Well, sort of. Who are you thinking of?"

"I'm thinking of someone who has a grudge against me but I do not think he would do something like kill someone just to get at me." Donaldson leaned back against the wall and crossed his arms.

"Never can tell, doc. Who's the guy and what's the story?"

Donaldson shifted around on the bunk and both Ron and Gene pulled out their note pads. Donaldson took a deep breath and said, "This is silly."

"Talk," Ron said.

After a short pause, Donaldson began, "His name is Terrance Raganathan." He waited for a moment and then spelled the name. "Terrance is a drug rep who works our area …"

Gene jumped in, "A 'drug rep'? What's that?"

"He works for one of the large pharmaceutical companies and he goes to hospitals and doctor's offices to advertise their drugs. He came to New City and put on some luncheons for the housestaff …"

"Who are we talking about there, the housestaff?" Gene wanted to know.

"That's the residents and interns in our training programs."

"The young doctors, right?"

"Yes."

"Okay. Sorry. Go on."

"The drug reps often set up a speaker to come in and push one of their drugs and they get the housestaff to attend the talk by buying them lunch."

Gene nodded, "That would work for me."

"Well, it works for them, too. But once, Terrance didn't have a clinician speaker; he was doing the touting himself."

"And, is that bad?"

"Not necessarily. Most drug reps have a degree in pharmacology, and they know what they're talking about. But their information isn't clinically-based many times, and he was pushing something that I consider wrong."

"What was that?"

"He was telling the housestaff to use a powerful diuretic for patients in heart failure." Donaldson quit trying to be balanced and let his disdain show.

"And that's wrong?"

"Many times it could be. Conventional practice at this time favors using a more gentle drug and adding drugs with a different actions and only moving to the powerful diuretic when others have failed. Jumping straight to a powerful diuretic may have serious side effects."

"And Terrance didn't like your opinion?"

"He not only differed in opinion on the choice of drugs, but he also went so far as to challenge me as interfering in the medical education program of the hospital."

"So, I guess he would be pretty mad at you for that."

"I rather imagine he was even angrier after I went to the Pharmacy Committee and had him removed from the list of approved sponsors of medical education seminars."

"Wow. That does sound like it would piss him off." Gene made an emphatic mark in his notebook.

"I know it did. He called me names and said he would go to the Medical Board about my action. But he didn't. I think someone in his company called him off."

Ron got Donaldson to identify the company Raganathan worked for. Donaldson did not know the man's address or telephone number but suggested that such folks were usually well known to both the chief of staff and the members of the Pharmacy Committee.

In the end, Donaldson shook his head, "I just don't see anyone killing somebody to get at me for that, though. I hate to make an accusation."

Gene commented, "Well, if that's the only guy you've pissed off, I'd say you were way ahead of the two of us. Any chance this drug rep would have a keycard to Railway?"

Donaldson shook his head and started to smile but stopped and got a faraway look in his eye. Ron noticed and said, "What is it, doc?"

"He was not the only one. I just remembered another person upset with me. His name is Dickie Overhart. He's a technician in the surgery department. Runs the heart-lung bypass machine."

"Why is he upset with you, doctor?" Gene asked, his notebook back open.

"It's about his mother. She was a diabetic and had a lot of medical problems, and the final blow was kidney failure. Dickie asked me to accept her on dialysis, and I examined her and talked to her about her condition. She wasn't immediately going to die, but it wouldn't be many months. And I turned her down for dialysis."

"Why did you do that? Can you even do that?"

"Before we start anyone on dialysis, we have to answer two critical questions. The first is, 'does this patient need dialysis?' And we include the near future in answering that question. Mrs. Overhart met the first criteria. She had end-stage kidney disease from her diabetes and would probably require dialysis in the next 3 months. But not immediately."

"Why didn't you accept her to the program, then?"

Donaldson continued as if he had not been interrupted by Gene's question. "The second question we ask is 'will dialysis benefit this person?' And the answer for Mrs. Overhart was no, it would not."

Gene was quite puzzled by this. "Why wouldn't the treatment benefit her? This dialysis is a kind of artificial kidney, isn't it? And if she didn't have good enough kidney function on her own, why wouldn't the treatment be of benefit?"

Donaldson nodded at Gene and explained, "It's a difficult thing to explain, Detective. Mrs. Overhart had severe disease in the blood vessels of her arms and legs that made access there to perform dialysis in our usual way impossible. We would have had to use a plastic access tube stuck under her collarbone; such devices have significant infection problems and often get clotted up.. Her diabetes was so uncontrolled she probably would have had an infection in her bloodstream within a week or two."

"But you could have tried, right?"

"Oh yes, and we would have made some money from trying, too. But that was not in Mrs. Overhart's best interests. She wanted to stay at home."

"So, what happened?"

"Dickie convinced his father to take her elsewhere. They tried to put in an access in her arm, and it clotted and got infected, and she lost three fingers. They didn't want to try the collarbone access, so they put her on peritoneal dialysis and admitted her to the hospital on bed rest. She got bedsores and then developed an infection in her belly and died a month later."

"But this Dickie is still upset with you?"

"Yes. I understand Dickie says his mother would not have died if she had been at New City."

"Okay. We'll talk to Dickie. Does he have a keycard to Railway?"

"I don't know."

Ron turned back from the door to the cell to ask, "Have you gotten an attorney, yet?"

Donaldson said, "Oh, yes. Tom found a criminal lawyer for me and we met yesterday. He's very encouraging but he doesn't know what you told just me about the keycard system."

"You can tell him, but ask him to keep that under wraps for a while. You understand that Gene and I are on the other side of this business. I can't go telling your lawyer anything."

"I understand. Thanks for telling me." Donaldson with a degree of genuine relief as the detectives left his cell.

CHAPTER 24

Their lunchtime did turn out to be well past the noon hour when they arrived at the café. The detectives' favorite booth was empty, and they slid into the seats almost unnoticed. Sandy did see them, however, and was soon at the table taking orders.

"I thought maybe you went somewhere else today," she said, teasing Gene.

Ron said, "He would not allow me to go anywhere else, Sandy. If I tried that, he would be arrested."

"Arrested?" she asked. "What in the world for?"

"For shooting me," Ron said. She giggled and left with their orders. And, per routine, they watched her walk back to the kitchen.

As they waited for their food, Ron asked his partner, "What do you think of these two new leads?"

"Not much. Well, maybe the drug dealer has a big enough motive. Both of them sound rather weak to me."

"I thought the same. Tom certainly likes this guy Donaldson so maybe he doesn't make a lot of enemies."

"I'm still suspicious that he is keeping something from us," Gene sipped his drink.

"Huh. I guess Donaldson could be hiding something. I'm not sure why he would do that, though. Seems like he trusts us, and it's not in his interest to keep something back if it would clear him."

"Yeah. But maybe whatever it is would be a major embarrassment. He might hide that until all other avenues have been closed."

They didn't talk much while they ate. As Ron finished his sandwich and pushed the plate to the center of the table, he commented, "Let's hold off on coffee until we get to New City."

"You bet. I'm sure that Nick is waiting for us."

A casual observer would have concluded that Nick was waiting for them. He waved as they entered the lobby and made a motion like drinking from a cup. They both nodded, and Nick turned to the machines with a big grin. By prior agreement, Gene went to the cashier and paid for their drinks while Ron stood at the end of the counter to collect them. But Nick, breaking habit, stepped out from behind the counter carrying their cups and indicated they should follow him to the seating area.

He handed each man a cup and said, "You wanted me to tell you if something came up, right?"

Ron nodded.

"Well, there was a guy in here yesterday, one of the representatives, and he said something I thought you'd like to know."

"What was that?" Gene probed.

"He ordered a latte, and I was steaming the milk. He came down where I was and was talking to one of the residents. He said something like 'Locked him up for murder?' and the resident said 'yes' so this guy goes on and says 'Right thing, that. Proper comeuppance, I say." Nick delivered these lines with his best imitation of an English accent.

Gene grinned at the accent and asked, "Was he British?"

Ron said, "What's this guy's name?"

Nick said, "British schooling, I think. In India." He turned to Ron and said, "His name is Terrance Raganathan. He is a pharmacy representative, and he's around here a lot. I had no idea he was on the outs with Donaldson."

Ron nodded, "That's good information, Nick. Thanks a lot. Do you know where this guy is now?"

"No. He's here often like I said. I see him in the lobby. I think he buys a coffee every time he's here, and I haven't seen him today."

Ron looked at Gene and then said to Nick, "Well, thank you for that information. We will certainly look this guy up and see why he's so sure that Donaldson got what's coming to him."

Nick shook their hands and went back to the kiosk. Gene said, "When it rains, it pours."

"That would be a more appropriate comment if Nick had given us a name we didn't already have."

"More reason for us to find this guy, though."

Tom was not in his office. Mary Brighthouse looked up when they came to her desk and asked, "Was he expecting you?"

"No, ma'am," Ron said. "We were stopping by to see someone here and thought maybe he could give us information about where to find one of the drug representatives."

Mary smiled at him, "We keep a list of all frequent outside visitors and their contact information. Maybe I can help you."

"That would be first rate! This man's name is Raganathan. I imagine there's not a lot of people around with that name."

"No, there's not," Mary said, shuffling through the pages of a large three-ring binder. "Here he is."

She placed the book on the counter in front of her desk, and Ron copied the information into his notebook. Then he asked, "Where is the surgical department? We want to talk to Dickie Overhart."

They followed Mary's direction and came to the office of the department chair, Dr. Samuel Newberry. Newberry's secretary was very helpful; she located Dickie and asked him to come to the office, and she arranged a room for the interview.

Dickie Overhart was a skinny thirty-year-old with blond hair in a buzz cut, sunken dark brown eyes, and a set of narrow lips that appeared set in a consistent frown. He was wearing green scrubs and running shoes. Ron indicated he should sit and then introduced himself and Gene.

Overhart asked, "What's this all about? Two homicide detectives don't pull me away from machine maintenance every day."

"Mr. Overhart, do you have a keycard to the Railway Building?"

"Huh? No. Why?'

"Do you often go to the Railway Building?"

"No. All my work is here in the operating room. I've been in that building maybe twice since I started working here. Why?"

"We are interested in your movements and whereabouts on the evening Dr. Alexander Abbate was killed."

"What? You're not serious. You think I killed him?"

"Mr. Overhart, please answer the question. Where were you that evening between six and ten PM?"

"Oh man, I don't know. Let me see. Are you serious?"

"We are very serious, Mr. Overhart," Gene said.

"Stop with the Mr. Overhart stuff, will you? That's my Dad. I'm Dickie."

"All right, Dickie. Where were you between six and ten PM the night Alexander Abbate was killed?"

"I think I was at home."

"Can someone corroborate that?"

"What? You mean like an alibi?"

"Was anyone else there with you?"

Dickie paused for a moment, then a small grin crept onto his pale lips. "Yeah, someone was there with me. My son."

Suspecting something fishy about this support for his alibi, Ron asked, "Can your son support your story that you were at home during that time?"

The grin got larger. "Nah, not really. He slept most of the time. Plus, he's only six months old. His vocabulary is limited."

"You were home alone, caring for your six-month-old son during the period from six to ten PM that evening?"

"Yeah. I remember now. My wife was at a meeting, and I was there with the kid. Heard about Abbate the next morning."

"Can your wife support your story?"

Dickie sat up and leaned forward. "Look here, I answered your questions. You tell me what's going on. Yes, Julie can tell you where I was, but I want to know why all these questions?"

"Did you have any hard feelings toward Dr. Abbate?" Ron asked conversationally.

"What? Dr. Abbate? No. He took care of my aunt. I liked him."

Without indicating that this was news to them, Gene leaned in and said, "Tell me about that."

It was apparent that Dickie had told this story before. His voice became steadier; he didn't pause to consider what he was saying. The story just flowed out. Five years previously, shortly after Dickie came to work at New City, his mother's sister was diagnosed with non-Hodgkin's lymphoma, Stage 3. When Dickie mentioned this at work, several others in the department recommended a referral to Dr.

Abbate; he was among the best in the city. Abbate saw her and made a treatment plan of outpatient chemotherapy infusions every three weeks throughout the summer. She gets a scan every year and has remained free of disease. Abbate recently told her she was a 'five-year survivor' and could consider herself cured.

The story had obvious emotion behind it, and neither Gene nor Ron doubted Dickie's gratitude to Abbate. They watched him for a moment after he finished the tale of his aunt's treatment and cure. Then Ron asked, "How about Dr. Donaldson? Do you feel as positive and friendly toward him?"

Dickie's face changed completely. In a heartbeat, his face hardened, his lips pulled back, and he asked, "What about him?"

"We have heard that you are somewhat at odds with him. Is that right?"

Dickie nodded, and when prompted, said, "Yeah. I don't like him. He didn't help my mother."

This time Dickie delivered the story with more emotion and with bursts and pauses in the narrative. The story about his diabetic mother and her kidney disease was less detailed than what the detectives had heard from Donaldson. And the description was more slanted toward a view that Donaldson should have helped avoid all the problems that occurred at the other hospital.

"Do you blame Dr. Donaldson for the problems your mother had?" Ron asked.

"Yeah. Well, mostly. I wanted Donaldson to take care of her and put her on dialysis, and he wouldn't. He said it would end up losing her fingers and having a terrible infection."

"Sounds like he was right," Gene added.

After a pause, Dickie shrugged and said, "Yeah, I guess so."

"But you've been very upset with Dr. Donaldson, haven't you?"

"Yeah, sure. Of course, I have. I lost my mother."

Ron looked at Gene, who shook his head.

"All right, then, Mr. Over …Dickie. That's all the questions we have for you. You may go," Ron said, standing and offering his hand. Dickie Overhart got up and took the offered hand briefly, and left.

Ron looked at Gene and commented, "Not exactly a criminal mastermind, is he?"

Gene said, "No access that we know of, a wobbly motive and a strong reason not to be killing Abbate. Not our best suspect."

Ron said, "Yeah, but he's also got a weak alibi. And a weak handshake."

CHAPTER 25

Rather than go back to the office, Gene suggested they stop at the coffee shop to discuss their Knowns and Unknowns. Ron agreed they needed to have that discussion, and he certainly didn't want to get coffee in the break room.

With their respective cups, Gene started the discussion with, "I'd say our knowns are few but important in the broad scheme of things. For instance, we know that Donaldson was in the building when the murder occurred, and ..."

"Hold on," Ron said, stopping Gene. "We don't know that at all, partner. I submit that it is most likely that someone set the time on that watch to indicate Donaldson was in the building. But the murder and the watch setting could have happened at any time."

Gene paused and nodded, "Yeah, right. Okay, I'll start all over. We know that Donaldson was in the building the night of the murder." He looked expectantly at Looney, who nodded and indicated he should go on.

Gene took a sip of his coffee and went on, "And you have shown how someone else could have been in the building and not left a trace on the keycard system." Looney nodded again.

Gene hesitated and then said, "We may have reason to suspect that the circumstantial evidence was planted, but we have no suspect to blame for that." Looney made a slight nod and bowed his head.

"We now have two names of people that may have had a grudge against Donaldson, but we have to stretch things to believe they would murder Abbate to frame Donaldson. I don't like where this is all going, Ron."

Looney replied, "No, I don't either, Gene. I think we are off the main road, slipping and sliding around on these muddy side roads. We may have created our diversion by looking for motives against Donaldson. We have to run those down, but our need, as you said, is to refocus on motives against Abbate."

"Okay. That makes our Knowns list down to Donaldson was in the building that night and possibly so was someone else. Not particularly helpful."

"Well, I think that person you call someone else was a keycard holder. And that person likely was in the Railway Building that day."

"That doesn't fit Dickie Overhart."

"Nope. But he has a weak alibi and doesn't like Donaldson. We need to run down his alibi. We need to talk to his wife."

"Okay, that's one thing on the To-Do List. What about this Raggy guy?"

"Raganathan. We certainly need to interview him, too. I have his telephone number. I can get him in to the station for an interview."

"What about Dickie's wife? He said she's a teacher."

"Right. So, she ought to be at home by now. Let's go by there as soon as I get Raganathan scheduled." He pulled out his notebook and phone and dialed the number Mary had given him. The call was answered after three rings.

"Hello?" came the slight British accent.

"Mr. Raganathan?"

"Speaking."

"Sir, my name is Ron Looney. I am a detective in the Homicide Division, and I am investigating the murder of Dr. Alexander Abbate."

"I thought you people had already arrested the culprit."

"There are some loose ends, sir. Would you please come to the station downtown to help us clear up a few things?"

"I'm afraid I have no information that would assist you, Detective."

"We believe you can add some substance to the circumstances, sir. Please come to the station at ten o'clock in the morning. Ask for me, Detective Looney, and we can clear these things up promptly."

"Tomorrow? Well, that's not convenient. I have a meeting scheduled and …"

"Tomorrow morning at ten, Mr. Raganathan. If you are not there on time, I will issue a subpoena for your arrest."

There was a slight pause on the other end of the line, then, "Right. Ten o'clock." Both men disconnected.

Gene said, "You're playing hardball quite early in this interview aren't you?"

"It seemed necessary. He was resisting."

"Maybe the school teacher will be more accommodating."

Julia Overhart was a slim thirty-something brunette wearing a plain straight polka dot dress and house shoes. She met them at the door and explained that Dickie was still at the hospital and the baby was asleep.

"I just picked him up from the daycare and fed him," she explained. "He will probably sleep for a couple of hours now."

Ron said, "I'm sure we won't take long, Mrs. Overhart."

"Okay," she said, leading them to the living area and indicating they should take a seat. "Would you like something to drink? Coffee?"

"No, thanks, ma'am, we won't be long."

She sat across the coffee table from them, folded her hands in her lap, and looked at Ron expectantly.

Ron spoke, "Ma'am, as we explained at the door, we are investigating the death of Dr. Alexander Abbate at New City Hospital."

"Yes, that was terrible."

"What we need to know right now is where was your husband that night?"

"What? Dickie? You think he had something to do with that?"

"Ma'am, as we said, we are just collecting information right now."

"But why are you looking at Dickie?"

Ron ignored her question and continued on his line of questioning. "Do you know where he was that night, ma'am?"

"Well, kinda," she said. "He was babysitting here with Georgie."

"Where were you?"

"I had a parent-teacher meeting at school. There were two meetings, actually. And Dickie stayed in that night and took care of Georgie."

"How do you know that?" Gene asked in a calm voice.

"Well, where else would he be? He was taking care of the baby."

"Could he have taken the baby and left for a while?"

"No. That's completely crazy! Taking the baby means taking all those diapers and a bottle and all that."

"I see," said Ron, also trying to calm the conversation. "Did you call him at any time during the evening?" Ron remembered how his wife, Meg, called the babysitter two or three times any night she was away from her infant children.

"Uh, yes. I called him between meetings to see how things were going."

"And, what did he say?"

"Uh, well, he didn't say. I mean, he didn't answer. He told me later that he was asleep and turned the ringer off."

Ron looked at Gene. Gene asked, "What time was that?"

"Probably a quarter to nine."

"What time did you get home that evening?"

"I think it was about half-past ten. My second meeting was short."

"What was Dickie doing when you got home?"

"He was asleep on the couch. I woke him to talk about not answering the phone, and he told me he had been asleep."

"And Georgie? How was he?"

"Perfectly fine. Dickie told me we didn't have to watch him sleep."

"But you were worried?"

"Well, I know about those crib deaths, and, yes, I worry."

"But he was fine that night?"

"Yes. Slept through a feeding, it seems. He woke up about a half-hour after I got home and needed feeding then."

"Had Dickie fed him anything while you were gone?"

"No. They both slept, it seems. Why are you asking about this?"

"As I said, we are tying up some loose ends, that's all. And I think we have everything we need. Thank you for your time," Ron said, standing up.

She ushered them to the door and said good night. They walked to Ron's car in silence, but once Gene had fastened his seat belt, he asked, "Could he have done it?"

"Seems unlikely," Ron said, starting the car. "I doubt he could have taken the kid."

"Well, think of this, maybe he didn't take the kid. Left him at home and maybe gave him something to make him sleep."

"Gene, while I'd have to give that a 'possible', it doesn't ring very true. First, they're worried about crib death. Second, I don't know if he could have gotten out of the building that early. I'm sure that Hector goes out for a smoke more often than just at eleven-thirty, but I don't know when those times occur. Dickie would be lucky to use that way to get out early."

"Okay, but maybe he was lucky,"

"Remember, partner, he would also have to be lucky to find a way to get into the building, too. He doesn't have a keycard."

"Hmmm. That's a hard one to get over."

"Well, you can keep worrying about that. I see a weak alibi but also a weak motive. I'm just glad you're not complaining about something in my car."

"I wasn't going to mention it, but I think this seat belt has been tampered with. Have you noticed? It's too short."

CHAPTER 26

Terrance Raganathan appeared at the office right on time. He was five foot, six inches in height and about 130 pounds, and dressed in a three-piece suit with shiny shoes and a handkerchief in his breast pocket. His skin had the café-au-lait coloration of the subcontinent, and the expected black hair was slicked down on his head. He was clean-shaven, and his most prominent feature was the open expression on his face. Coupled with his engaging smile, that expression created a feeling of friendliness from first contact.

Ron was engaged with the smile and the friendliness, pleased that the man had decided not to bring a hard pucker to the interview room. He asked, "Would you like something to drink? Coffee?"

"No, thanks. I had a cup on the way over here. I'm fine."

After introducing himself and Gene, Ron said, "As I told you yesterday on the telephone, we are still investigating the murder of Dr. Abbate, and we believe there are some circumstances you could help us clear up."

"Yes, that's what I heard you say. What can I tell you? I wasn't there."

"Well, that certainly clears that up very nicely," Ron said, with a broad smile. "But there are a few other things, too. For instance, where were you around seven that particular evening?"

Raganathan cocked his head slightly and, still smiling, asked, "When was that again?"

Gene answered, "Ten days ago. Between seven and eight that evening."

Raganathan smiled directly at Gene, "That was a Thursday, as I recall. Thursday evenings, I have a set appointment to play poker with some friends."

"And you will give us their names so we can validate your presence at the game, right?"

"I will not be giving you their names. I do not know the names of most people in the game. There is commonly a different set of people each Thursday night. I imagine there are only one or two people at the usual game that I have ever seen before. Even then, all I know are first names or nicknames. Certainly, I do not know telephone numbers or addresses."

Gene pressed, "That's an interesting game. Regular time, irregular attendance, and no name exchange. Perhaps you are aware, but that sounds very much like an illegal gambling activity."

Raganathan shrugged, "I know nothing of the sort. It's just a poker game arranged by an acquaintance."

Ron pulled out his pen and pad, "And the name of this acquaintance?"

Raganathan looked at Ron, then broke the eye contact and looked around the room as if seeking the way out. After several seconds, he said, "Sid."

"Last name?"

"Don't know. He's just Sid."

"Uh-huh. Do you meet 'Sid' or does he send a limo around to pick you up?"

"It's not like that, detective. Honestly. I go to him, or rather to his place."

Ron put his pen down and stopped smiling. "Are we going to have to pull this out of you, or are you going to cooperate?"

"I'm thinking about my options."

"You don't have many options here. You can tell me where 'Sid' runs this game, or you can spend some time in our cells downstairs for obstruction of justice."

"Obstruction of justice. What a phrase. Sounds like that would give me far more credit than is appropriate for just failing to give you an address. What do you need to talk to Sid about anyway?"

Both detectives sat back in their chairs, looking puzzled. Ron asked, "Have you not been paying attention, sir? We want to check out your alibi for the night of the murder of Dr. Alexander Abbate."

"Alibi? Me? I didn't kill him."

"So you said. We will want some verification of that assertion. Where do you meet 'Sid'?"

"Wait a minute here. I have no reason whatsoever to kill Dr. Abbate."

"What about framing Dr. Donaldson? You got any reason to do that?"

A pause, then, "I don't like Jim Donaldson. He has messed with my reputation in the hospital. But that's no reason to kill somebody. Especially not somebody I hardly know."

Gene pressed on this point, "Why not? You were overheard saying that the arrest of Donaldson was a 'right thing'. That seems to us as a motive enough."

"Well, it's not. I didn't killAbbate. I wouldn't do that under any circumstance. I told you, I was playing poker."

"You didn't tell us where or with whom you were playing poker. Therefore, we can't check your story and, frankly, in a murder case like this one, we don't trust anybody. We check everything and everybody. So, now, where is this game 'Sid' runs?"

Raganathan frowned. "If I tell you, I probably won't be allowed in the game again."

"Again, that sounds like an illegal activity."

"Well, of course, it is. That's why I am hesitant about telling you its location."

"Then you will have no alibi for the time of the murder and we will have to start a much more thorough investigation into your activities." Ron turned to Gene and asked, "Should we start first with interrogating his neighbors or going to his company and explaining our concerns to his co-workers and supervisor?"

Raganathan said, "Oh, come on."

Gene allowed, "Neighbors, I think. They probably have an idea about things that go on in his home."

"All right, cut it out!"

"Just doing our job," Ron said.

"Look, if I tell you can you check it out without, you know …"

"Without letting them know who disclosed their location? Of course not. You may not be able to go there and gamble anymore, but you'll be out of jail and still employed. If your alibi holds, that is." Ron was having a good time with this press.

Raganathan looked at his shoes for a long moment and then nodded dispiritedly, "Sid runs a game twice a week out of his arcade downtown."

"Address?"

An hour later, sitting at their desks, Gene said, "You know, that was a little bit of fun. Hassling that stiff-necked self-absorbed guy. Twice I thought he was going to ask to make a run to the toilet."

Ron nodded, "I agree. I don't mind giving guys like that a little what-for. Now we need to decide whether we're going to tell the boys over in the federal building about this den of iniquity we have uncovered."

"Why would we do that?" Gene wanted to know. "They never tell us anything except to back off."

"Yeah. I agree. This is clearly a local level problem. It's too small to interest the Feds."

"Speaking of small …" Gene let the sentence hang in the air.

"Are you referring to the size of the pastry you had this morning?"

"I am not. I am suggesting how small the return, in this case, is from spinning around looking into people who might hate Donaldson enough to kill Abbate, just to get Donaldson framed for it."

"Gene, you and I have the same opinion about that. We need to get some real probabilities to work on."

"And not spend time on these peripherals."

"And not spend time on these peripherals. At least not after we've cleared up the alibis for Raganathan and Overhart."

"How're we going to do that? We can't question Dickie's baby, and it is unlikely we will get a straight answer from this 'Sid' person if we ever can find him."

"We'll have to think on both those questions, partner. Something will turn up. I think I know how to leverage 'Sid', however. The first question is can we find him?"

CHAPTER 27

They went back to New City and took advantage of their schedule to stop by the Green Bean kiosk to thank Nick for his tip. They smiled nicely when he asked if they wanted their 'usual' coffees. Then, well supplied with a Red Eye each, they dropped in to see Tom Bolling.

Mary looked up as they entered and cocked her head. Ron understood the unasked question and said, "No, we didn't call for an appointment."

She smiled and waved them on. Tom answered the knock on his door; soon the three of them were planning their next steps.

Ron explained, "As I said before, Tom, we will need to do the usual detective stuff, talk to all the people and things like that while you're looking into the medical aspects of Dr. Abbate's activity in the clinic and the hospital. Can you give us the big picture on his work?"

Tom explained that Alexander Abbate had been recruited to New City several years before he became chief of staff. Abbate was a graduate of SUNY Upstate Medical College and did his post-graduate training at the Cleveland Clinic. After completing his residency and fellowship, Abbate opened a practice in Akron. Four years afterward, he was recruited to Cincinnati and New City Hospital to develop the hematology and oncology program for Southwest Ohio Medical School. As an academician, Alex Abbate was outstanding. Initially, he obtained funding for research on the molecular abnormalities associated with sickle cell disease but soon became a noted expert in treatment of certain solid tumors. In each of those instances, he quickly recruited a younger colleague and slowly gave the developed program to the associate. He continued to refine his tumor interest and became one of the state's experts regarding lymphomas.

More than seven years ago, Abbate joined a group of scientific oncologists in a national cooperative study on patients with non-Hodgkin's lymphoma. The multiple ground-breaking papers from this group helped propel Alex to a full professorship at the Medical School. In the last two years, he expanded his research funding with grants from the National Institutes of Health to study Hodgkin's and other rare forms of lymphomas.

Tom said that Alex Abbate was a national treasure for his knowledge and research ideas about lymphomas. At the same time, he was not skilled in teaching medical students. His 'explanations' of diagnostic reasoning were circuitous at best; students and residents did not seek him to discuss cases. He was meticulous in his medical documentation, often keeping two sets of records, one for the clinical record, and one for his research notations and thoughts. He had a wheeled walker in his office for use at clinic time. He would put an old wooden desk drawer in the walker seat to hold all the research files on the patients scheduled for the clinic that day. When he had finished examining a patient, reviewed their laboratory results, and discussed everything with the residents, Alex would make a lengthy note in the electronic record and then put a handwritten note in the research chart before moving to the next patient.

As previously noted, Abbate used Thursday evening to review the research records and update the major report forms for the grants he held. His habit of documentation and entering research findings into his electronic databases was well known throughout New City.

As far as personnel in the department were concerned, there were three other physician staff and the nursing staff of the chemotherapy infusion unit. Tom was not aware of any departmental friction among the faculty physicians, but he noted to Ron and Gene that he had been wrong about that once before. The nursing staff in the infusion unit was notable for its lack of turnover. Tom took that as an indication of a good working relationship between the doctors and the nurses.

Tom's last point was that he had reviewed all cases of lawsuits against the hospital in the past five years and had found none that involved Abbate or the infusion unit.

"Wow," Gene said as he threw away his cup, "I personally know more people that should be killed than this guy."

Ron pushed, "Are we straight about you and Dr. Song looking over the medical care pieces? Gene and I will take the personal approach."

"Yes," Tom said, "I've asked Beverly to pull the cases from the last two years from Abbate's clinic activity, consultations, and research enrollment. Monica and I have set aside an afternoon to get the review started."

Howard Kindall, associate chief of the hematology-oncology division, was a bright-eyed, blond-haired athletic man. He was five foot eleven, 175 pounds, with wide shoulders and a deep chest. He wore round-rimmed black-framed glasses that he frequently removed, examined, and then put back on. He sat slumped in a conference room chair when Ron and Gene entered. He looked up and asked, "Is this going to take long? I have several patients to see."

Ron replied cautiously, "I don't think we'll be long, Dr. Kindall. We have only a few questions about Dr. Abbate and how he got along with everyone."

"Oh, looking for the proverbial enemies list, eh?"

"Is there such a list?" Ron asked.

"Well, not to my knowledge. Alex was not the type to make a lot of friends. He was a quiet guy, sorta intense, I guess you'd say. That might have given some people the idea that he was unfriendly, but I don't think that would make them his enemy."

"Do you know of anyone that would want him 'out of the way'?

"Interesting phrasing there, Detective. I think that question is aimed at me, the next in line, as it were."

"Did you?" asked Gene.

"Did I what?"

"Want him out of the way?"

"Absolutely not. I wouldn't call Alex one of my close friends, but he was a friend. More than a friend, he was a mentor. He recruited me here straight out of my fellowship, and part of what he promised me was support in my career. He allowed me to take over a highly productive research program and clinical care effort for patients with sickle cell. He also continued to give me advice and counsel whenever I asked. If you are looking for who will benefit from his death, it will not be me; I'm likely to lose the most."

"Were there others who felt differently about him? Maybe someone jealous of his success?"

After a short pause, Kindall said, "I don't know of anyone in that category."

Ron handed Kindall a card, "Here's my contact information. If you happen to think of something that might help us, please give me a call."

Kindall took the card and nodded to the detectives as he left.

Jeremy Beason was five foot seven, 150 pounds, and dark black-skinned with short cut black hair. His eyes were also dark and seemed to have a light burning behind them. Clean-shaven, without glasses, he also appeared to have no nervous mannerisms. He came into the conference room after Kindall left, exhibiting no self-consciousness. He walked directly to Gene, who happened to be closest to the door, and stuck out his hand, "I'm Jeremy Beason, director of the solid tumor program. I understand you want to talk about Dr. Abbate."

Gene said, "I'm Detective Gene Novalchek, and this is my partner, Detective Ron Looney. Yes, we are trying to find out why Dr. Abbate was murdered. Do you know why?"

Beason made a slight shrug with his shoulders and a shake of his head, "I'm afraid not. Alex was not big on close personal relationships, good or bad. He was good to all of us in the division, and his patients loved him. I can't think of anyone who would have hated him enough to kill him, though."

"Do you think Dr. Kindall might have wanted him dead so he could become the leader of the division?"

"Howie? No way. We all know that wouldn't happen. Howie becoming chair of the division, I mean. That's not what is generally done here at SWOMS and New City. There would be a national search, and the next hire will probably be from another medical school."

"Huh," Ron offered. "How does that make you feel? Getting passed over like that?"

"Hey, we understand the rules. Alex was helping us build our careers so someday we would be recruited by someone else. Besides, knowing there wasn't going to be an internal candidate meant we weren't competing with each other."

"Huh." Gene offered. Ron looked at him, but Gene just shrugged.

"If it's not someone in the division, who do you think would have reason to kill Dr. Abbate?"

"Beats me. Bea and I talked about that yesterday. We have no idea."

"Bea?"

"Beatrice. The other staff physician in the division."

"How did Dr. Abbate treat you?"

"Is that a loaded question?"

"It was not. Why would you think so?"

"Because I'm black. Many people think I got this position because of some diversity action."

"Was that true?"

"Of course not. At least, I hope not. It never seemed that way. Alex made a hard push to recruit me here, and after I came, we had long discussions about my career. He wondered if I felt like the sickle cell program should be mine to run instead of Howie."

"Why?"

"Again, because I'm black and sickle cell disease affects mostly black individuals. But, I said I didn't think that and did not want to be a disrupter in the division. So he offered me the solid tumor program instead. That's a seriously bigger deal than the sickle cell program."

"So you don't have resentment toward Dr. Abbate?"

"Absolutely not. I'm going to be the big loser here. I have no backup on the solid tumor program with him gone. The day-to-day care piece will be full-time, and that means the research program will suffer. And that's my ticket for academic advancement. To fracture a quote from John Donne, Alex Abbate's death diminishes me."

"Can you think of anyone who might want him dead?"

"No, sir, I cannot."

Ron did his thing with the business card and asked Beason to give him a call if he thought of anything in the future.

Beatrice Mullinax was not waiting around for her interview. The division secretary paged her, and she arrived a few minutes later. Bea had her stethoscope around her neck and appeared the rushed but precise and busy physician. Her brown curly hair was swept back into a ponytail, and her slightly freckled face was open and inquiring. Ron noted she was wearing sensible shoes, a pair of silver-colored ABEO Discovery running shoes. She smiled politely at the detectives and introduced herself and "Bea Mullinax, Assistant Professor."

Gene decided to cut to the chase and asked directly, "Did you kill Dr. Abbate?"

She appeared puzzled by his question and answered promptly, "Of course not. Who said I did?"

Ron held up his hand, "No one has accused you. My partner is sometimes too direct in his questioning. But, now that we are assured of your innocence, who do you think might have killed him?"

"Not a clue," she replied. "Jerry and I talked that over yesterday and neither of us has the faintest idea."

"How did Dr. Abbate get along with people?" Gene asked.

She made a slight upward gesture with her eyebrows and said, "Well, there were probably three ways. For his patients he was 'all in', he gave them all the time they needed, day or night, and they loved him. For the three of us, he was a mentor, advisor, and counselor. At least during the regular work hours. That was kinda the way he was with the unit nurses, too. Patient, listening, and coaching when needed. Everybody else got the 'I'm busy' attitude and body language."

"Anybody get angry about that treatment?"

"Again, not that I know of." She fixed the two detectives individually with wide eyes for a moment each and then pointedly looked at her watch.

Ron caught the hint and said, "Thank you, Dr. Mullinax. Here's my card. Please call me if you think of anything else."

Bea took the card, looked at it, nodded, and left the room.

Gene looked at Ron and said, "Rocky's looking smarter and smarter all the time."

CHAPTER 28

The nurses in the chemotherapy infusion unit agreed to meet briefly with Ron and Gene as a group during their lunch period. Without much discussion, the detectives found their way back into the lobby and over to the Green Bean kiosk. Several other people had the same thought about getting their coffee around that time of day. The detectives were slow in getting through the line, asking for their 'usual' drink, a Red Eye, and paying before moving to the stand where sugar and cream were available.

Gene asked, "Do you know where we're going?"

Ron said, "I have the room number. It's up in the tower. I doubt we will need Waze to find it. C'mon." He headed for the elevators. After a short wait, they got into an elevator cab holding several young people in green scrubs and white coats, also holding cups of Green Bean coffee.

One of the white coat wearers said, "I'm just saying, I've never seen that much blood in a belly before."

Another one said, "Harry, we'll talk about it later." This comment was accompanied by a head gesture indicating the presence of people on the elevator wearing civilian clothes.

Another white coat noted, "That's not saying much, Harry. You don't have even a full year of experience yet."

Harry made some gesture toward the second speaker and scrunched back against the wall of the elevator.

On the third floor, Ron and Gene exited, and each pointed simultaneously at the sign on the wall indicating the direction in which they could find the Chemotherapy Infusion Unit.

The unit was part of the most recent construction of New City, the Medical Tower. Its location on the third floor provided a panoramic view of the Interstate to the east of the tower. The unit had eight treatment areas, or 'chairs'. Each set in a small three-sided cubicle facing the central nursing station. The cubicle could be closed to observation with a curtain on the fourth side. The treatment chair was a large, comfortable, and adjustable lounger, and the cubicle had ample space around the chair for various medical machines and intravenous poles.

When Ron and Gene arrived and were allowed into the infusion unit, nurses were completing their treatments on five patients in the second shift of the day. Many patients had treatment schedules that required less than six hours for infusion. Two patients were quietly resting in their chairs, not yet finished with their treatment. The detectives were impressed with the cleanliness and brightness of the unit. There was little to no clutter on the nurses' desktops and all machinery was against the wall, leaving a broad, open walk space around the central nurses' station. The high windows allowed sunlight into the room to hit the yellow and off-white walls and reflect around the unit brightening everywhere.

Gene looked around and said, "Do you think we could get the decorator from here to do something in the Dick Pen?"

Ron laughed at the idea, and said, "Of course not. Too much light and airiness in our work area and we'd never get out enough to solve anything."

"Yeah, but I'd like to work in an area like this. Lots of space to walk around."

"And close to the Green Bean and Nick's 'usual, too."

"Right. So, can you explain why our work area is so dark and dismal? Why are great things expected of us when our work area is crowded and oppressive?"

"Gene, let's hold off on the metaphysical questions for right now. We have a job to do." He recognized the head nurse from her badge and introduced himself and Gene. The head nurse of the unit, Lena Wilmette, had arranged some cross cover in the unit for the shift of patients and began to herd the unit nurses down a short hallway. Within three minutes she had assembled the unit nurses in a nearby conference room.

Lena introduced the detectives and told them each of the nurses' names as the interview began. Ron explained, "We are continuing the investigation of the murder of Dr. Abbate. I know you are aware that an arrest was made, but we are examining the strength of that case. Let me start by asking whether any of you are aware of any circumstance where a patient or a family member exhibited anger toward Dr. Abbate."

The nurses looked at each other and exhibited a gaggle of puzzled looks before one spoke up, "Everybody loved Dr. Abbate. He explained how the drugs worked to the patients, and I always learned something from listening to him."

Another one contributed, "I think the patients thought he was wonderful. Families have sent us cards and mentioned how much they thought of him."

Several nodded, and Ron looked at one of the nurses who was staring straight ahead. "Susan," he said. "It is Susan, isn't it?" She looked at him and nodded.

"It seems like you don't agree with the sentiment expressed so far about Dr. Abbate. Do you have something to share?"

Susan looked down at her shoes before looking up and saying, "Well, no, I don't completely agree with that general sentiment about not saying anything bad about the dead."

"Could you expand on that, please?"

"Listen, we all know that Dr. Abbate could be abrupt and dismissive." She looked around the group, and a few nodded gently. She went on, "If he felt rushed, he would say he would explain things later. And he always used a tone of voice like he had to explain things to children. I didn't like his attitude."

Ron looked around the group and noted a couple of heads bowed. Others shook their heads. "Is that a general opinion of Dr. Abbate's interaction with nursing?" he asked.

When no one else immediately answered, Lena said, "No, it's not. But Susan's opinion and experience are not solitary examples of Dr. Abbate's interactions with nursing. I have had some less than friendly exchanges with him, too."

"Huh," Ron said, more to Gene than anyone else. "Could you explain?"

Lena went on, "Yes, I think I can. Alex Abbate was a superb physician and a very compassionate and caring treatment specialist. From what I understand, he was highly respected in his field by other physicians." She paused for emphasis. "But, he had a degree of tunnel vision in coming to the correct diagnosis every time."

Gene noted two of the nurses nodding as they watched Lena talk. He tried to remember their names as he made an entry in his notebook.

Lena went on, "Every now and then, he became engaged in a heated discussion with other physicians about the diagnosis for a particular patient. Sometimes it was more about the treatment of a known diagnosis. But whenever it occurred, Abbate got testy with everyone for a day or two until the issue was resolved."

"What if he turned out to be wrong?" Ron asked.

. Lena paused and grinned, "Then, he was all smiles and friendly comments, right ladies?"

The nurses nodded, some more vigorously than others. Gene asked, "And what if he was right?"

Lena answered, "Pretty much the same. As long as there was no question in the air, he was a gentleman to us, and a teacher and friend to patients and their families."

Ron paused and asked, "So, do any of you have an example or maybe a name of anyone Dr. Abbate might have angered enough to make them want to kill him?"

Again, the nurses seemed to pause to reflect before they individually began to shake their heads. Ron looked at Lena, who said, "Okay then, back to work."

"Thank you for your time," Ron said as the nurses passed by him and out the conference room door on their way back to the infusion unit. When they had all left, he turned to Lena, "Could you spare a little more time?"

Without hesitation, she said, "Certainly."

CHAPTER 29

After the nurses left for the infusion unit, Lena closed the door to the conference room and returned to the chair where she had been sitting. She looked at Ron and waited for him to begin the conversation.

He did, asking, "Did we get the real picture from the nurses? Sometimes I think interviewing a group like that doesn't allow us to get beyond superficialities."

Lena nodded, "Oh, they were superficial all right. But, truthfully, that's about all they knew of Dr. Abbate. They usually saw him at his absolute best, when he was with a patient or talking with a family."

"So, can you tell us more about his dark side?"

"Let me be clear, detective, I am a fan of Dr. Abbate. I did have opportunities to see him at a deeper level than most of the unit nurses. But I still saw a basically patient, caring physician. Those other times when he was upset, it was because a system or process error impaired his ability to provide care or delayed treatment. Even then his manner of reproach centered on the process error and not on the individual involved. His personal arguments were almost always with decision makers, not with staff."

"Can you give us an example?"

"Certainly. About a year ago we began noticing that laboratory values were late in coming back to the unit. Dr. Abbate called …"

"Wait a minute, please. What laboratory studies were involved?

"Let me go back a little. When a patient arrives in the unit for their scheduled chemotherapy infusion, we, that is, the nurses, draw whatever blood work has been ordered and send that to the lab. Usually the treating physician, say Dr. Abbate, would come by to check on the patient a few hours into their treatment. Part of that examination involved checking on their laboratory values, particularly their level of hemoglobin and platelets. Those values are directly affected by the chemotherapy and if we need to treat the patient we want to have time in the regular day to do so. That involves calling the blood bank and ordering a cross-match on blood and …"

"But recently those reports were late in coming back?"

"Yes. And that lateness pushed our requests to the blood bank toward the end of their day and led to overtime. Plus, we didn't get blood for transfusion while the patient was still on treatment so they had to stay later than usual and some missed their transportation. The late results were causing problems in several places."

"What did Abbate do?"

"He took the time to walk backward in the process and find out what had changed and why. It turned out that the senior laboratory technician had interpreted a discussion with the laboratory supervisor concerning inappropriate orders for STAT lab results. Orders for STAT results from the wards had increased in July and August because of the new house staff, the interns, and the supervisor determined not to perform STAT requests unless they were signed by a staff physician."

"And, I guess they were unaware of the new requirement."

"Right. But the change meant that our requests were also delayed."

"Okay. So, Abbate figured out the problem with the process, but it wasn't his process. What did he do about it?"

"He took our data and what he could find from the laboratory technicians and talked to the chairman of the division and the supervisor. They decided the problem was coming from the interns ordering everything STAT and took that to the chairmen of medicine and surgery. They cleared the issue up in a few days."

"Pretty clever."

"That was Dr. Abbate's way. He simply did not work through confrontation."

"Did he deal with many of the other doctors here?"

"Oh, yes. That's another thing about Dr. Abbate. Or was. He saw a lot of different abnormalities in our patients in the unit. When he didn't know what that abnormality was or what it represented in risk to the patient, he would call for a consult from another specialist."

"Did that happen often?"

Lena made a small coughing smile, "It seemed we had a consultant in the unit every day. Abbate was almost obsessive about seeing that his patients got the best possible care."

"Did that ever cause trouble?"

Lena thought for a moment. "No," she said, "I don't remember any issues because of consultants."

Ron cocked his head at her choice of words, "Were there issues for other reasons?"

"What? Oh, you thought I was being careful with my words. No, I don't really recall any difficulties or arguments. We had a few patients who turned out to have medically interesting complications and that engendered a parade of folks wanting to come through and look at them. I had to put my foot down since I couldn't keep up with the infection control protocols."

"How did Abbate take your decision?"

"He agreed with me entirely. All those people tramping through the unit was creating a risk for all the patients."

"How did the others take their exclusion from the unit?"

"Oh, a couple of them complained about missing out on some teaching aspect."

"Who were these doctors?"

"Uh, the major one to complain was the dermatologist. She said that her students needed access to see the various skin changes that accompany certain types of cancers. I think Dr. Abbate made some accommodation for her. But that occurred outside the unit."

"Did anyone get very upset with him?" "Look, detective, I know you want to find someone mad enough to kill him. But I just can't see it from the perspective of the infusion unit. He solved issues without causing anger or anyone feeling targeted."

Ron paused and then stood and handed Lena his card. "Thank you for your time. If you think of anything else, please give me a call."

As he and Gene headed for their car, Gene said, "I hate to say this, but Rocky looks like he knew what he was doing."

CHAPTER 30

Tom Bolling had a headache. There was no mystery about the cause; he had reviewed more than 100 cases of Alex Abbate's cancer patients' electronic records. Tom had reviewed the diagnosis, the planned treatment, the actual treatment given, and whether any complications occurred. Most patients had developed some complication that led to an alteration in the planned treatment schedule. There were several cases where an offending drug was omitted from the regimen, many others where doses were adjusted downward, and others where the overall treatment period was lengthened.

Plus, he categorized the complications and tried to assign cause to each. This was a struggle for an orthopedic surgeon, and Monique Song took charge of this part of the review. Monique also did her share of primary reviews; she and Tom had planned a fifteen percent overlap to check each other's findings and conclusions. The two had spent most of their unobligated time in the last few days on the reviews. Even with frequent breaks and visits to the Green Bean kiosk, the work was mind numbing, repetitive, and tedious.

Tom leaned back in his chair and said, "I think I have caught a carcinoma of my memory cells. And it's painful."

Monique nodded but did not comment. She was staring intently at the computer screen in front of her. Both physicians were doing their reviews using the hospital's electronic medical record system; Tom had the Information Technology staff wire a second terminal in his office for Monique so they could talk about cases easily. Monique had asked for dual screens and often had microscopic slides on one screen and clinical notes on the other. When Tom spoke, she was staring at a chest radiograph on one of her screens.

After a brief lull, Monique asked, "Tom, what does this look like to you?"

Tom got up from behind his desk and moved to stand behind her chair. He looked at the radiograph for a moment and asked, "Is this a trick question?"

"No," she said, continuing to stare at the screen.

"Okay, then. It looks like a consolidated left upper lobe. Pneumonia, I'd guess. What's odd about that?"

"This was taken mid-morning when the patient was having trouble breathing. Blood cultures were drawn at the same time, and sputum showed gram-positive cocci."

"Alright, then. This patient has pneumococcal pneumonia. What's your question?"

"The patient is an 82-year-old man under treatment for chronic myelogenous leukemia."

"That can't be good for him."

"It's worse than that. His white count is almost 100,000 but he has no mature white cells."

Tom shook his head. "If you want to play 'Can You Top This?' I think I can find a case that looks just as bad. What are you trying to prove?"

Without speaking, Monique flipped through a series of additional radiographs and put one on the screen that showed no evidence of disease in the left upper lobe. She said, "Are you going to show me a case where the patient survived and cleared his pneumonia?"

Tom squinted at the digitized picture. "Is this really five days later?" he asked.

"Yes."

"That's remarkable. How did Alex accomplish that?"

"I don't think he did."

"What do you mean? Wasn't he taking care of this man?"

"Oh, yes, he was. But he was completely surprised as well. I just read his notes. He was puzzled. Now, let me tell you a couple of other things about the case. The blood cultures were positive for Type III pneumococcus."

Tom stood straight. "Lobar pneumonia, sepsis with the worst form of pneumococcus and no white cells, yet he recovered! That's amazing. What did Alex say about it?"

"Same as you. He called it amazing, and inexplicable."

"He had no explanation?"

"Not in this chart."

"Well, this is certainly out of the ordinary. What do we know about this guy? Is he still alive? Can we talk to his family? Maybe Alex told them something."

"I've got the man's name, but he has since died. His address is from one of the shelters downtown, and there are no next of kin listed."

Tom returned to his desk and took his seat. He stared at Monique for a moment and then said, "Monique, I think I saw a case much like this one. I can't remember it exactly now, but I think there was a serious pneumonia that cleared but the guy died. Wait a minute, I'll look in my list of complications." He turned to the handwritten file he had on his desktop and began flipping through the pages. More than once he stopped, copied a patient record number, and turned to pull up the record on his computer only to shake his head and return to searching the file.

More than fifteen minutes passed before Tom said, "Got it!" He began searching through the electronic record and finally located a chest X-ray that showed a large, dense infiltrate in the right middle lobe. Tom turned his screen so Monique could see. Then he advanced the screen through several other similar radiographs and stopped on one that showed no infiltrate.

"See?" he said. "A big serious pneumonia that was cured! I thought that was strange, but then the guy died, and I thought that was the end of that."

Monique did not move. "What was the cause of death?" she asked.

Tom said, "Uh, I don't know. Just a moment and I'll see." He turned to scroll through the patient's record and fairly quickly had the death certificate for viewing.

"It says he died from profuse hemorrhage from the lower bowel, no definite lesion was found. You did the autopsy, Monique."

"Hmm. When was that?"

Tom checked the date. "Five months ago."

"I think I remember that one. I spent a lot of time looking for a bleeding point. What was his diagnosis?"

Tom went back to the death certificate and read, "Primary cause of death was massive gastrointestinal hemorrhage secondary to thrombocytopenia from chemotherapy for chronic myelogenous leukemia."

"Same diagnosis," Monique said, staring at Tom.

"How many charts do you have left to review?"

"Fifteen or twenty."

Tom nodded, "And I have less than twenty. Let's go through them quickly and see if there are any other cases of this diagnosis."

Their search was completed in less than thirty minutes. They identified only one additional case of CML, and it was in Monique's stack. She pulled the full chart up, opened it, and then searched and found a death certificate.

They read it together, "Primary cause of death was subdural hematoma secondary to thrombocytopenia from chemotherapy for chronic myelogenous leukemia."

"Bingo!" Tom said. "Three cases of CML, all died from low platelets due to chemotherapy."

Monique said, "Wait, Tom. There were some other cases of CML in my stack, and I bet there were in yours."

Tom nodded gingerly.

"Before we jump to any conclusion on this, I think we have to look at all those cases to see if there is a difference between them and the three we have identified."

"Monique, we have three cases that all died from low platelets."

"I think I have seen others die from that without this diagnosis. Remember, we identified the first two because they had this peculiar recovery from a usually fatal circumstance. Let's at least start with looking at the third case to see if he had anything like that."

Tom agreed and turned to his assignment of searching for other cases of CML in the review charts allocated to him.

Half an hour later, Monique interrupted him, saying. "That's it! Got it!"

"Got what?"

"This guy fits. While he was in getting chemo, he developed a flaring urinary tract infection. Little fever, some flank pain but there was pus running out the catheter. He had just gone into a blast phase of the disease and had almost no mature white cells at the time. Sixty or seventy thousand immature ones, though."

"I thought those immature white cells were ineffective in fighting infection."

"Everybody knows that. But this guy recovered in two days, blood cultures went from positive to negative and did the urine culture."

"What was Alex giving him?"

"It appears he had been treated with one of the TK inhibitors but was failing, and Alex admitted him to start chemo and to talk about marrow transplant."

"So, we've got three cases and …"

Monique interrupted him, saying, "We aren't sure what we have until we examine all the cases of CML. I will only be certain these three are outliers after we've looked at all the others."

Tom's face did not indicate pleasure with this plan, so Monique went on, "C'mon. Let's divide them up and get started."

CHAPTER 31

ooney parked his car and walked back to the café where he had dropped Gene to secure their usual seating. They had timed their arrival to occur before the lunchtime rush, and Gene had successfully staked out a claim to their favorite booth.

Ron slid into the booth seat across from Gene and noted that Sandy had already provided them with glasses of water. He took his glass and had a long draught. Gene asked, "How long do you think Thor will allow us to look into this locked room case before he and Rocky get fed up?"

"Dunno. I haven't seen any sign of impatience yet. The guy that Rocky thinks is guilty is locked up and waiting for formal arraignment, so Rocky isn't creating any pressure on us."

"But this can't go on forever, partner. You know that Thor is going to show up at your desk someday soon and say 'Huh?' and you won't be able to answer him."

"Yeah. I know it seems like we haven't found out a lot of new information but ..."

"Actually, we haven't," Gene said, switching to a broad smile as Sandy arrived to take their orders.

"'Y'all have no menus, so I'm guessing it will be the usual orders," she said with her order pad in hand.

Still smiling broadly and not moving his eyes from hers, Gene said, "Of course."

Ron smiled briefly and said, "You know, I don't feel so hungry today. I'll have a bowl of the clam chowder, please."

She made a note and asked, "Anything else?"

Both men shook their heads, and she walked off. Despite the conversational tension that existed, neither spoke until they had watched her walk back to the kitchen. Then Gene continued his line of thought.

"Look," he said, "we don't have anything concrete to present to Thor as a reason to keep looking into this case. You know that."

Ron shook his head, and replied, "That's not strictly true, partner. When we took over to look into Rocky's case, he and everyone else was convinced that Donaldson was guilty based on the 'locked building' feature. All the available evidence then indicated that Donaldson was the only other person in the building at the time of the murder and closed the case. At the very least, we have shown that another person could very well have been in the building. Further, I think we have raised a significant question about the so-called 'supporting evidence' with the watch damage and the directionality of the blood drop on Donaldson's shoe."

"Wait. What are you talking about?" Gene asked.

"Didn't we talk about that?" Ron asked. "The blood drop on the shoe came straight down. That's not what would have happened if it were throw-off from the weapon hitting Abbate in the head."

"That has not been mentioned that in our conversation before," Gene said, scratching his chin.

"Huh. Well, I spent a lot of time in the Railway building hiding from Hector, and I did a lot of thinking about the mechanics of the murder. I'm convinced the watch was broken to give a false time of death and the direction of the blood drop is unnatural."

Gene looked steadily at his partner for several seconds and then slowly nodded before saying, "You won't mind if I go back and check on the blood drop, I know. And I am going to do that. But I do agree about the watch, and now that you've demonstrated how someone could be in the building undetected, we do have good reason to doubt the guilt of Donaldson. I think we need to run the Knowns again."

Sandy appeared at their table right then with their orders. She said, "There you go again, honey. Talking about those gnomes. Somebody else might think you had a serious fixation on short people."

Gene grinned, Ron muffled a laugh, and Sandy looked at them wide-eyed. Then she blew a kiss in Gene's direction and left. Conversation again came to a halt until she finished her trip to the kitchen.

Then Gene said, "You know she doesn't mean 'gnomes', right?"

"Of course. Now you were saying we need to run the Knowns." Ron paused to put some pepper on his chowder. "It may be easier to convince Thor to leave us on the case if we present him with a list of significant Unknowns."

"What are you thinking?"

"We have a ton of information regarding people whose loved one had cancer and died when Abbate was the doctor of record. All those people have praised him and the care he gave. When you think about the number of cases he took care of over the past few years that adds up to a strong lack of motive coming from that angle. We have collected a pretty good list of people who would attest that Abbate was such a nice guy he wouldn't have people standing in line to kill him. Further, we could not corroborate Donaldson's so-called motive, nor could we find any other person or motive. That has to call the prosecution's case against Donaldson into question. We have also looked for motive to frame Donaldson without any significant reason popping up."

"Wait a minute," Gene said, "I agree we haven't found anything that looks like a real motive there, but we also haven't cleared those two guys that we identified having a grudge against Donaldson."

"Another reason for us to continue on the case."

"Oh, right."

"So, the motive is a zero in the case. And, as far as opportunity is concerned, our interpretation that the killer set the watch and broke it to raise doubt about the actual time of death and that creates doubt about Donaldson."

"And now," Gene said, pointing at Looney with a potato chip, "You have raised the forensic doubt about the blood drop on the shoe and cast doubt on the 'locked room' theory completely."

"Right. However, all we have accomplished by that last step is increasing the potential pool of killers to everyone with a keycard to Railway."

"Thor is not likely to see our findings as definitive steps on the way to finding the killer."

Ron pushed his chowder bowl away and said, 'I intend to take the approach of Thomas Edison."

"What's that? Going to 'shed a little light on things'?"

"Cute. No. I'm thinking of his comment about how long it took for him to find the right filament for his light bulb invention."

"What's that?"

"Edison said he didn't fail, he found 10,000 things that didn't work."

"Oh, I get it. We are going to claim victory by failing upward."

"I agree. My point is that the opportunity piece now seems incredibly weak, doesn't it? Maybe there's not 10,000 other possibilities but our field of suspects is no longer limited to James Donaldson.""

"I don't see Thor being enchanted that we've weakened Rocky's case with possibilities of alternative activity."

"C'mon partner, it's all in the telling, isn't it? If and when Thor pushes for a brief, I intend to make the case that what we have accomplished is sufficient to put a stay on the arraignment of Donaldson and bring more manpower to the search for the real killer."

"Let me get this straight. You intend to dance with Thor by telling him all negative information and getting him to see that as progress. And then, you think he will let Dr. Donaldson out of jail."

"Yes. You understand my plan exactly," Ron said with a broad smile.

"I think we should plan to have another talk with Tom. We need to focus more on finding some positive information about Dr. Donaldson not being the killer," Gene commented.

"You know you're suggesting we need a positive-negative?"

"Huh. Well, maybe that's exactly what we need at this time."

"I agree we should go back to Tom and look again at Abbate. Maybe Tom and Monique have found something for us to work on," Ron agreed.

"And we can put your so-called 'plan' on the shelf?"

"Absolutely not. If Thor wants a briefing, my plan is what we'll give him."

"What gives you any encouragement that it will work?"

"Trust in my eloquence, logic, and persuasive manner of presentation."

"Have you tried any of that on Thor before?"

"Uh, not exactly.

"Uh-huh. Will you give me some time to rally up a pool in the Dick Pen? I'd give eight-to-one odds right now that your plan is a flop."

"C'mon, partner. You're supposed to back me."

"Look at it this way, Walker. If I can set things up, it'll be a win-win."

"How do you reckon that?"

"If Thor buys your story, you win, and our partnership wins. But if he doesn't, and he shuts us down, I win, and our partnership wins. Win-win, all the way."

CHAPTER 32

The crowd around the Green Bean kiosk was numerous and Nick did not see the detectives until they had worked their way to the front of the line to order drinks. He signaled his recognition with a head nod and raised eyebrows. They responded with raised thumbs and moved on to the cashier.

"Odd thing, that," Gene noted as they paid for their drinks.

"It is no longer odd or strange that Nick knows us or that he knows the drink we favor," Ron replied.

"How about the fact that we can order without speaking?"

"Oh, well, that is odd, come to think of it."

They picked their drinks off the counter, waved to a busy Nick, and headed for the chief of staff's office.

Mary Brighthouse told them that Tom was out in the hospital. She put them in his office and said she would let him know they had arrived.

This time Ron took the overstuffed chair that Tom kept for VIPs, leaving Gene to sit in the straight-back chair at the side of Tom's desk.

Gene looked at the array of medical texts in the bookcase behind Tom's desk. "I wonder how much of those books Tom has read," he mused.

Ron said, "Tom once told me a story about his first day in medical school. The Professor who taught Anatomy wheeled a cart full of big, heavy books into the lecture hall and proceeded to slam them down on the lecture desktop one at a time. When he finished, he pointed at the line of four-inch-thick volumes and told the class, 'This represents part of the material you will be required to master before you can get a passing grade in Anatomy.' Tom said two young men got up and left the room."

"What? They were quitting on the first day?"

"Tom said that's what everyone in the class thought. But, it turned out that the two guys were assistants in the Anatomy lab. The Professor had put them up to the walkout to get everyone's attention."

"Huh. That's still not as hard as the Academy. They use live rounds."

"Tom said the failure rate was 25% from his class. Anybody in your Academy class that got shot?"

Before he could answer, Tom came through the door asking, "To what set of fortunate events do I owe the honor of this visit?"

Both detectives silently raised their Green Bean cups. "I see," Tom said, sitting behind his desk. "Clearly, my helpfulness on this case is in second place."

Ron interjected, "It's a close second, General. Very close."

"Whatever. Why are you here today?"

Ron commented, "We are here to do several things. First, we want to tell you what we have discovered or figured out. Second, we have additional questions for you. And, third, we hope to hear about any progress you have made reviewing the medical aspects of Dr. Abbate's activities."

Tom nodded and said, "You go first."

Ron spent the next twenty minutes going through the discussion he and Gene had gone over at the Café earlier. He referred to the information Tom had provided them about the putative motive Rocky had identified, and he quoted Tom's information about the legal meeting where that concern was put to rest. Then, Ron provided middling detail about the information he and Gene had obtained, showing a universal lack of motive from any of Abbate's patients or their families. He paused to sip his coffee, and Tom asked, "Is that it?"

"Oh no," Gene said, "He's just getting started."

Ron grinned and went on. He developed the theory he and Gene had concocted that perhaps Donaldson was the intended target and mentioned how Donaldson had suggested Dickie Overhart. Tom frowned at the mention of Overhart's name but kept his silence and Ron continued. He explained how Nick had come to tell them about the conversation he overheard where Terrance Raganathan expressed some pleasure at Donaldson's plight. Ron detailed the initial conversations he and Gene had with those two individuals and ended his storyline saying he thought both individuals had weak motives for going after Donaldson coupled with a lack of access to the Railway Building. Nonetheless, he emphasized, he and Gene had not eliminated either Overhart or Raganathan from suspicion. When he paused this time, Gene quickly said, "That's it for the first part."

Tom nodded and said, "I presume you do intend to follow through on the alibi for each of those last two people."

"Oh, yes. Certainly. They just aren't on the top of the list right now. And there's the question of how, exactly, we could go about that anyway."

"I see," Tom said, leaning back. And what else is it that you want to know from me?"

Gene looked at Ron and then said, "We haven't made any progress to speak of. Despite that long intro by my partner, we have no leads and no other suspects."

"Except for everyone who has a keycard to the Railway Building," Ron interjected.

Tom understood their concern and said, "I guess you would like for me to give you a couple of leads or names of some suspicious characters."

"Yeah, that would be good."

Instead, Tom stood up and said, "How about I show you something that Monique and I discovered going through Abbate's cases?" He walked over to the credenza and opened the doors. He extracted a thick pile of papers, put them on the top of the credenza, and began sorting pieces into various piles. Ron and Gene got out of their chairs and went to stand beside him and watch the piles grow.

"Is your explanation going to involve polysyllabic words?" Gene asked.

"Probably," Tom answered. "That's the only language I've spoken for over thirty years."

When he had finished placing the papers into the various stacks, Tom began his explanation, "These files represent every one of the cancer patients treated by Alexander Abbate in the past five years at New City Hospital."

"There are only about fifty pieces of paper here," Ron started to say.

"Each of which contains information on twenty-five to thirty individual patients," Tom interrupted. "More than thirteen hundred cases of cancer seen by Alex in consultation or treated by him primarily. Monique and I have reviewed every single one of them for any irregularity of diagnosis, treatment of outcome."

Gene whistled. "Nice job, doc.

Ron asked, "What did you find?"

"First and foremost, what we found was a pattern of sophisticated thought processes in diagnosis, current knowledge in the application of treatment and, in general, respectable and noteworthy outcomes."

"No help, then?"

"Not exactly, but pretty close to nothing helpful."

"So, what did you find, Razordoc?"

"We found a minimal anomaly. Three cases that are different but that's all we can say."

"Different how?"

"All three cases were men with the same diagnosis." Tom turned to Gene and said, "They had polysyllable disease, Gene. Chronic myelogenous leukemia."

"I know that last word," Gene said.

"What's odd about that," Ron wanted to know. "Is that a rare disease?"

"No, not rare. The disease is not what caused us to stop and consider these cases of some interest."

"Then what was?"

"Each of these men had no family, for one thing. The phase of their disease was similar for another. Also, each of them had a serious infection that should have killed them but they completely recovered."

"And that's what you think is noteworthy?"

"Yes, and we don't know why. Let me explain. I'll try not to use too many big words, Gene. These men had a disease of the white cells in their bodies. Their leukemia pushed very immature white cells out of the marrow, and those cells never become competent to fight infection. The immature cells cannot help in the defense against infection, so when these men developed serious life-threatening infections, including bacteria in the bloodstream, the condition is almost 100 percent fatal. But these three survived."

"Why them? What was so different about them?"

"We don't know. There is nothing in these charts to suggest anything unusual in their treatment. They just recovered."

The detectives were quiet for a moment, then Ron asked, "Can we talk to them?"

"No. They are all dead."

"Wait, you said they recovered."

"They did recover. From that serious infection. But then, they died of other complications from treatment."

"Which were?"

"Bleeding. Two developed bleeding from the gut, and one hit his head and bled in his skull."

"Is that rare?"

"No, not really rare. These men developed very low platelet counts, and we caught that side effect too late to stop the bleeding. We could have given them platelets. We even have a drug to stimulate marrow production of platelets if we had known."

"You say 'we' like you were part of it, General."

"I was not part of their team, but I mean 'we' as in the team of all physicians at New City."

"Are there any other reports that Abbate might have? You said he had research projects. Wouldn't he have to make reports on those activities?"

"That kind of data or report would still be in his office in Railway. We haven't cleaned that room up yet."

"Have you looked through the papers in his office, Tom?"

"I have not. I understood your request was for Monique and I to go through the medical material."

"Won't the research reports be medical, too?"

"Somewhat. I believe most of the data are reported in graphic format. And, there will be a summary that might require a little translation."

Ron held up his hand and said, "Tell you what, Razordoc. Gene, and I will take a look at things in the professor's office and we'll call if we need a translation."

"All right. Anything else?"

"Were there other physicians involved in the case? Other than Abbate, I mean?"

"Yes. Alex was noted for calling in consultants to help when patients did poorly. Several others saw these men. But to no avail."

"Same doctors see all three men?"

"Uh, no, I don't think so. Let me check."

They waited as he flipped through a spreadsheet.

"Yes, there were. All the leukemia patients had consults by several different doctors. But Beauchamp and Wannamaker each saw these three."

"And not others?"

"No. These two saw several others. They were the only physicians that saw all three of our interesting patients."

"Who are these doctors?"

"Dr. Denis Beauchamp is a young cardiologist, and Dr. Cole Wannamaker, the infectious disease specialist, is one we would expect to see these infected patients."

"I believe we need to talk to these two doctors ourselves," Ron said, making an entry in his notebook.

CHAPTER 33

Tom agreed to ask Mary to set up interviews for Beauchamp and Wannamaker. He admitted that he did not know either of them well. Both doctors already had left New City for the day, however, so the detectives decided to return to their office.

They were in Ron's car and had not driven more than a hundred yards when Gene asked, "Do you keep an armadillo in there?" He pointed at the glove compartment.

"What are you talking about?"

"That noise. It's coming from the glove compartment, I think. Sounds like something scratching to get out."

"I do not hear a noise, my friend. Perhaps you are having some kind of early sign of a stroke."

"I'm not making this up. There's a skritching rattle-like noise in here," Gene declared as he opened the glove compartment.

"Hey, leave that stuff alone," Ron said, irritated by the distraction.

Gene found only an operator's manual and folded sheets of paper from the mechanic documenting service on the car. "It's still here," he said. "I think it's coming from inside the hood."

"Put those papers back in there," Ron said.

Gene held up a thickly packed envelope. "This looks like all your safety checks."

"So? Put everything back in the glove compartment. Now."

"I'm wondering how you can pass the safety checks when your passenger seat is broken, and the engine makes that horrible noise." He put everything back in its place.

"I've got an idea. Why don't you find your own way to crime scenes from now on?"

Gene was not subdued by what he gathered was an empty threat. "Nah, someone needs to be with you when this buggy breaks down. One of the perks of the job."

As they exited the parking garage on foot, Gene pointed out that quitting time was still an hour away, and their Green bean coffees were several hours in the past. Ron agreed, and they turned away from the office and headed for the small coffee shop. Waiting in the short line for their drinks, Ron said, "Let's hope Thor is out of the office and we can sneak in and finish the paperwork before he wants a briefing." Gene nodded and commented, "I tell you, he's not going to be happy with our progress. All we've done is punched a hole in Rocky's case without finding an alternative."

Ron countered, "Earlier, you were saying we had identified a whole hospital full of alternatives." Each of them ordered a Red Eye and ate separately. Thus fortified, five minutes later, they went up the back stairs and opened the door to the Dick Pen.

"Huh," came an authoritative comment from Thor's office as they passed.

They turned and saw Thor at his desk, mounting a halfway Look.

"Hey, Captain," Ron said, with a lift in his voice. "We were hoping to find you still here."

'Hmm," Gene mumbled while nodding and smiling in the direction of the Captain.

Thor did not speak, but he did look at the chairs in front of his desk. Ron took the one on the right, and Gene took the other.

There was a brief moment of silence as Thor stared at each of them, then Ron took charge.

"We've just come back from New City, and we have made a lot of progress on this case, Captain. Let me explain." He sipped on his coffee and began the story.

Over the next twenty-five minutes, Ron set down the major findings he and Gene had uncovered. He started with the 'motive' that led Rocky to arrest Dr. Donaldson. The incident was true in all the parts Rocky had gathered: Donaldson had been the doctor of record for Abbate's mother on dialysis. Donaldson did allow her to stop her dialysis treatment and that did cause her death. Abbate did voice ethics violations about Donaldson's role. But what Rocky had not uncovered was a meeting arranged by Tom Bolling of the two doctors and the hospital attorney. That meeting cooled the charges and ended with a written document signed by Abbate admitting that no ethics charges were warranted.

At this point, Captain Thorason tucked his chin and said, "Huh."

Ron nodded vigorously and agreed, "Yes, that does make the arrest seem premature, but don't forget Rocky had another reason for making that arrest."

Thor's eyebrow rose, and Ron went on, "It appeared that he was facing a locked room scenario. And Dr. Donaldson was the only one in the locked building who could have murdered Dr. Abbate. In that circumstance, Rocky was justified in making the arrest."

Thor's expression didn't change but he leaned back in his chair and the atmosphere lightened.

Gene said, "However, we have now determined that the 'locked building' wasn't completely locked. Ron has figured out how someone other than Dr. Donaldson could have been present and done the murder."

Thor made a slight motion with his lips and said, "Huh."

Ron picked up the story again, telling Thor how someone else could have been in the building undetected. He went on to say that such a finding had widened their pool of suspects and he and Gene were working their way through this collection.

Gene understood his cue and took control of the conversation. "We have gone back to the hospital staff to seek individuals with a motive for killing Abbate. We even raised a possibility that Donaldson was the primary target and identified a couple of guys with motives against him."

Gene quickly explained the putative motive for Overhart and Raganathan. Thor's response was to shrug his shoulders. Gene then told how Tom had identified three of Abbate's cancer patients that died under suspicious circumstances and brought the investigation up to date by outlining the plans for interrogation of two other physicians involved in the care of those patients.

Thor was silent when Gene finished, but his eyes moved from one detective to the other. Ron answered the unasked question, "No, sir, we do not have a better suspect than Dr. Donaldson at this point."

He continued, "As Gene pointed out, we have primary interviews set up with those two doctors tomorrow. We also need to review Dr. Abbate's research notes; nobody has done that yet." He paused and waited for Thor's response.

After a moment, Thor asked, "Those guys with motive against Donaldson need to be pinned down."

"Yes, sir."

"How long will all this take?"

"Can't be sure, Captain. At least a few more days."

Thor was silent for a moment, then said, "Huh."

"Yes, sir," Ron said with enthusiasm, pulling Gene from his seat and heading for the door.

Once back in their desk chairs, Gene asked, "How do you know that's what he was saying? I mean, giving us the go-ahead."

Ron looked at his partner and cocked his head, "What do you mean? You were right there, You heard him. He said, 'huh', plain as day."

Gene leaned forward to speak less loudly, "That's exactly what I heard him say. I'm asking how you know what he meant when he said it."

Ron answered, "Truthfully, that was a gut feeling. But, one thing I'm certain about is that if he was giving us an order to stop what we're doing, it would have been much clearer. And probably louder, too."

CHAPTER 34

Looney had decided to interview both Beauchamp and Wannamaker at New City Hospital. He hoped the setting would lower their anxiety and facilitate their answers. He and Gene collected their second coffee of the morning from Nick, told him they were conducting routine interviews, and let Mary Brighthouse take them to the Executive Suite Conference Room.

Cole Wannamaker was in the waiting area and smiled at them as they went through. He was thumbing through a magazine on hospital administration. Mary had the room set up with a carafe of water and four glasses set on the table. After she checked around the room to assure herself that everything was in proper order, she asked if she should bring Dr. Wannamaker in. Looney agreed and asked her to do so.

Cole Wannamaker entered and impressed immediately with his height. He was six-foot-two inches tall and filled out his blue blazer with broad shoulders. He was clean-shaven with light brown, slightly curly hair covering his head. He was wearing a lightly patterned blue shirt, and striped tie under the blazer. His khaki-colored gabardine pants and black loafers completed the common 'uniform' worn by physicians. He greeted each of the detectives with a warm, firm handshake and took the offered seat.

Ron began the conversation, saying, "Dr. Wannamaker, as I mentioned, my name is Ron Looney; I am a detective in the Homicide Division of the Cincinnati Police Department. This is my partner, Gene Novalchek. We are carrying out further investigation into the death of Dr. Alexander Abbate."

Wannamaker nodded solemnly. "Yes, I know. Mary explained that to me. But I thought you had arrested Jim in that case."

"Well, yes. An arrest has been made. But the arraignment is pending our completion of the facts in the case." He looked casually at Wannamaker and said, "As you may have heard, there is now substantial evidence that the man arrested was not alone in the Railway Building when the murder occurred."

Wannamaker blinked and made a slight sideways movement of his head. "No, I didn't know that. When did that come to light?"

"Very recently. But I'm sure you can see how that information increases the need for a complete story, including anyone with dealings with Dr. Abbate recently."

"Uh, well, I guess so. How can I help?"

"We have some specifics to go over, but let me start with the usual generalities. Where were you when Dr. Abbate was killed?"

Wannamaker paused before asking, "Do you mean that day or at the specific time?"

"The time."

"I don't think I know what time he was killed. But I can say I don't think I was in the Railway Building that day."

"I see. Your keycard will show that you did not enter the Railway Building at all on that Thursday?"

"I didn't know it showed that kind of information, detective. But I had no business to be over there that day, and I don't think I was. Do you want to check my keycard?" He began reaching for his wallet.

Ron stopped him with a gesture and said, "That won't be necessary, I'm sure. We may have to ask for that later, but I don't need it right now."

Wannamaker nodded and sat back in his chair.

Ron went on, "We have reason to believe that Dr. Abbate was killed between seven and eight PM that Thursday evening. Can you tell me where you were at that time?"

Wannamaker's face made a slight frown and stared over Ron's right shoulder as he said, "Well, I had been seeing a couple of patients in the hospital earlier, then I went to my office and checked my emails. I grabbed my coat and left, and went home. Got there about half-past eight."

"Did anyone see you?"

"Uh, well, yes, I'm sure there were some who saw me on the ward seeing those patients."

"And after you left the ward?"

"I don't recall running into anyone."

"Where is your office, Doctor?"

"It's, ah, down the hall from the library on the third floor of the old building."

"Sort of out of the way, isn't it?"

"Yes, I suppose. I rather like it because of the view."

"Did anyone see you there?"

"Oh no, everyone had left by then."

"What time did you get to your office?"

"Look, detective ah, Looney is it? I wasn't checking my entry and exit times that evening. I didn't know I would need a minute-by-minute alibi."

"Calm down, doctor. I'm simply doing my job, and if you knew the times of these events, it would help me, that's all."

"Why are you asking me about all this? I wasn't anywhere near Alex that day."

"We will get to that in a moment. So, no one saw you in your office?"

"As I said, no."

"About how long were you there?"

"I read my emails. I don't know how long that took. Maybe fifteen minutes."

"And then you left?"

"That's right. And I didn't run into anybody getting to my car."

"What route did you take to get to your car?"

"I took the back stairs. They come out near the Nursing Home entrance. I park in the Doctors' Parking area right in front of the Nursing Home."

"And did you then drive straight home?"

"I did."

"No stops for groceries or gas?"

"No. Directly home."

"And you said you arrived there," Ron checked his notes, "about eight-thirty, is that right?"

"Yes."

"Can anyone corroborate that?"

Wannamaker shook his head. "You could ask my dog. He seemed very happy to see me. But I don't think he can tell time."

"Your wife was not there?"

"No, Detective. She was not. She had taken dinner to a friend who had broken her hip and had just come home from the hospital. I found out about that when I found her note when I got home."

"When did she return?"

"I think it was shortly before ten. She left me some supper, and I was reading. We always watch the news together, and that came on just a little bit after she got home."

"All right, Dr. Wannamaker. That's all I need to know about your alibi, right now."

"When are you going to tell me why I need an alibi?"

"Let's talk about that right now, sir." Ron asked Wannamaker if he recognized the names of the three cancer patients treated by Abbate who died from bleeding. As Ron read out the names, Gene was closely watching the doctor for signs of anxiety.

"Yes," Wannamaker said. "I recognize all three of them. They were patients that Alex asked me to see because of their serious infection."

"Do you remember how they were treated?"

"Pretty much. I mean, I know what I used to treat their infection. And I know they all recovered completely to the surprise of all of us."

"Why were you surprised?"

"Detective, I don't expect you to understand this off the top. These patients had a disease that virtually prevented them from fighting infection. Then they got an overwhelming infection that has a high mortality rate in normal patients. They had a death sentence. And yet, they recovered. It was astounding. Of course, I remember them."

"Uh-huh. Was there anything unusual about their treatment?"

"Not from my perspective. But I don't really know about those chemical poisons Alex gave. Are these patients the reason you are suspecting me of killing Alex?"

"In a manner of speaking. Everyone agrees these three patients should not have recovered from their infection, and that is unusual. We are looking into the unusual in Dr. Abbate's life, and since you also saw all three patients, we wanted to know your role in their care."

Wannamaker smiled for the first time since the interview started. "I see," he said. His shoulders rose, and he went on, " We all talked about it, but we have no answer. I'm sorry. I apologize for being so abrupt. Alex was a friend, and I have no reason to want him dead. He helped me with my dog, and I can't believe you thought I might have something to do with his death."

"We are checking everything, Dr. Wannamaker. I thank you for your time."

"I can go now?"

"Certainly." Ron pushed back his chair and stood, holding out his hand. Wannamaker shook his hand and turned for the door as Ron asked, "What did Abbate do for your dog?"

"Oh, nothing direct. Alex gave me the name of a vet expert in German Shepherds. Alex had one, and mine got super sick. His reference helped my dog recover."

"That's great," Gene said, also coming to shake Wannamaker's hand. "I've got a neighbor with a very old German Shepherd, and he's looking for a specialist. What's this guy's name?"

Wannamaker looked at Gene for a second and then pulled out his phone. He thumbed through the contacts and showed Gene the information. Gene thanked him again, and everyone said goodbye. Wannamaker left, and moments later, Mary Brighthouse entered.

"Are you ready for me to call Dr. Beauchamp?" she asked.

The detectives looked at each other, and Gene said, "I think we need a break. The coffee has gone through me."

"But we need some more, anyway," Ron said and headed for the Green Bean.

CHAPTER 35

Twenty minutes later, they were about to start a new interview. The detectives felt refreshed; with empty bladders and full cups of hot Red Eye, they were ready to take on any task. Before they signaled Mary to call Dr. Beauchamp, however, Ron wanted a brief chat with his partner.

"What did you think of Dr. Wannamaker?" he asked, taking his first sip.

"Hmm. Everything seemed just a little too right, you know?"

"Specifics, Gene, please."

"Well, the cooperation at the beginning felt genuine. The barely suppressed anger at being considered a suspect seemed a little overdone, though. But, I didn't see any panic when you dropped the keycard business on him or when he learned we no longer believe in the 'locked building' hypothesis."

"Did you see what he did when I asked him for an alibi for the time between seven and eight-thirty that evening?"

"No. What?"

"He looked up and to the left. I think he was making stuff up."

"What should we do about it?"

"Nothing right now. Let's just keep him on the list. Maybe follow up and drop in on him later and see how he reacts without time to plan his response to our questions."

"Okay. I'll tell Mary we're ready."

Denis Beauchamp was an assistant professor of medicine but he looked like he was worried about getting turned down for a date to his senior class prom. Denis stood five-foot-ten inches but weighed less than 160 pounds. His thin neck and wrists made Gene think of the kid at the beach who always got sand kicked in his face. Beauchamp's hair was carefully in place, a dark red cap covering a low forehead. His eyes appeared green and widely dilated. His face was moderately freckled.

"Dr. Beauchamp, I'm Detective Ron Looney of the Homicide Division on the Cincinnati Police Department, and this is my partner, Gene Novalchek."

Each man stuck out their hand, and both were surprised by the dry, warm, and firm grip they received. Ron asked, "Do you know why we are here?"

"Yes. Mary Brighthouse explained things to me yesterday."

"Are you aware that we discovered the possibility that someone else was in the Railway Building when Dr. Abbate was killed?"

"Uh, I guess so."

"Would you explain that answer for me?"

"Well, it seemed to me that Dr. Donaldson was arrested quite soon after the murder. But that also appeared rational once we learned that there was no one else in the building that night. So, if you're here asking new questions there must be something wrong with the theory that Dr. Donaldson was the only possible culprit."

"Logical and well-parsed. And, by the way, absolutely correct. We do now know that Dr. Donaldson was not the only person in the Railway Building at the time of the murder."

"I see."

"Can you tell me where you were when Dr. Abbate was killed?"

"Possibly. What time was he killed?"

"Between seven and eight-thirty that Thursday evening."

Beauchamp had already pulled his phone out of his coat and was clicking buttons. After several seconds he looked up and said, "Sorry, I was checking my schedule. That afternoon I was asked to see a Juan Padrosa in the intensive Care Unit. He was a 69-year-old man with a new MI and congestive failure and …"

Gene raised his hand and interrupted to say, "we don't need all the particulars, doctor."

"Oh, right. Well, ah, he was an older man who had a heart attack and his heart was failing. I thought we might need to put him on ventricular assist …"

Gene's hand was up.

"Sorry again, that's a habit of presentation of cases. We were worried we would have to put a pump in his heart to do the job."

"Wow. You can do that?"

"Of course. But it's a big deal and kind of a last resort. So I was trying to get the right medicines to do the job first."

"How long did that take?"

"I think I went to the Unit about five o'clock and didn't leave for home until maybe nine-thirty. The nurses would probably know."

"Were you there the whole time?"

"Yes."

"Okay. Do you know why we are here asking you for an alibi?"

"Not exactly. I gather you think I might have some reason to kill Alex, but I can't think what it is."

"Margaret Dean was your sister-in-law?"

"That's right. Married my older brother."

"And Dr. Abbate was her physician when she had brain cancer?"

"Yes, that's right," Beauchamp spoke with little emotion regarding his sister-in-law.

"Were you close to Margaret?"

"Molly. We all called her Molly. Yes, I was very close."

"What did you think about the care she received from Dr. Abbate?"

"Oh, I see where you're going with this. Fact is, we all thought he was excellent as a caregiver. Many surgeons and oncologists will distance themselves from patients whom they can't save. I suppose it's a form of defense. But that wasn't Alex Abbate. He visited every day, sometimes twice. He gave advice and changed drugs and support systems often, trying to get her the best comfort. He spent hours sitting on her bed, holding her hand and answering as best he could her questions about heaven and the afterlife. If you think I had a grudge against him because Molly died, you are very mistaken, Detective."

"Uh-huh. Well, we had to talk to you about it, anyway."

"Really? Unless you heard about Molly's death from the newspaper, anyone here could have told you our family felt indebted to him for the time and quality of that time that he gave us. There's some other reason you put me on your suspect list, isn't there?"

Ron looked at Beauchamp and realized he had underestimated this young man. The physician who looked like he belonged in high school had discerned why he was being interviewed from some minimal information and was telling him a believable story, refuting any possible motive for killing Abbate. This fellow deserved his respect. Ron nodded in response to Beauchamp's question and asked if he recognized the names of the three cancer patients.

"Yes, I do. I consulted on each of them in hospital, and Alex asked my opinion about improving their cardiac function."

"What was wrong with them?"

"I assume you mean other than a perfect storm of cancer and overwhelming infection."

"Yes, we are aware of those conditions and the treatment they were receiving. What were you asked about?"

"Each of these patients was extremely short of breath. And that existed before they developed pneumonia. Alex wanted me to determine whether they also had heart failure causing the breathlessness."

"Was that the problem?"

"No. Their symptoms were related to their severe anemia. Alex and I have seen many patients like that in his cancer unit. These were no different. I convinced him to provide some limited red cell transfusion of fresh blood and their symptoms became much less troublesome."

Ron paused in his note-taking to ask, "Was that the only treatment you gave them?"

"I didn't give those patients anything. I recommended to Alex they receive blood; he gave it to them."

Ron closed his notebook. "I think that clears up all the questions that we had for you, Dr. Beauchamp. Thank you for your time and cooperation." He stood and extended his hand. As Beauchamp shook Ron's hand, Gene asked, "Do you have any idea who killed Alex Abbate?"

Beauchamp turned to Gene and answered softly, "I do not, Detective. If I had a serious concern, I would have mentioned that earlier."

"Of course. Thank you for coming," Gene also stood and shook hands before the doctor turned and left.

The detectives waited until the door closed behind Beauchamp before heavily retaking their seats, accompanied by audible sighs. Ron shook his head before commenting, "I felt a little like I was the one being interviewed."

"I noticed that. He seemed honest and forthright though. I believe him."

"I do too. But remember what the old newspaper editors used to tell rookie reporters, 'If your mother tells you she loves you, check it out!'.

"Okay, I agree we got some checking to do. But right now, I don't see any forward progress."

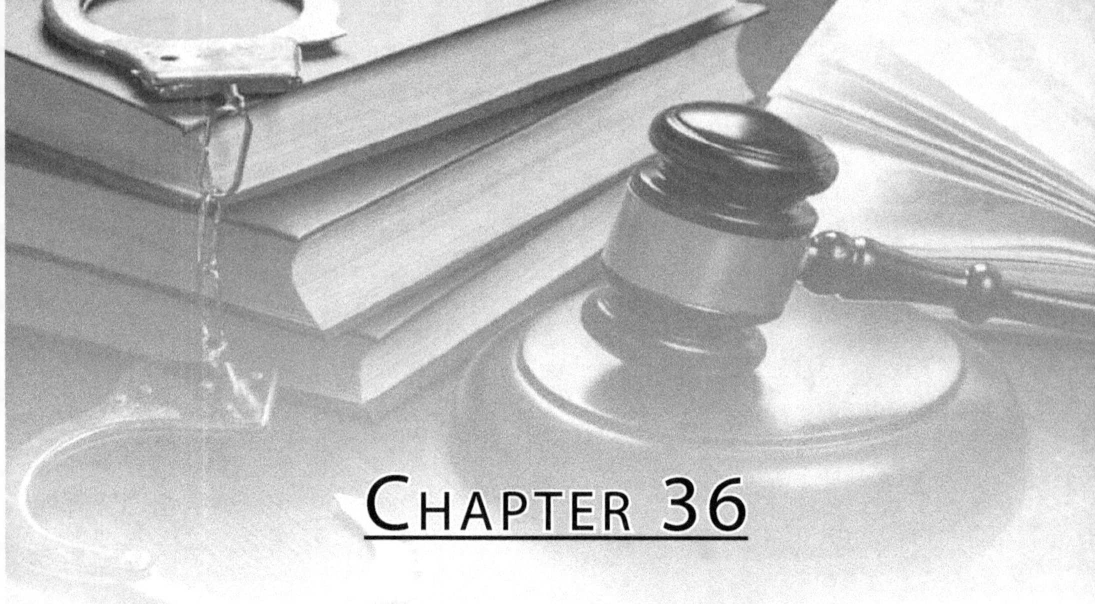

CHAPTER 36

They sat in the same chairs as last time, Tom at his desk in his Herman Miller Aeron, Looney in the wing-back chair usually reserved for VIPs, and Gene sitting in the straight-back wooden chair at the side of Tom's desk. Ron had given Tom the short story on the formal interviews with Cole Wannamaker and Denis Beauchamp, and the three men were considering whether they had learned anything of assistance in the case of Dr. Abbate's murder.

Tom asked, "Learn anything?"

"Nothing much useful," Ron replied.

"Gene added, "They have alibis for the time of the murder, but we haven't checked them completely yet."

"So, they both remain on the list of potential suspects, then,"

"Right, but not with a lot of hope."

Tom asked Ron, "Were you suspicious of either of them? You know, their story sounded weak, or they acted deviously?"

"No. They both seemed to be honest with us. Wannamaker's alibi is largely unsubstantiated. Beauchamp was moving around but mostly in the ICU."

"So, the nurses can vouch for him, right?"

Ron shook his head, "In my experience, alibis that depend on a crowd of witnesses are not usually very solid. It's hard to account for one person's time for every minute."

Gene added, "That turns out to be true, especially when the guy we're interested in is moving around a good deal."

Tom chuckled lightly and noted, "I understand. I've had people who were assigned to work in my area for part-time. They had another part-time job elsewhere. I found it difficult to deal with them. It always seemed that they were not present when I needed them, and somebody had to spend time telling them what went on when they did come back. Part-timers don't add much to the workforce, in my opinion."

Ron turned to Gene and said, "The General is being polite in his phrasing. In the Air Force, he was well-known for considering his forty-hour workweek employees as part-timers."

Gene grinned at Tom, who made a comic frown at Ron, and said, "That was supposed to be a secret."

Everyone grinned and took a sip of their coffee. Then Ron asked, "Any thoughts about these two or their possible motives against Donaldson? We don't seem to have anything on them against Abbate."

Tom nodded and put his cup down. "There's one minor little thing. And I do mean minor. But that's like the definition of minor surgery."

Gene asked, "How's that?"

Ron said, "I know this one." He turned to Gene and gestured with his hand, "Minor surgery is done on other people; major surgery is done on me."

Gene nodded, "Got it. So, what's this minor little thing?"

Tom said, "Every year, the medical school gives awards to those instructors that the students have chosen as outstanding teachers. There's an award for the pre-clinical courses and an award for the clinical teacher in each discipline they think is the best."

"Is this that Golden thing?" Ron asked.

"Yes, the award is the Golden Apple, awarded for excellence in teaching. Jim Donaldson won the award each of the last two years."

"And that's causing trouble because …" Gene inquired.

"Because both years, Denis Beauchamp was in second place in the student voting. And I have heard that he has expressed a little jealousy."

"Over a little award?"

"Major and minor, Gene. Many of the faculty here considers their teaching position as what defines them. It differentiates them from the physicians who are here "simply" practicing medicine. The teaching award is evidence of their being on the right side of that line and, of course, also being good at their job."

"And, missing out might be enough to push someone to murder?"

"I wouldn't think so," Tom said. "But, full disclosure, I have won two Golden Apples in my career. A jury might think I couldn't see things from the perspective of a two-time loser."

Ron spoke up, "So, maybe we need to probe Dr. Beauchamp a little on his feelings about Donaldson. We focused on Abbate in the interview, and we may have missed something. What did you hear about him being jealous?"

"It was a casual remark. Something someone said in passing. I can't quite remember the phrasing. It was something like 'Donaldson thinks it's big stuff winning two times in a row' or something like that. I'm quite sure no threat was attached to the statement."

"Still," Ron commented and cocked his head.

"I'm not disagreeing," Tom said, "You do what you think is right. I'd just be surprised, that's all."

"Uh-huh, well, that's happened before."

Gene broke in, "Remember, we also need to check his alibi about the ICU."

"Right. Tom, can we get a list of the nursing personnel in the ICU the night of the murder? We especially want to interview those who were involved in the care of," Ron flipped through his notebook, "Juan Padrosa."

"Sure. I can take care of that right now." Tom picked up his phone and hit a key. When answered he said, "Bev, Ron and Gene are here and would like a list of the nursing personnel on duty in the ICU the night Abbate's murder. Can you get that for them?"

After a brief interlude, Tom went on, "They are checking Denis Beauchamp's alibi. Ron said they are most interested in talking to the nurses caring for Juan Padrosa." Another pause for her to ask a question, then "No, I imagine they prefer to ask about those things themselves." Finally, "Okay, Thank you."

Tom smiled at Ron, "Bev says 'Hi' and that she will have that list right away."

"She's great," Ron noted, "I wish we had such a function in the Division. We could probably get our job done more quickly."

"I dunno about that, partner," said Gene with a vigorous shake of his head. "That would likely mean that Thor would just give us more cases."

Ron shrugged and asked Tom, "How would we check on Wannamaker? He seems to have left the ward about the time he could have slipped in the Railway Building. His story from that point until about ten that night involves checking his email, walking out the back way, and driving home without seeing anyone who could corroborate his presence."

Tom pondered the scenario a moment before agreeing, "I don't think there's a way we can prove that. Sam and I have talked about security cameras on the back entrance, but they aren't there yet."

As he finished speaking, there was a firm knock on the door, and Beverly stuck her head into the room. "Hey, guys," she saluted Ron and Gene and then came into the room. Bev was carrying a printout from her computer, and she handed it to Ron. "This is the roster from Nursing Service of the assignments in the ICU that evening," she said.

"Great," he responded, scanning the document, "Only thirteen more interviews. Gene, we're going to enjoy several more 'usuals' from Nick."

CHAPTER 37

Ron sat at the back corner table at the coffee shop and waited for his partner to join him. Gene was buying a pastry to go with their late afternoon coffee. Ron was thinking of getting home and having dinner with Meg, and he was beginning to feel hunger deep in his gut. In a couple of hours, Ron knew he would be ready to eat a meal. But if he ate a pastry at this hour, Ron knew he might not be hungry again for four or five hours. And yet, he knew that Gene would not be deterred from eating a solid meal later by having this pastry now. He wondered how that could be.

So, he asked Gene as he came to the table with an apple fritter, "Do you have a medical condition that I should know about?"

"What do you mean?"

"Malabsorption, perhaps?"

"Don't know what that is."

"Tapeworm?"

"Not if they cause any kind of pain."

"Then how do you keep your trim weight and eat all the time? You come to work interested in a little something after breakfast. You snack in the mid-morning and have a sandwich with chips at lunch. Then you nibble all afternoon, including that fritter. And I'm certain you will not skimp on dinner tonight, right?"

By the time he finished talking, Gene had taken a large bite of the fritter and looked at him with his mouth full. He gestured for a break in the conversation and increased his chewing.

Ron continued, "I've known you for several years now, and you are wearing the same belt size as when we met. I've gone up a notch."

Gene took a swallow of his coffee, wiped his mouth, and replied, "I can't help it. In college, I tried to gain weight into the heavyweight class, and the only way I could gain any weight at all was to lie around for a week eating ice cream. But all that gained was five or six pounds, and I lost all muscle tone."

"So, you're telling me that you are cursed with a metabolism that doesn't gain weight?"

"Yeah, that's it. Cursed," Gene grinned as he took another bite of the fritter.

Ron's eyes went upward, and he sighed, "It's like we're both cursed with doing interviews that tell us nothing."

Gene nodded but did not try to comment.

Ron frowned at Gene and said, "We are here to discuss the interviews, not to ruin my dinner."

Gene finished the fritter and wiped his hands and mouth. "Sorry, partner. I needed a little burst of sugar for proper brain function."

"Well, what's your brain function tell you about the interviews with the ICU nurses?"

Gene pulled out his notebook and flipped through some pages. "I initially thought we were going to get a minute-by-minute report on Dr. Beauchamp. The first three nurses I talked to were helpful, but their memories were mostly about the medical care for the guy with heart failure. They remembered the doctor only when he did something."

"I had that same impression. I talked with five others, including the charge nurse, and they were very certain about what happened to that guy in the bed but not so much about where anybody else was at any given time."

"Well, one of them told me that the doc left the ICU once."

"I heard that, too. The nurse said Beauchamp was on his way to the laboratory to check on some lab results."

"Hmm. The story I got was Beauchamp said he was running down to radiology to look at the chest x-rays."

"What time was that?"

"She didn't know. She said everybody was running all over the place at the time, and I figured that he left for that purpose early in the course of treating the heart failure."

"I agree about the timing thing. I did not find one person who could tell me what time anything happened, but they could all tell you what the sequence of events was."

"Disappointing."

"But not unexpected. While you were talking to that last nurse, I called Tom. He said we would have had a complete timesheet if anyone had bothered to call a code. That brings in surgeons and others, and somebody has responsibility for writing everything down and timing it. This guy just sorta slid off the edge of the world, and the ICU crew took care of it. No code."

"The timeline of events we do know about and the presence of Dr. Beauchamp at a couple of those instances does not provide absolute proof of his presence for the entire time."

"That's what I thought, too. I don't know how long some of these things take or how long they wait to see if there's an effect, but it seemed to me Beauchamp was 'out of sight and out of mind' at least once long enough to get to the Railway Building and kill somebody."

"I think there are two such gaps in the record," Ron said, leaning back and rubbing his eyes.

"But I don't see the guy getting over there and waiting until eleven-thirty to get back. That doesn't fit at all."

"Gene, I didn't check on Hector all night. I'm pretty sure that a smoker like he is would take a break for a cigarette more than just that one time all night. If our killer got out of the Railway Building the way I did, it could have been as early as eight-thirty. It could have been at any time after that."

Gene was silent for a moment before, "Meaning …?"

"Meaning it's exactly what we didn't want. Beauchamp is not alibied out, and he remains on our suspect list."

Gene made a note in his book and asked, "Same for Wannamaker?"

Ron slowly nodded his head. "Yeah, I think so, at least for now. I'd like to see the note from his wife about the friend with a broken leg. Or hear her side of the story. But, push comes to shove, she was not at home when he arrived, so we cannot get an accurate read on that."

"But she was there by ten, so they watched the news. And I was going to bring up the problem of the eleven-thirty door thing, but you have already explained that to me."

"And that brings us to a big fat zero for suspects."

"Not so, my pastry-eating brother-in-arms. It's not a zero in terms of candidates for suspects. It's almost an infinite number of people."

"Do I have to say again that Rocky is looking pretty smart on this one?"

"And do I have to remind you that we are certain of one thing, and that is that Dr. Donaldson is not the killer?"

"Oh, right. There is that little detail. What's next?"

"My gut tells me we have come in contact with Dr. Abbate's killer already in our questioning. I want to talk to Wannamaker again, and I think we need to check on Raganathan's and Overhart's alibis. Plus, we still need to go through Abbate's lab books and reports. We still have a lot to do before Thor pulls the plug."

Tom took Looney's call at his desk. He had been reviewing a dozen applications for privileges at New City and wanted a break; the phone call gave him the needed excuse.

"What's up, Ron?" he asked.

"We're just treading water here, General. We have now talked to all the nurses on Beverly's list. Both Gene and I now have a new insight into the stuff that goes on in the ICU, and we are impressed."

"Well, that's good news for me, at least. Did you find what you were looking for?"

"Uh, part of the impression we walked away with was how incredibly focused you medical people are on the sick person at the center of the care."

"Again, a nice thing for me to hear about our people."

"But …"

"Of course, there's always a 'but' with you, isn't there, Ron?"

"But, your people are so focused on what they're doing about that crashingly sick guy that they don't pay attention to anything else around them."

"What do you mean?"

"I mean, a troop of gorillas could walk through the ICU, and they wouldn't notice. Unless they got in somebody's way."

"Meaning?"

"Now you're starting to sound like Gene, asking me for the ultimate meaning of things."

"Did you get the information you needed, or not?"

"According to your people, Dr. Beauchamp was there for the resuscitation except when he wasn't. And they don't know when either of those periods occurred."

"So, you didn't get a solid alibi for Denis."

"Yes, General, that's what I said. He was there, except when he wasn't. We have sightings of him at certain times, but no one can say they saw him present in the ICU for the entire period."

"I'm sorry our highly trained professionals don't have the skills of observation needed for your job. We hire them to do exactly what you saw them doing - patient care."

"Well, they are quite good at it. And, they are no help to me investigating a murder at all."

"What's next?"

"I was calling to see if you had any more ideas or theories about these suspects. Our inability to track Beauchamp in the ICU leaves him on the list. Wannamaker's alibi doesn't leave us any method of checking. Both of them have plausible stories about why they would not kill Abbate. You know, he took care of someone they loved. Is it possible there's some other reason they might have?"

"Why are you focusing on the two doctors? Didn't you have a couple of other people with more obvious motives?"

"You mean the drug pusher and the heart technician, right?"

"The pharmaceutical representative and the heart-lung technologist, yes. Those are the people I mean."

"Well, yes, they're still on the suspect list. But, c'mon, Tom, how did they get entrance into the Railway Building? Yes, they have a motive to be upset or angry with Abbate, but I'm not convinced either motive is enough to kill. And I still have trouble getting them in the building in the first place."

"Look, Ron, I don't have any more insight into this than what we've already talked over. I feel like I know the two doctors better than the other suspects. I don't see either of them as a killer. I think you need to look elsewhere."

"Can I get access to Abbate's research notes? Maybe there's something in there we can use."

Tom thought for a moment, and then replied, "I can make that happen. I need to clear it with the Research folks. I know those files and papers haven't been removed from his office yet. Let me make arrangements, and I'll call you back."

"Thanks, General. And please think about those guys a little more, for me, okay?"

"Okay. Ron. But only because you asked politely."

Tom hung up the phone and sat looking at the pile of paperwork on his desk. For some reason, he remembered a sign he had seen posted above a toilet paper dispenser in a military men's room. The sign read, "Remember, the job's not finished until the paperwork is done!" Tom decided he wasn't ready to get back embroiled in paperwork. He picked up the phone and pushed the button for Beverly's office.

She answered, "Yes, sir?"

"Bev, could you please make arrangements for Ron to review Alex Abbate's research files and notes tomorrow? I gave him a keycard, but he will need access to the office and someone to show him the files."

"That shouldn't be a problem. Is this going to get us closer to knowing who was responsible for Dr. Abbate's death?"

"Well, that's the premise."

"I'll do it right away."

Tom thanked her and hung up. He leaned back in his chair and tried to recall any incident involving either Beauchamp or Wannamaker, or anyone else for that matter, which might have engendered a motive to kill Alex Abbate. Nothing particular came immediately to mind; soon, Tom's mind wandered to thinking again about the charts he had previously reviewed on the three cancer patients who died after recovering from what should have been a fatal infection. As he remembered their clinical course, something struck him as a little out of the ordinary. Tom had a clear memory of some progress notes made by physicians as the patients recovered from their infections. Both Beauchamp and Wannamaker continued to visit the patients and make notes in their charts.

Such ongoing encounters from consultants were not, of themselves, odd or rare, except these consultants continued to follow the course of these patients' care when their reason for consultation had ended. Tom decided that was unusual enough for him to engage in some additional follow-up of his own. He asked Mary to remind him of the medical record number of those patients and then to get Monique Song on the telephone.

A few minutes later, Tom was thumbing through one of the charts on his computer and confirming the visits by Beauchamp and Wannamaker after recovery when his phone buzzed.

"Hello?"

"Dr. Bolling, I have Dr. Song for you."

"Thank you, Mary." A pause, then Monique asked, "Do I need to come up there?"

"No, I don't think so. I wanted to ask if perhaps you had any additional laboratory results on those three leukemia patients that recovered from their infections so dramatically. Ron called and is getting nowhere with interviews. For some reason, I think those patients have something to do with Abbate's death."

Monique was quick to respond, "Sure, I can look around. You know I collect and keep a lot of material."

Tom responded, "And, I don't want this request to create a perceived need for additional storage for more material than you already keep."

Tom thought he might have heard Monique smiling as she said, "We'll see." Then she hung up. Tom turned back to thumbing through the medical charts, looking for a clue that he couldn't describe that would help him fathom a situation he didn't understand.

CHAPTER 39

Tom thought about the three patients who had recovered from a usually fatal infection. He had never seen a circumstance like that in his many years of practice and had no frame of reference for the continuation of visits by consultants. He knew that some consultants continued to visit patients during a hospital stay, but those visits were part of the observation of continued care. Beauchamp had recommended transfusions for the patients' anemia, and their shortness of breath improved. Wannamaker might have had a professional interest in their recovery from infection, but he had visited every day, even after the infection had ceased to be a problem. What were they looking at?

Tom also wondered why he should care. He did not have any indication that the consultants had played any role in Abbate's death. Tom wasn't sure that the three patient cases were connected, either. He decided he needed advice from a more objective observer. He pushed the intercom button on his phone and heard Beverly Hancock answer from her office, "Yes, sir?"

"Bev, could you come in here and chat with me about a puzzling issue?"

"Certainly. Give me a minute to finish these forms."

Tom leaned back in his chair and thought about the best way to present the question to Bev. He often sought her advice in matters where the clinical and the administrative facets of medical practice intersected. By appearance, Beverly might lead one to mistake her for a librarian seeking an overdue book. She was, however, the strong right arm for Tom since he became Chief of Staff. Beverly's experience working in several departments in New City over the years provided invaluable insight into the processes behind these support services. She also knew the thinking that drove most of the activity in the administrative services. Early on, Beverly explained to Tom that she felt aligned with him on the 'clinical side', but she considered herself an administrator and a very good one. Tom had long ago agreed with her assessment. His opinion of her capabilities was she represented his best chance of succeeding in his job.

Tom decided he would present the issue to Beverly as an administrative question, not a clinical one. Beverly's experience in the New City Fiscal Office would give her the background for his concern.

Beverly came into the office with a smile, asking, "What's up?"

"I want your thinking on an administrative thing."

"A thing? I don't think we've had one of those lately."

"An issue, then."

"But not a question?"

"If it looks like one to you, that will be fine."

"Okay. What is the 'thing'?"

"We have three patients here who were treated by Abbate. They each had chronic leukemia and died. Abbate asked both Denis and Cole for consults on the three patients. And, after they completed their recommendations, each of the consultants continued to see those patients every day. They made notes, but no further orders, and they made no recommendations to Abbate. At least, their notes made no suggestions for care." He paused and looked at Bev.

"Isn't that something that all consultants do?"

"What do you mean?"

"Don't they often continue to see patients on whom they consulted, as long as the patient is in the hospital?"

"Well, yes, that's true when the reason for their consultation remains a clinical issue. That's not what happened here."

"Do I need to dig that out of the chart?"

"No. Each patient developed shortness of breath that Abbate thought was unusual. He asked Denis about it, and Denis pointed out the relationship of that symptom to the patients' anemia. He recommended transfusion, and that was done. The symptoms went away. Yet Denis came by to see each patient every day for another two weeks."

"Until they died."

"Exactly. What do you think?"

"You said Dr. Wannamaker did the same? What was he asked about?"

"All of the patients developed a serious infection, and Cole consulted about the choice of antibiotics."

"And …?"

Tom spread his hands and replied, "And, the patients got better and he kept coming around every day."

"Maybe they just wanted to know that their recommendations had the desired effect."

"Beverly, I considered that explanation. And that may well be the right one. But something about their actions didn't seem totally explained by that motive. I'm wondering if there is some other justification."

"You mean something administrative, like charging for their visits?"

"Well, we know that does happen."

"Why are these visits concerning you so much, then?"

Tom made a half-hearted grin, leaned back in his chair, and said, "Probably because the odd visits involved these three patients and they were treated by Abbate."

Now Beverly sat back in the chair and fixed Tom with a steady look. "So what? Why are these three patients worrying you? Is it the consults, or is it the consultants?"

Tom took a deep breath before answering, "It's both. Each of these three men had an infection that normally is fatal. For some reason, all of them recovered completely. One such patient gets reported in the medical literature. Three suddenly looks suspicious."

"Why?"

"As I said, one case would get attention in the literature, a second case should have been the talk of the hospital. The third case begins to sound like a major scientific breakthrough."

"But?"

"Exactly. I heard absolutely nothing about any of these cases. I've looked at the medical records, of course. Three of our staff physicians saw these patients every day and made notes to the effect that the patients were recovering from their infection, and no one indicated any surprise."

"You think something covert was going on?"

"I asked you for your opinion, Beverly."

"And you framed that as an administrative question. Do you really think this is administrative? It sounds more clinical to me."

"Other than the billing aspect, is there any administrative reason you could imagine for their behavior?"

"Not right now. Why don't you ask the two of them why they were following these patients for so long?"

"I believe it will finally come down to that. However, I don't feel confident that these guys will tell the truth."

"Oh? Now we are getting down to the brass tacks, aren't we? What are you afraid of, Tom?"

Bolling crossed his arms and responded, "I'm more than a little suspicious that something unethical was going on here."

"Why? Because a couple of physicians saw patients more than usual?"

"No. Because each of these patients was enrolled in a clinical research protocol and they had no family. Because each of them had an infection that should have killed them. Because they each recovered from the usually fatal infection and because three of our intelligent staff physicians were aware of all that and watched those patients daily. But most of all, because no one told me about the miraculous recovery of each of these patients." Tom had become more energetic in explaining his reasoning as his explanation proceeded. He lightly pounded his fist on his desk to emphasize his last point.

Beverly nodded and sat back in her chair. "You also are concerned that it may have something to do with Abbate's death, aren't you?"

"Yes, I am. If you can't think of an innocent administrative reason for the action of these two physicians, I have to conclude the event is clinical and something they didn't want me to know. And I can't defend us from things I don't know about."

CHAPTER 40

Looney arrived at New City hospital just after eight that morning. He timed his drive and arrival to the usual lull in business at the Green Bean. Nick smiled at him when he entered the lobby and turned to his espresso machine without a word. Accepting their new mind-reading association, Ron paid for his Red Eye and thanked Nick as he gathered his drink. As Ron turned to walk away, he almost ran into Cole Wannamaker, also heading for coffee.

"Oops," Ron said. "pardon me, Dr. Wannamaker."

"Hmm? Oh, no harm."

Ron waited until Wannamaker had given his order and then asked, "I wonder if we could have a brief chat, doctor?"

"Ah, sure, whatever."

"It's nothing much. I was reviewing some of Dr. Abbate's patients' records and noted something odd. I wonder if you could help me out."

"I don't know. I mean, oncology is not my field."

"This isn't about cancer, doctor. It's about you."

"Me?" Wannamaker took his coffee and headed for the cashier. "What about me?"

Ron smoothly continued, "My question is about your visits to three of Dr. Abbate's patients." He mentioned their names and watched Wannamaker for a reaction.

Wannamaker shrugged and said, "Yeah, I remember them. Lots of patients get infections during their chemotherapy. Those guys had pretty bad pneumonia, I recall. Alex asked me to recommend treatment. That's pretty much it." Wannamaker nodded dismissively and headed for the elevator.

"One more thing," Ron said, halting the doctor's progress. "You continued to see each of those patients every day after that. Why?"

"Detective, that's not uncommon. Many consultants continue to see patients during the hospital stay. I wanted to follow their progress. I might need to recommend a change in antibiotics."

"I see." Ron waited for a second and then asked, "And, how did they do?"

"Uh, I'm sure you noted in their chart. They all died."

"Did you think there should have been a change in the choice of antibiotics??"

"No, no, no. Their infections cleared. That was no longer a problem. They died of something else."

"Was that common, doctor?"

"Actually, I was surprised they survived the infection. Most cancer patients in that state do not recover."

"Do you have any idea why these cases were different? Why they recovered, I mean?"

"Where is this going, detective? I have some patients to see, and I already told you I don't know much about cancer or chemotherapy."

"Any idea why they recovered?"

"No. I do not. Now, please excuse me." Wannamaker stepped over to the elevator as the doors were about to close, entered the cab, and turned to smile at one of the occupants. The doors closed without his eyes making contact with Looney's again.

Ron stood quietly for a minute or two, thinking about the response he received from Wannamaker. Then, he took a sip of his coffee and headed for the Railway Building.

In Abbate's office, Ron cleared off the top of the desk and replaced items with a single legal pad. Ron had asked Tom for access into the clinical records of not only the three patients who died but also other patients seen by Abbate in the last three years with the same diagnosis: chronic myelogenous leukemia (CML). Tom had arranged for Ron to get that information earlier, and Ron now took the paper listing those patients' accession numbers from his pocket. He tapped the Bluetooth mouse pad and typed in the password identification number Tom gave him.

Over the next several hours, Ron searched fourteen medical records of patients with CML. He carefully read Alex Abbate's first note concerning each patient's diagnosis and treatment plan and carefully made his notes on the legal pad about questions to ask Tom. There were several similarities and differences among the cases. Well before noon, he had three and a half pages of notes and questions.

Shortly after noon, Ron realized he was hungry and he thought of Gene, probably already at the café where Sandy worked. Gene likely had a tall tale about why Looney wasn't with him. Those thoughts reminded Ron of the pastrami sandwich he enjoyed there, and he hustled himself to the hospital cafeteria. The cafeteria did not boast pastrami sandwiches, but there was a choice of three soups, a salad bar, and a man who offered to cook him a medium-rare hamburger. He chose the hamburger, dressed it with onions, lettuce, and tomato at the salad bar, grabbed a bag of potato chips and a can of soda. As Ron paid and looked for a seat in the area, he noted Monique Song sitting at a table by herself. Ron went over and asked if he could join, and she smiled and said, "Of course."

They shared their thoughts about Abbate's death as they ate. When they finished, Ron realized he wanted another cup of coffee and offered to buy Monique one, too. She demurred and returned to the laboratory, so Ron found his way to the lobby and waited through the post-lunch line to get another Red Eye before heading back to Railway.

By mid-afternoon, Ron had finished his assessment of all the CML cases, keeping the three patients of interest until the last. The electronic medical record was a prime source. But Ron also could access Dr. Abbate's research records. These came in two arrangements. One format was a typed report sent to the review body at regular intervals. These reports included aggregate graphs and tables of responses to treatment and complications: Ron had no way to identify individual patients in the typed, aggregate research257. The second record set, however, contained dated, patient-specific, handwritten notes in a bound logbook. The entries were all in the same hand, presumably Abbate's. Unfortunately, the entries were often made in shorthand that Ron did not recognize. Abbate apparently saw patients and made notes on progress, changes in treatment, and the like in the bound notebook and later translated the key points into the electronic record. The reports to oversight and review committees later were extracted from the electronic record.

Ron found the notes regarding the three patients of interest with some difficulty. Abbate's notes on the first case contained exclamation points dated about ten days before the man died. The second case, a month later, also contained some exclamation points. The third case, six weeks after that, also contained exclamation points and the word, "terzo" circled in ink. Ron noted that at the end of the third patient's entry in the research log, Abbate had written "chee" and circled that in ink.

When Ron finished reviewing all records, he had five pages of notes and questions. As he read them he realized that he had discovered the answers to some of his earliest questions; he drew lines through those entries. Ron looked at the thicket of notes and questions and knew he would have to do some cleaning and rearranging before his legal pad would be of any help.

He found some colored pencils in Abbate's desk drawer and went through the pages marking questions in red and facts in blue. Finished with that, Ron tore off the pages he had written and created a new list of questions on a new page of the legal pad. He realized that his questions fell cleanly into three categories: the diagnosis of CML, which seemed based on less evidence in some patients than others, the treatment for the disease, which was sometimes oral and sometimes intravenous, and the outcomes, which varied from alive and well to dead. Ron identified several questions relating to infections suffered by certain patients; he made this a stand-alone category.

When he had completed that task, Ron checked his watch. Nearly four PM. He decided he had time to put his notes into a similar order and started anew on a fresh page on the legal pad. He quickly found no order to the notes that would allow categorization as he had done with the questions, and he decided to do something different. He reviewed the questions he had and the notes he made reviewing the three particular patient charts. Then he searched through the notes and added to his list those that addressed issues or findings from the three patient charts.

Ron realized his back was aching, and he stood and stretched. Then he again checked his watch. Six-thirty! He remembered he had promised Meg not to be late for dinner, so he quickly packaged up his notes and pads, turned off the computer, and headed for home.

CHAPTER 41

They took their usual seating arrangement: Tom at his desk, Ron in the overstuffed chair, and Gene in the straight back chair beside the desk. Each man was fortified with one of Nick's special drinks, and their topic of conversation was familiar.

"I just can't put my finger on it, Tom," Ron said, "Nobody sticks out of this crowd as a murderer."

Ton nodded and asked, "From what you've said, it seems like the Overhart chap has the weakest alibi. I mean, 'Home Alone' sounds more like a movie than a solid defense."

Gene replied, "In point of fact, neither of the doctors has a better alibi. Both of them claim they were involved in patient care at the time, but no one can vouch for their presence every minute. Wannamaker went off to his office to read his mail and Beauchamp left the ICU several times to check on other things. Both of them had an opportunity to get to the Railway Building and back unobserved."

Tom frowned, then asked, "But what about getting back to the hospital in time to appear as if they had never left the ward or the ICU? Ron showed us how to do the 'vanishing act' and be inside the building without a trace, and I'll grant that someone could have done that but getting back out depended on Hector taking his after-lunch smoke break around eleven-thirty."

Gene nodded vigorously, looked over at Ron, and then said to Tom, "Yes, I know that, and I have argued that with Walker for several days now." He looked back at Ron and went on, "Why don't you try your argument on Tom? Explain to him how someone might get out using Hector and not have to wait for eleven-thirty."

Tom looked expectantly at Ron, who sat unperturbed, sipping his coffee. He leaned back in the overstuffed chair and explained, "Smokers don't go for four hours without taking a break for a butt, guys. Hector is a smoker. He goes through a pack a day. That's twenty cigarettes in sixteen hours. So, the likelihood that he doesn't slip out onto that loading dock a couple of times before eleven-thirty is vanishingly small. I think our killer knew of Hector's habit and was down there ready to sneak out within a few minutes after he took care of the upstairs business. All he had to do then was wait for Hector."

Ton and Gene were both quiet for a moment, pondering what Ron had said. Tom finally asked, "What is your timeline for events, then, Ron?"

Looney leaned forward and gestured with his hand as he spoke. "The only restriction on when the murderer entered the building is that it had to happen unobserved. So I won't put a time on that. I believe the actual murder occurred very shortly after Jim Donaldson left the Railway building. We have his word that he left around seven-forty, so I put the murder at seven forty-five to seven-fifty." He stopped and raised his hand toward Tom, who was about to speak.

"Yes, Tom, I know Abbate's watch stopped at seven-thirty-four and that everyone presumes that to be the time of death. I think the killer bludgeoned Abbate and then set the watch to a time when Dr. Donaldson was still in the building and then smashed it to implicate Donaldson."

Tom indicated his surprise at this assertion. He looked at Gene, who nodded and shrugged. Tom looked back at Ron, who then proceeded, "The fact that the smashed watch was on his left arm is what initially made me think Donaldson was being framed."

Tom said, "This is very interesting."

Ron continued, "So the actual murder, I think, was around seven forty-five to seven-fifty. Then the murderer obtains a drop of blood and takes the stairs to Donaldson's office. As we've seen, gaining entrance takes no time at all. The murderer puts a spot of blood on Donaldson's shoes and heads for the loading dock. I can easily put him in the closet before eight p.m."

Gene picked up the narrative, "And, if the conditions were right for the murderer to get in the building between seven-thirty and seven-forty, he could have observed Donaldson leaving, kill Abbate, plant the evidence and be ready by eight for Hector's next smoke break. That's the way Walker sees things right now. If Hector really did take a smoke break around eight that night, our murderer would only be missing from observation for about half an hour."

"Leaving well-meaning nursing staff to give us his alibi as having been 'present but on and off the ward' over a several hour period," Ron finished the theory and leaned back in his chair.

Tom said, "Of course, you don't have to posit such a tight timeline if one of the other suspects committed the murder."

"That's true," Ron said, looking steadily at Tom. "But it would raise another difficulty, wouldn't it?"

"What's that?"

"How would one of them get a keycard for entrance in the first place?"

Tom was quiet and then, after a short nod, asked, "What did you get from the research record review?"

Gene indicated he needed to step out to the toilet while Ron went through his findings. Gene had already heard the story.

Ron said, "Not very much, but there were some things I found confusing and that I don't understand. In thumbing through the research notes on those three patients who died, I found some annotations by Abbate that do not appear on other charts."

"What kind of annotations?"

"Nothing cryptic. He put an exclamation point at the end of a note on the second case and then did the same on the third, plus he wrote a couple of words that I think are Italian."

"Well, he was Italian, first-generation. What were the words?"

"On the third case, he wrote in the margin of his note "terzo". I looked that up, and it means 'third', so I figure he had put the whole picture together."

"What else did he write?"

"I haven't figured that one out yet. It was also on the third case. It was down under Abbate's signature at the end of the note. It said "chay", and he circled in ink."

"You looked it up?"

"Yeah. It must be slang or something. It literally translates as "which is' and I can't figure if that's a question or a statement. There's a couple of guys down at the precinct with Italian backgrounds, and I'm going to ask them about it tomorrow."

"Well, I can't help with that. Is there anything else you need?"

"Yes. The more I think about this, the more it seems to me that Abbate's research holds some kind of clue about what happened to him. Could you give me a list of every person at New City with a research activity?"

"Certainly. I can get Beverly to provide you with a copy of that information in the morning. Do you want just researchers or support staff or administrators?

"Well, after that last case, I think I'd better have a list that includes them all."

Gene appeared in the doorway and inclined his head toward the outside. Ron nodded, got up, threw his coffee cup in Tom's wastebasket, and followed Gene out.

CHAPTER 42

aptain Thorason was not in his office when Looney arrived the following morning so he and Gene took the opportunity to make a coffee run to the shop down the street. Several others were also getting their morning caffeine fix and the line moved slowly. When it became their turn, both detectives ordered Red Eyes and Gene added a morning bun.

With drinks in hand and their favorite table occupied, Ron grabbed a seat at a small table close to the door. He wouldn't mind entering the office after Thor did but not with Gene eating a pastry. Uncomfortable about discussing much in the exposed environment and any conversation hampered by Gene's eating, most of their interaction was composed of coded questions from Looney and head movements from Gene.

Ron asked, "What can I tell him about the interviews?"

"Need more."

"Yes, we need to go back to both of them. But what can I use to convince Thor that we should go back, not Rocky."

"Dunno."

"That's not helpful, Gene. We are very close to our deadline. If we can't impress Thor with our progress, he may tell us to break camp and go home, or maybe we'll be assigned to the suburban bank robbery where the teller was killed."

Gene washed down the last of his morning bun, wiped his mouth, and said clearly, "I don't know, Ron. Maybe we should tell him we have narrowed the field and want to focus more on these four."

"What if he wants to know how we ruled others out?"

"No keycard?"

"Two of the guys on our list have no keycard."

"Yeah, right. What about mentioning that everybody's alibi needs multiple interviews, and we just aren't finished yet."

"You know, that may be the very way to gain more time. Tell him we have identified more people to interview."

"Right, partner. Let's tell him the job is too big for us to get done in the short amount of time we had."

"I don't like that presentation, Gene. It makes our situation appear like he was the culprit by setting too short a timeline."

"Well …"

"Nope. I've seen Thor ask people who told him a story like that, whether they were saying they couldn't do their job. I'll push the need for more time, but only because we did such good work in uncovering the need for these interviews."

"I'm glad you settled on a process. Let's go get this over with."

Thor was back in his office when they came out of the stairwell. Ron waved at him and asked, "How about a briefing, Cap'n?"

Thor nodded, so Ron and Gene entered the office and sat in the chairs in front of his desk. Thor eyed each of them separately before nodding to Ron, who opened the discussion by saying, "We're making some progress, and I thought you would want to hear about where we are."

"Huh."

"The last time we briefed you, there was concern about two specific suspects. They each have a motive, although they seem rather weak reasons for murder. You probably remember that our interviews found each to have an unconfirmed alibi, and we need more digging in each case."

Thor nodded.

"Well, we have now uncovered two additional suspects; both are physicians. Neither of them has an identified motive for killing this Dr. Abbate, but neither of them has a solid alibi either."

"Huh."

"Well, the basic reason we have these two under suspicion is that they were closely linked to Abbate in the care of three patients with very unusual circumstances."

"Huh."

"Yes, sir. That drew us to them right away. These cases involved an unusual form of leukemia and recovery from an infection everyone expected to be fatal."

Thor did not speak, but his raised eyebrows indicated both surprise and a question.

Gene picked up the narrative, "Even Dr. Bolling is concerned that these cases are very unusual. He thinks the cases might very well have a connection to Abbate's death."

"Huh."

"Uh, well, none of us are exactly certain how they are connected. Dr. Bolling thinks one such case would be reportable in the medical literature, and three of them together is unheard of. He wasn't aware of the cases before the murder, and that makes him think there's something under the surface that is linked to the murder."

This time Thor took several moments before speaking. He said, "Two other physicians?"

Ron answered, "Yes, sir. Both are keycard holders and would know how to frame Donaldson. Now that we think Donaldson had no motive and may have an alibi, these two seem high on the list."

"The others?"

"Well, we haven't closed them out. Their alibis are going to be difficult to prove, and their motives seem weak."

"Huh."

"Okay. Weak motives are better than no motives, I agree. I admit we don't have the slightest inkling about motives for the two doctors yet. But I haven't told you about my review of Abbate's research files. I went through his records on these three patients and several others and found some notes in Italian where he …"

Thor interrupted, "Italian?"

"Yes, sir. Abbate was a first-generation Italian immigrant. Probably raised in a home where English was the second language."

"Huh."

"So, I'm running down the possible meaning of these notes. I think Baldacci in Robbery knows enough Italian to help me out."

"You want more time, right?"

"Yes, sir."

"Go on."

"Right, Captain." They left and hurried over to their desks.

Gene said softly, "Good plan. That went well."

"Maybe. It will not be well in the future if we don't come up with an alternative suspect for Donaldson."

Chapter 43

They arrived for lunch and found their booth was unoccupied. Ron slid into his side of the seating, facing the entrance from the street. After the discussion at the coffee shop about Wild Bill Hickok, Gene had developed an interest in not having his back to the door either. He had asked Looney to change seats with him to no avail. Recently, he discussed the possibility of them both sitting on the same side, facing the door. Looney refused to discuss that idea. They agreed that Looney would do double duty and watch the door for both of them.

As usual, neither man needed a menu. They patiently waited until Sandy had time to come to their table.

"Hey, honey," she said to Gene.

"Hey, Ron answered quickly, and everyone laughed.

"The usual today, boys?" Sandy asked.

"Yes," Gene agreed.

"I'll have the cheeseburger, today, please Sandy," Ron said. Adding, "and iced tea."

"Be right back, fellas."

Again, as usual, they both watched her walk back to the kitchen.

Ron spoke without moving his head, "Are you going to marry that girl?"

"That's a very personal question, sir?"

"So is watching your back, but I'm doing that."

"Not the same."

"Not saying they are. I'm asking about your intentions."

"What is this? Are you now going to play like you're her father?"

"Gene, this has been going on for close to two years now. She is still calling you 'honey', but I had to force you to take that vacation together. What's up with you, man?"

"Can we talk about this some other time?"

"Can you promise to think about it and actually discuss it later?"

Gene paused and looked Ron in the eyes, "Yes. I promise. Just leave it alone right now, okay?"

So, they sat facing each other with their hands on the table until Sandy arrived with their drinks. She looked at each of them and asked, "Is this a staring game?"

Gene answered, "No, Sandy, we're just thinking about a case. That's all. Thanks." He lifted his drink in a mock salute. Ron nodded and did the same with his glass. Sandy smiled and went back to get their food orders.

Ron said, "Okay, then let's talk about where we are and where we need to go."

"Knowns first."

"Got your list?"

"Sure. Right here," Gene said, as he took out his notebook. He thumbed to the right page and quickly scanned his notes. "First thing should be a correction, I guess."

"About what?"

"The locked building mystery."

"Oh, yeah. We have to keep the memory of that in the back of our minds because others are still considering that to be a reality. Actually, some are basing their case on it."

"Rocky will be so disappointed."

"He'll recover. Probably will convert the whole idea to being his thinking all the time."

"The rest of the list looks pretty much the way it was the last time we discussed it. We've got the cause of death is blunt force, an assailant with a keycard and known to the victim, the blood on Donaldson's shoe likely was planted and four suspects with minimal motive and poor alibis."

Ron shook his head, "That's pitiful. We've got to up our game."

Sandy arrived with their sandwiches at that moment and commented, "Not until you eat your lunch. We can't have you out there doing your detecting game on empty stomachs."

They smiled at her and tucked into the food, pausing their discussion briefly.

After the third bite, however, Ron said, "Let's review the basics, Gene. We've got Method. The murder was definitely done by blunt force using that arm statue. That leaves Motive and Opportunity."

Gene grinned, swallowed, and added, "What we have over four motives doesn't add up to killing a howling cat."

Rod nodded and munched a handful of fries. "We are much better on the Opportunity piece."

"I think your trick shows that the Opportunity came with a keycard."

"Meaning?"

"Meaning I don't think we should spend much effort on Raganathan and Overhart. They don't have cards of their own and would have to depend on someone else letting them in."

"Unless they have come into possession of a keycard somehow, someone lent it to them, or they found it dropped on the ground."

"Stretching."

"Yeah, I guess."

"Given the time crunch, we need to focus on the two docs."

After a short pause and another bite of his cheeseburger, Ron agreed, "Okay, let's keep Raganathan and Overhart on the suspect list but inactive. I want to check up on that story of Raganathan's about an illegal gambling table downtown. But that can wait. I've had a second short talk with Wannamaker that got me nowhere. I suggest we set up at Beauchamp's and tail him when his wife goes to Bible Study."

"Fine."

"And I want to try another little trick. Let's exchange our notebooks. You read what I wrote in all our interviews, and I'll read what you wrote. Maybe that will jog our memories about some small thing."

"Clever idea, partner."

"Not clever enough to think of a way to check out Overhart's story, though."

"Something will turn up. If we don't get anywhere with the doctors, we can have another talk with him and maybe catch a break."

Ron pushed his empty plate away and said, "I'm going to have to have coffee, or I won't get anything done this afternoon."

Gene nodded and suggested the coffee shop. They agreed to use that time to review each other's notes, as well. This time as Gene paid, and chatted with Sandy at the cashier's, Ron made a stop in the Men's Room and they then walked to the car together.

CHAPTER 44

Tom Bolling was reviewing a report from the Operating Room Utilization Committee. The most recent findings indicated the turn-around time between operations had increased from less than 35 minutes to almost 50 minutes in the past quarter. Tom made a note in the margin to check with the chief of surgery, Sam Newberry, and the head nurse in the operating room, Janet Pilman. He was jotting down some topics to consider such as staff shortages, nursing turnover, need for education, etc. when a loud knocking on his office door interrupted him.

Tom looked up to see Monique Song peeking in with both eyebrows raised.

"Come in, Monique."

"Mary wasn't at her desk, and I just barged on in."

"So I noticed. What can I do for you?"

"Have you got a few minutes?"

"Sure, what is it?" Tom put his hands behind his head and leaned back in his chair.

"Well, you have to get up and come to the laboratory. I have something I think you need to see."

"Huh. Okay." He heaved himself out of the comfortable chair and followed her, grabbing his white coat from the rack near the door. Once she was certain that he was following her, Monique did not look back nor make small talk. She proceeded at a quick pace to a nearby staircase and descended to the basement, then down the hallway toward the laboratory.

Tom followed along and entered the hematology section several seconds behind Monique. He found her seated at a double-headed microscope used for teaching. She waved him to the student seat and bowed her head over the eyepiece on her side.

"What do you see, Tom?" she asked.

"Hmm. I didn't know this was going to be a test."

"Just tell me what you see."

"This is really strange, I see nothing but white cells here. What am I supposed to be seeing? Is this pus from somewhere?"

"It is not pus, although I can see why you might think so, all those white cells." Monique paused a beat and then asked, "Do you see anything in those white cells?"

"Uh, yeah. Most of the cells contain some black granules. What is this slide from, anyway?"

"This is a buffy coat smear. Oncologists make these when they are following someone with a condition like acute leukemia. It's most useful when the patient's white count is low because they can look at a large number of cells quickly."

"Okay."

"This is a buffy coat preparation from one of our three leukemia patients. As you know, my policy is for almost everything we do in anatomic pathology, we keep a copy for reference or teaching. I went through our records and found this slide. According to the date, it was prepared the day after he was discovered to have lobar pneumonia."

"Oh, wow. So, what are those black spots?"

"Spot on, Tom. That's exactly what is important about this slide. First, look again at the white cells."

"Yes, Okay. What about them?"

"Do you see anything funny about the nucleus?"

"Hmm. Wait. Yeah, these are immature cells."

"Right. Those cells have nucleoli. These are myeloblasts, and they should not exist outside the bone marrow. This many out in the periphery indicates the presence of leukemia."

"Wait. You brought me down here to confirm the diagnosis of leukemia?"

"No. I wanted you to see the black dots in those cells. I did other examinations on these slides. Those dots are bacteria, Tom. The same bacteria as in his pneumonia and that he had in his bloodstream."

"That's unusual to see bacteria in the blood."

"Those bacteria are in the white cells, Tom. Those very immature myeloblasts have ingested bacteria. That's not supposed to happen. Those cells are incapable of that function. They only gain that function later in their life span."

"Well, those cells quite clearly are doing their job. Do you think this is why those patients recovered from their serious infections?"

"I do. And it is something completely unheard of in medicine. People with myeloblastic leukemia and no mature white cells often die from overwhelming infection. Because they have no functioning white cells!"

"But ..." Tom started to interrupt.

Monique did not pause. "But this patient, at least, with no difficulty, cleared his pneumonia and recovered. And now we have evidence that he accomplished that because his myeloblasts developed the ability to fight infection by ingesting and killing the bacteria, just as if they were mature!"

"And …" This time, Tom let the implied question hang in the air.

"Something happened to this patient, and it made his leukemic cells capable of fighting infection, even serious infection. Whatever it was that happened, it saved this man's life! And the evidence is right here on the buffy coat preparation. I'm certain that Abbate saw it. Why didn't he say anything to anyone?"

"Do you have similar information on the other two patients?"

"I don't know yet. I just started looking when I found this slide and decided to look at it."

"What material do you keep? I know your background as a medical examiner has made you feel obligated to keep copies of specimens and …"

Monique interrupted, "No, I'm keeping things now because I want the teaching material. There's a difference with samples like this, however. We, that is, my laboratory technologists don't make buffy coat smears. The oncologists make the preparation, at the bedside. So, the only way we in the laboratory would see a slide like this is if they had brought it here for staining. I know that's what happened with this slide. I don't know if that happened with the other patients."

"What are you going to do?" Tom asked.

"Well, you asked what material we keep. We should have slides of routine blood smears. With this high white count, I should be able to find enough white cells to examine. Plus, I always have the technologists save a tube of serum every other day or so. We should have frozen aliquots from all three patients."

"Rather like Dija tubes, eh?

"Sorry. I don't know that term."

"Surprising. Interns get a Dija tube on every patient at admission. Then, the following morning, when the attending asks "Dija get some previously unknown test?" the intern can honestly answer 'yes' and then orders that test on the 'Dija tube' of serum."

Monique shook her head. "I don't think I want to know about that."

"And you're certain this is not something ever seen before? Maybe just a rare occurrence?"

"Oh, no. I looked in the literature before I came to get you. Hard documentation exists that immature myeloblasts definitely cannot ingest or digest bacteria.

"So this provides us with a reason why this patient, and maybe the others, were so interesting to Alex and the others. And it raises another problem question about why no one wanted to tell me about the startling recovery," Tom said, beginning to sort out in his mind the implications of this discovery and the need to share it with Ron.

CHAPTER 45

Gene hung up the phone and stared across the desktops at his partner. Ron was thumbing through the notes he had taken regarding Abbate's research. After a few seconds, he became aware of the silence across the desk and raised his eyes to meet Gene's.

"I'm guessing that means you got something."

Gene nodded sideways, "Sorta. I've set us up for an interview with Mrs. Beauchamp at their home."

"Hey, good job. When?"

"This afternoon. She says she knows about Dr. Abbate's murder and wants to be of help."

"Help?"

"Well, she wants to assist us in our investigation."

"Does she know something?"

"She said we should come by this afternoon."

"Well, I can read these notes anytime. Let's go now." Ron stood, grabbed his jacket off the back of his chair, and started for the stairs to the parking garage.

"Shotgun!" Gene claimed.

"Agreed."

Mrs. Claire Beauchamp was a match for her husband. Slim, five-foot-six in stocking feet with brown hair pulled back into a ponytail. She looked like the date Denis Beauchamp would have worried about. Her face was oval and unblemished, wearing no makeup. She wore sweatpants, a sweatshirt, and white athletic socks. She opened the door, said, "Come in," then turned and retreated into the living room without asking for their credentials.

Ron looked at Gene and smiled, then allowed his partner's first entrance. They entered the living room to find Claire seated in the middle of the couch facing two stuffed chairs across a low, narrow coffee table.

"Can I get you something to drink?" she asked, with no body movement to indicate that she was interested in doing so.

"No, thank you," Gene said and continued, "Mrs. Beauchamp, my name is Detective Gene Novalchek, I'm the one you spoke with earlier on the phone. This is my partner, Detective Ron Looney. As I said on the telephone, we would like to talk to you about Dr. Abbate's death."

"Oh, yes," she said with no visible emotion. "That was so horrible."

The detectives sat in the chairs across from her. Gene went on, "Do you remember where you were the night of the murder?"

"Me? Uh, well, let's see. That was a Thursday, wasn't it? I was here, at home, probably grading papers or reading."

"Was your husband here also?"

"Yes, of course."

"What time did he come home?"

"Uh, I don't remember. It was later than usual, though."

"Any idea how late?"

"Do you think Denis had something to do with that man's death?" She delivered her question in the same calm and almost disinterested voice as before.

"We are making sure that we know where everyone was at that time. Routine questions, that's all."

"Where does Denis say he was? You have asked him, haven't you?"

"Yes, ma'am, we have. We are trying to get corroboration of everyone's whereabouts that evening. What time did he get home?"

"I'm not sure. I think it was later than usual. We didn't eat dinner until Denis came home, and I remember that the food I had prepared was cold, and I had to reheat it."

Ron asked, "What time does he usually get home?"

She swiveled her attention to him. "Almost always by seven o'clock."

"And do you usually have dinner ready at that time?"

"Well, yes, why?"

"Did you know he was going to be late that particular evening?" Gene asked.

"No, I'm sure I didn't. I mean, why would I prepare a meal for seven o'clock if I knew he was going to be late?" She looked at Gene as if he had asked whether she ever grew horns.

Ron asked, "Did you know Dr. Abbate?"

"I met him at one of the parties at the hospital>"

"What did you think of him?"

"Pleasant little man, I guess. We didn't talk much."

"What does your husband think of Dr. Abbate?"

"Didn't you ask him?"

"Yes, we did. Did your husband ever mention Dr. Abbate to you in any conversation here at home or away from the hospital?"

"I don't recall. No, I'm sure he didn't. We don't talk about things at the hospital much at all. I don't understand what he does. My field is mathematics, not biology."

"Mrs. Beauchamp, when we talked on the telephone, you said you wanted to help with our inquiries," Gene probed.

"Yes. And I would."

"The best information you could provide us is the time your husband came home the night Dr. Abbate died."

"Well, I can't do that with the precision and accuracy you are expecting. I've said that I have no recollection of the exact time Denis came home. If that is all you have come to collect, it appears that I cannot help you at all." She stood up.

The detectives also stood, thanked her for her time, and were ushered to the door.

Standing on the short sidewalk from the porch to the street, Ron said, "Well, Gene, I think we should let you make all the arrangements for our interviews from now on."

"Who knew? She said she wanted to help. I thought that meant she had a piece of information we could use."

"That was a very bright woman, Gene."

"You think she was toying with us?"

"No. Mrs. Beauchamp is a mathematician. People in that discipline operate on a different plane from the rest of us. I think she was sincere in saying she would like to help, having no real idea what that meant."

"So, we aren't any better off as far as his alibi."

"Not so fast, grasshopper. The dinner that she was ready to serve at seven was cold when the husband got home. How long would that take? An hour? Two?"

"I don't know. Probably more than an hour. Maybe two."

"I'd think so. And I believe that puts Beauchamp home after nine that night. He said he left the hospital around nine-thirty. It might take him thirty minutes to get home. Ten o'clock, and his food definitely would be cold."

"So, how does that help us?"

"It surely doesn't help Beauchamp. Nobody can vouch for his continual presence at the hospital, and his wife just said he came home much later than seven. This guy stays on the list, Gene. Good work."

CHAPTER 46

Monique Song took her refreshed cup of oolong tea back to her desk and began reviewing the results of her actions in the past several hours. She started reviewing the notes she made after reading the electronic medical records of the three patients of concern. Each of the men was older than 65 years of age; one was 81. Two men, including the oldest, had been referred to New City by the medical team in the health clinic associated with one of Cincinnati's homeless shelters. The third man presented in the Emergency Department one afternoon 'feeling poorly'. The third patient was also homeless, and the records did not provide information about where the three had been sleeping for months before admission. So, she had no information to trigger an environmental study, but that was not surprising.

Monique went back over the records of the physical examination and initial laboratory results for each of the men. Again, she found more similarities than differences. The men were malnourished and underweight for height, and they all had complained of various aches and pains in joints like most individuals their age. The baseline laboratory studies also were similar: significant anemia and peripheral white cell counts above sixty thousand were universally present. Also, each man showed more than 90% of their white cell count to be composed of immature myeloblasts. Monique knew this meant they were probably incapable of mounting any response to an infection. Most individuals with these findings usually died from infection.

The medical records showed that the three men were admitted separately over several months. The resident physicians that admitted them and cared for them on the wards were different in each instance. Each patient, however, was admitted to and treated on the same ward, 4C, and so shared a few instances of care by the same nurse. However, Monique had studied the nursing notes for these admissions carefully and there was no instance of a single nurse caring for all three of the patients.

Monique found similar results from searching the schedule and records in the Hematology/Oncology section regarding the residents rotating through that service. The usual three-month rotation for residents resulted in each of the three patients being seen and treated by a different resident. Monique had to conclude that the record contained no indication or hint of any person associated with the care of each of these three patients except for Alex Abbate. She noted that Alex saw each of the patients early in their hospital course, made specific recommendations about their treatment, and then followed the patients daily, visiting them at their bedside and making a progress note regarding their treatment and response.

At that point, Monique had opened her laptop computer and used Excel to create three separate time courses, one for each patient, plotting treatment and laboratory results by day of hospitalization. She highlighted the time on the graph where each patient became infected, noting the general lack of fever at the time and seeing, in retrospect, the beginning of the fall the patient's platelet count. That fall appeared to be unnoticed by the clinical team until it had reached severely low levels in the first two patients; treatment with platelet transfusion was begun too late to affect the gastrointestinal hemorrhage that caused the patient's death. That course was different, however, in the third patient. Clinicians recognized the falling platelet count much earlier and began platelet transfusions. That patient, however, fell and hit his head causing intracranial bleeding and death.

Monique placed the three timelines together and overlaid them. The similarities in the courses once the patient became infected were striking. After that point, the clinical events and the platelet counts overlaid on all three graphs almost perfectly. Monique thought that pattern was significant, and she thought she knew what it meant.

Monique converted the three timelines back to separate documents and studied the actual dates of clinical events for each patient, especially the dates of laboratory testing. She made a few notes and then got up and left her office, heading into the clinical laboratory.

Using her keys to the storage section, and to the freezer where she kept secondary samples, Monique was able to find and extract several saved tubes of serum from the three patients. She closed and locked the freezer and went to the hematology section. After searching through the drawers of saved slides, she found three buffy-coat smears, one from each patient. She took the results of her treasure hunt back to her office.

Monique turned to her special two-headed microscope for inspection of the buffy-coat slides. She was disappointed about the limited set from which to choose. Monique had come to New City from Cleveland, where she trained and served as the medical examiner for Cuyahoga County for four years. During those years, she became known, and respected, as very organized and thorough. The District Attorney viewed her as a reliable witness and Monique was frequently called to testify. But Monique came to dislike the courtroom. When her research interest evolved to center on cytocellular damage from chemotherapy agents, she realized she needed a different work environment and decided to move. New City provided her an academic setting and an opportunity to pursue her research and the two were a good fit.

From the outset, however, she organized the clinical laboratory, the morgue, and all technicians there as if she were setting up a medical examiner's office. Duplicate samples were obtained from everywhere during an autopsy. Because of her interest in cytotoxicity, it was almost universal that a sample tube of blood and other fluids available for testing also accompanied every autopsy. Two of her autopsy technicians had come with her from Cleveland, and they knew her habits and procedures by memory – they considered the protocols a semi-religious set of steps. Microscopic slides from unusual cases were kept in storage after documentation and filing of typed reports. If Monique's technicians had made the buffy-coat slides, they would have kept a copy. But Alex Abbate considered the technique a teaching point for his residents. Consequently, almost all such slides were made and discarded by the residents. The few slides that came to the laboratory were for teaching purposes, and Monique ensured they remained. But now, she faced the reality of having a single slide for each of the patients. She and Tom Bolling had already reviewed one of them. She took the other two and started her meticulous examination.

An hour later, Monique appeared in front of Mary Brighthouse's desk.

"Is the boss in?" she asked.

"He is, and probably not very busy. Let me check for you, Dr. Song." Mary moved to the doorway and knocked, She opened the door a crack and said, "Dr. Song is here to see you."

Getting the approval sign from Tom, she turned back to Monique and said, "Come on in, Doctor."

Tom looked up and asked, "Have you got good news, Monique?"

"I don't rightly know, Tom. But I do have news."

"Well, let's hear it, and then we can decide."

Monique chose to sit in the straight-backed chair at the side of Tom's desk. She laid her notebook on the corner of the desk and said, "I spent the afternoon reviewing these records and some of the lab work on these three patients. I have some new information but I'm not certain what it means."

Tom leaned back and smiled. "Let's hear it," he said.

"First, I created a timeline for each of our three patients starting with their admission. As you would expect, none of their clinical courses was exactly like any other, until they got infected."

Tom sat up, "What happened then?"

"It appears that on the day they first manifested infection, two of the three had shortness of breath, and the third was flushed and tachycardic."

Tom nodded, "Two had pneumonia, and the third had sepsis. Makes sense."

Monique nodded back but said, "But those symptoms were improved the following day. Much too fast for any of the treatment given."

Tom leaned back again and raised his eyebrows.

"No, I don't know why. But all three clinical courses were surprisingly similar after that. Within six days, they had cleared the pneumonia or the sepsis, and their platelets started a precipitous fall on day five. The two patients with GI bleeding died five and six days later. One of them received platelets for one day before death. The third patient was different only because his platelet count was starting to rise from transfusions. He never developed GI bleeding but died on day twelve from blunt force trauma to the forehead when he fell and struck the lavatory with his head."

"And that suggests what to you?"

"It looks like something happened, a procedure, a new medication or something on the day they got sick or maybe the next day. And whatever it was, it 'cured' their infection but suppressed their platelets to a lethal level."

"Cured?"

"Well, they improved symptomatically, and their infection was gone in five days. What would you call it?"

"What caused this?"

"As I said, I don't know. But, I do have some other information. You remember the slide I showed you with the blasts eating bacteria?"

"Right. Something you said doesn't happen."

"To my knowledge. And everyone else's. It's in the textbooks, for crying out loud."

"Okay, Monique, what about that slide?"

"It came from the second patient, and the buffy-coat smear was collected and prepared two days after the patient first began to have shortness of breath. The day before, he was known to have right upper lobe pneumonia and Type III pneumococcus in his bloodstream."

"What about the other patients?"

"That's where things get somewhat fuzzy. I do have a buffy coat smear slide from each of the other patients. The slide from patient number one was made early in the admission and several days before he got infected. There are no bacteria in his myeloblasts."

Tom made an unpleasant noise and Monique held up her hand.

"But," she went on, " I also examined a slide from the third patient. It was timed about five days after he became septic. The myeloblasts contain a few bacteria but nothing like what we see on patient number two."

"Sounds like an improvement," Tom said.

"Yes, but what is improved? The peripheral myeloblasts are still high in number so his disease is not improving. The decrease in bacteria may mean the infection is clearing, but why? What turned these myeloblasts into powerful anti-infection machines?"

Tom answered, "Okay, we don't know. What other material do you have in the laboratory to work with?"

"I have some serum on these patients before and after they improved. I'm going to run it through the gas chromatograph and the mass spectrometer."

"Big guns," Tom noted.

"Big question," Monique countered.

"That's almost like the quote from Hamlet."

"Which is?"

"Diseases desperate grown, by desperate measures are relieved, or not at all."

CHAPTER 47

Gene was grinning like a teenager after a stupid joke. He leaned back in his chair and made eye contact with Ron when he entered the Dick Pen. Ron twice tried to break the stare as he walked to his desk but without avail. So, before he even pulled his chair out, he asked, "What's up with you, partner? Did Sandy say 'yes'?"

"You need to broaden your horizons, Walker. You keep thinking about Sandy and me getting married and someone else will have to solve our case."

"What have you done, Gene?"

"I did what was needed. And it is possible. I have the proof of that."

"I believe you are talking a little in circles. I already have a headache forming, and your patter is not helpful."

"What I have to tell may give you a bigger headache."

"And you seem to be proud of that. Spill it, partner. What have you done?"

"Sit quietly and listen to my story. It will chill your heart and warm your loins."

"You're making that stuff up. Just give me the facts."

"Okay, okay. Here's why I'm somewhat excited. Last night I drove over to the Overhart's house and parked across the street from his front door." Seeing his partner's immediate frown and noting that Ron was about to interrupt, Gene went on hurriedly, "Hold on. You wanted to know. So, sit down and listen."

Looney closed his mouth and leaned back, but he didn't change the frown.

"So, I was parked there in front of his house, and I had my stopwatch in the front seat. At seven o'clock, I started the stopwatch and drove directly to the Railway Building. I did not speed, and I obeyed all the traffic laws. I got to the Railway building in slightly more than twenty-two minutes. I parked at the hospital and walked to the eastern door, used my keycard and entered, and immediately used the card to open the door and appear to leave. Just like you showed me to do, partner."

Looney nodded and indicated Gene should continue his story.

"I went directly to Abbate's office and jimmied the door as you showed me. I stayed in the room exactly five minutes and then used the stairs to get to Donaldson's office. I waited there for only three minutes and then hurried down to hide in the closet near the loading dock." He paused to catch his breath and assess his partner's reaction so far.

Looney cocked his head and looked up and to the right.

Gene understood that look to mean his partner was adding up the time, and said, "I got in there at seven thirty-nine, Walker. A couple of minutes to get into the building and a little more than a minute to use the stairs, and stay out of Hector's sight. Seven thirty-nine."

"Okay. When did Hector go for a smoke?"

"About seven-fifty. He was back in the building by eight-oh-three, and I was out by eight-oh-five. I made it to the car before eight-ten and pulled up at Overhart's house at eight thirty-five."

Looney stared at his partner and started to shake his head.

"Hey, don't do that. I just showed Overhart could have done it. I went at the same time of night, probably similar traffic, made all the moves, and got to the closet for the eight o'clock smoke break. Don't you go all negative on me."

"I'm not being negative, partner. I'm being surprised and amazed at your planning and execution. Well done, Gene. Well done."

"You're not thinking this through, are you?"

"What do you mean?"

"Well, I just showed that Overhart could have left his home, got to the Railway, killed Abbate, and got out and back home in plenty of time. And you want to drop him off the list of suspects."

"No, I get it, Gene. It's a good piece of work that the defense could put in front of a jury to confuse things. I don't want Donaldson to ever get in front of a jury."

"Well, yes, I agree. But, now we can put a little more pressure on Overhart. See if that story of his stands up."

"Okay, Gene. Why don't we push on this story ourselves first? Let's see what a good prosecutor would do. Okay?"

"Okay. What do you want to attack first? I've got my notes on the timeline."

"I'll take the timeline as absolutely correct, Gene. I want to question how Mr. Overhart got into the Railway Building. Where did he get a keycard like the one you had for entry?"

Gene swallowed hard and said, "I don't know. I doubt that he will tell us, but he could have picked one up along the way."

"Tom tells us that New City closely monitors those keycards. Anyone who lost one would report it immediately. Overhart doesn't have a card."

"Okay. Maybe he doesn't have a card that we know of. But if he does, he could have made that trip in the time needed."

"Second, what did he do with the baby, Georgie?"

"Well, I think he could have just left him at home. He wasn't gone that long."

"I'm going to do you a big favor and never tell Sandy about that comment."

"What? What does Sandy have to do with this?"

"She would drop you like a stone if she thought you had that little regard for an infant."

"What do you mean?"

"Most first-time mothers are afraid their child will die in their crib if they are left unattended."

"That's crazy."

"Another thing I will let you and Sandy work out in my absence."

"Okay, so he doesn't want to leave the child there. Maybe he takes the kid and leaves him in the car. How about that?"

"Possibly worse."

"Well, maybe he dosed the kid with a sedative and left him at home?"

"You are getting deeper and deeper into child abuse or neglect."

"If this guy's a murderer, why couldn't he be an abuser, too?"

"We don't have evidence he's a murderer, Gene. I appreciate you running the course and showing that it was possible. But, until we have reason to think he has a keycard, I don't think we have reason to pursue this right now."

"I think we have to keep Overhart on the list as a Possible."

"Okay, Gene. I will agree to do so, but way down the list. Until you find his keycard."

"Huh."

"However, because of the initiative you showed, I'll buy the first cup of coffee today."

"Deal. I want a Red Eye."

CHAPTER 48

Monique sat back in her chair and thought. She had performed the analysis twice and now was considering whether a third time would be beneficial or not. She had even taken the time to recalibrate the gas chromatograph and the mass spectrometer before the second analysis. And even then, both studies produced the same results. Results that she did not completely understand, at least at first.

Monique had pulled several reference books and drilled some websites while the second analysis was underway. Her findings were moderately clear but remained rather difficult to understand. She made another computer search, this one into the New City Pharmacy database before deciding that repeating the sample analysis was a waste of time. She needed to share her findings with Tom.

Tom responded to her telephone call by coming to her office in the laboratory. He arrived about fifteen minutes after she hung up and brought her a fresh cup of coffee from the Green Bean. Monique smiled her thanks and indicated Tom should sit where he could view her computer screen.

She said, "I definitely found something, but I don't completely understand it."

Tom looked at her and said, "That's going to be a first."

"I'm serious, Tom. Here's what's going on." She explained how she had followed her records back in time to the period when the three patients of interest were hospitalized in New City. Due to her protocols for saving samples, she was able to identify and test five samples from the three patients. Her testing protocol, Monique explained, used gas chromatography and mass spectrometry and was capable of identifying compounds not normally found in human serum. Her studies also allowed for such compounds to be further characterized, almost to the point of molecular identification.

Tom, with a typical surgeon's approach, wanted Monique to get to the end of the story more quickly than she did. He motioned with his hand for her to wind up the story. "So, what did you find, Monique?"

Monique frowned at being hustled through what she envisioned as important background information. But she pulled out two graphic printouts from the mass spectrometer and positioned them on the desktop in front of Tom.

"I found two samples from two of the patients but only one from the other," she noted as she displayed the individual patient's results.

"The first specimen on these two," she explained, "came from a point early in their hospitalization and before they were infected. I can identify some of their chemotherapy agents in the samples but I would like for you to pay specific attention to the area right here." She pointed to an area of the line graph that was flat and appeared to be at baseline.

"Why's that?" Tom asked. 'It looks like there's nothing there."

"That's right. There is nothing there in these samples. But that is not true of the other samples from these two patients. Look at these graphs." She added two additional graphs to the desktop and indicated the point of interest on the lines.

Tom nodded and commented, "Alright, now I can see that peak. It's clearly different. What is it?"

"Just a moment, Tom. Look at this last graph." Monique showed him the single printout from the third patient. "Notice the lack of any identifiable peak in the critical area.

"So, now I'm confused about what this all means," Tom said, sitting down heavily in his chair.

"Well, then, I'm not the only one," Monique said, smiling at him. Then, she went on, "I've put the dates of these blood samples on a time course with each of the patient's hospitalization. The negative samples on the first two were drawn 1-3 days before they became infected. The sample on the third patient was obtained after he recovered."

"And the other two samples?"

"One was drawn on the third day of infection, the other on day five."

Tom was quiet and reflective for a few moments. He looked at her and asked, "You think this peak represents a drug or compound or something that these men were getting during their infection, don't you?"

"Yes, I do. Perhaps it could represent some strange metabolite from the infection. I mean, it's only present during the time of the infection, and it was gone afterward. But, yes, I think this represents something administered to these men. And there's nothing like that mentioned in their medical records."

"Do you know anything more?"

"The characteristics of the peak indicate that the compound is relatively small molecular weight and has migration characteristics of an alcohol."

"Two-carbon type?" Tom asked.

"No. Larger. There also seems to be one or more halide ions. I will have to run more knowns to be more definitive."

"You mean chlorides?"

"I can't tell. Could be bromides. However, it seems clear this is something from outside and not something produced by the infection."

They looked at each other. Tom asked, "Do you think Alex was administering this compound?"

Monique held his gaze steadily. "I don't know, Tom. There is nothing in the chart indicating the administration of any drug or compound like this. I have combed through their medication lists and looked at all the progress notes, doctors, and nurses. Nothing."

"Could it be a metabolite of the chemotherapy they were getting? You know, something that may be there more than we know and we're just seeing it because you're looking for something out of the ordinary?"

"The chemotherapy for all three of these men was routine first-line therapy for chronic myeloblastic leukemia. None of those drugs contain halides or polyalcohol structures."

"Hmm."

"Meaning, 'no, this is not a metabolite of chemotherapy'."

"What's next, then?"

"As I said, I will run a battery of knowns to try to pin down the molecular weight and structure better. Then it's likely that I'll spend time running the possible configurations through the databases. It would help if maybe you could talk to Lena in the chemotherapy infusion unit to see if there is something they give that might not get charted."

"I can certainly do that. But let's just look ahead for a moment. If it's not charted and Lena says they don't give anything without charting, we are in a bit of a no man's land. Even if you can identify this mystery compound, and we feel certain that it was given to these men, and not recorded in the chart, we have no idea how that could happen."

"And no clue as to who might have given them the substance."

"And no idea why. We are heading for a giant headache, Monique, but your identification may be the first best step."

Tom stood and headed for the door as Monique noted, "I'm on it, Tom. This has me deeply interested now."

Tom stopped her before he left to ask, "Monique, do you think this compound could have anything to do with the recovery of these men from their infection or maybe something to do with the findings on those buffy-coat preparations?"

She took a deep breath before answering. "Tom, all we have right now are questions, and those are very good ones. But if we simply look at the overlap of the timing of the appearance of this compound in the patients' serum, the conversion of their myeloblasts to actually combat infection, and their recovery from very serious infections, I'd have to say I think those things are all related."

"And how do you think those events relate to Alex Abbate's death?"

"I don't have the slightest idea, Tom. Not the slightest."

CHAPTER 49

Tom Bolling took a long lunch; he got a Red Eye from Nick and wandered around the buildings in New City. He thought about the findings that Monique had shared with him. It certainly was odd for this unknown compound to show up in two of the three patients they were focused on. But the small sample Monique had studied gave him some pause. He wondered what she would have found if she had looked at ten additional cancer patients, choosing ones with infection at the time of the sample? What if she examined samples from other patients, ones without cancer but who had pneumonia? Would she find the compound there?

Tom knew that Monique had a research orientation to her work, and he guessed that she probably had the same thoughts. At the same time, Monique had some new information about the three patients that interested him and Looney. Tom thought about whether he should call Ron and share this new information. When he realized that his coffee cup was empty, he decided to go back to the office and call Ron.

Looney wasn't at his desk. Tom did not leave a message but hunted through his phone for Ron's cell phone number. Looney answered on the third ring.

"Hey, Razordoc. What's up?"

"Listen, Ron, Monique has brought something to my attention, and I'm wondering if you might be interested."

"If she brought it up, I'm interested. What is it? You want me and Gene to swing by for a chat?"

"Let me explain it to you first. Then, if you're interested in more detail, I'll get Monique to meet here with you."

"Okay. Shoot. What's the find?"

"Monique came to see me about a strange laboratory finding on one of our three men. In short, she found a microscope slide that shows the cancer cells functioning normally to fight infection. That's not something anybody has ever seen before. So, she …"

"Whoa, there. Hold on, Tom. This was something she found on one of these guys? What about the others?"

"Give it a break, Ron. I'm telling this story."

"Okay. Just get to the good stuff faster."

"This is all good stuff. I'm building a storyline here."

"Yes, General."

"That's better. Monique looked for slides on the other two patients and found something similar on one of them. We discussed this yesterday and she did some additional work today. She found something peculiar in the blood of two of the three men but only around the time of their serious infection, so we thought …"

"Wait a minute. Do you think somebody poisoned these guys?"

"Actually, we don't know what this compound is. But, no, we are not thinking poison. We are thinking that they were given something that helped fend off the infection. Something that may have saved their lives."

"Except that they died."

"Yes, there's that, of course. But first, they recovered from a serious infection. And that is a dramatic thing. Further, they were being treated with cancer chemotherapy drugs that may have caused their bleeding and even their death

"So, what?" Looney asked.

"Well, I'm guessing here, but if the unknown was given to help them recover from the infection, even if it caused the drop in platelets, we usually handle that problem with transfusions. This compound might be a real breakthrough in cancer chemotherapy."

"You're making that up, aren't you?"

Tom sighed audibly. "Yes, I am. But, there's something about the three men, and we think it could have something to do with Alex's death. Maybe he had discovered a new frontier in medicine. Something like antibiotics but without the resistance. Maybe he …"

"Wait a minute. Sorry to interrupt the Nobel laureate speech. Are you suggesting that Dr. Abbate knew about this stuff and was covering it up for some reason? Maybe because the guys died? And, if this compound is going to be so useful, maybe somebody killed him to get the secret?"

"Ron, all this is very new in my brain, right now. Everything you are saying is possible. Or maybe it's not. I'm not an expert in this area. However, these findings of Monique's seemed important, and I wanted to share them with you."

"I'd like to talk with Monique about this."

"Right. I agree. Do you want to come over to the hospital now?"

"Yes. We have finished our trips for the day. We'll be there in half an hour."

Tom arranged for Monique to join him in his office, and they were discussing the possibilities that Ron had raised when Looney and Gene arrived. Tom had added another chair to the seating arrangement in his office; they sat circling his desk.

After greetings, Tom said, "This is mainly Monique's show." He made a broad gesture toward her, and she picked up the conversation.

"I understand that Dr. Bolling has made you aware that we have strong clinical evidence that two of the three men we are focusing attention on were given a substance that helped them to recover from a usually fatal infection. Because of the similarity of the clinical course between them and the third man, I believe all three men received this substance. Whatever it is, I also believe this substance was responsible for the three patients' ability to clear their substantial infections. I also believe it possible that the substance caused their platelet failure and contributed to their deaths."

Gene, who had been briefed by Ron on the trip to the hospital, asked, "Any idea what this stuff is?"

"No. At least, not to put a name on it. It appears to be a short-chain alcohol containing one or more halide atoms."

"Well, now that we have that straightened out..." Ron let the comment hang in the air. "What did you just say?"

Monique smiled, "I'm sorry, what I mean is this compound is of small molecular weight and has some attached chemicals of either chloride or fluoride or maybe bromide."

"Is it a poison?" Gene wanted to know.

"No," Monique answered, "it seems to have good effects."

"And we're all interested in this 'compound' because . .?" Gene went on.

Tom interjected at this point, "We don't know the answer to that question, Gene. What we do know is that Alex Abbate seemed to have a lot of interest in these three men. They each suffered from chronic myelogenous leukemia and they each received the standard first-line therapy for that disease. Each patient had a poor response and each man then developed a serious infection. Instead of dying, however, every one of them recovered from the infection only to die from a bleeding disorder a short time later. Monique has found information supporting that two of these men had this mystery compound in their blood, and it appears that the compound was responsible for their recovery from infection."

Gene had been nodding as he followed Tom's explanation. Now he asked, "But only two of the men had the drug in their system, right? What are you thinking about that?"

Monique answered, "Since their clinical course and their recovery from infection were so similar, and so unexpected, I believe all three men received the compound during a short period. The specimens in my laboratory were collected randomly, and no samples from the third patient were collected during the short period when I think the compound or drug was being administered."

After a moment's silence, Ron probed what had bothered him most since hearing of this new compound. "And who do you think administered this mystery drug?"

Tom shrugged, and Monique shook her head, saying, "That is unknown. You looked at the charts, Detective. So did I, and there is no notation indicating this kind of drug administration."

Ron looked to Tom, "Do you think this is connected to Abbate's murder?"

"I don't know. It could be. The fact that Abbate was the treating physician and there is no note about administration suggests he gave the drug. But I don't know how that would lead to his death."

Gene spoke up, "Well, if it is a wonder drug of sorts and can help patients cure these deadly infections, maybe there some money in it. So, it might be a motive for somebody to try to get hold of it."

"That doesn't narrow the field of suspects much," Ron said and Tom nodded.

Ron looked at Monique inquiringly. She responded, "Well, I intend to continue trying to identify the compound. Perhaps that information might help determine who had access."

"We will still have to figure out how someone gave these men that compound without anyone noticing."

"If it was Abbate, he could have done it, and no one would have a second thought about it," Tom noted.

Ron scratched his head. "This may have opened the door to many more suspects. I think I need a list of all the keycard holders for the Railway Building."

Tom agreed, "Sure. Beverly can get that to you by email. We'll get you anything you think can help."

Ron got up and headed for the door. "I don't know if this information is of any use or not, doctors. Seems like we will only know when we figure out who the killer is."

Chapter 50

The following morning, Ron and Gene sat at their desks, finishing some paperwork and making covert glances in the direction of the Captain's office. The door to that office was closed because the Captain had not come in yet. As long as he was not in the office, with his door open, the path from Gene and Ron's desk to the corner staircase was open and available. If they waited until Thor was in his office, however, they would likely be seen going out for coffee and remanded to the Captain's office for a status report.

Ron decided they had spent enough time in the Dick Pen and signaled Gene to grab his coat. They walked without hurrying toward the exit and had gained the doorway when they heard from behind them, "Coffee?"

They turned slowly and guiltily and Ron agreed, "Ah, yes, sir."

Thor fixed them with a glancing blow of The Look, turned to his office door, and unlocked it. As he stepped inside, he said, over his shoulder, "Bring me one when you come back, and we'll talk."

Gene opened the door to the stairway and slopped through. Ron followed and they allowed the door to close before facing each other.

Gene said, "I swear he was waiting for us to move so he could catch us."

Ron noted, "That's the kind of thing he does, alright. But now we're caught and have a command appearance. We better plan our progress report to sound like we've been doing important stuff."

They continued down the stairs and out the door. At the street, they turned toward the coffee shop down the block and walked, matching each other's strides, without talking.

The line was short, and they quickly had their coffee, but a couple was sitting at the table they preferred. Ron looked around and indicated they should sit at another table, one against the outside wall. Once seated, each man looked around their immediate environment and then checked the line of visibility to the main door. Ron could see the doorway over Gene's shoulder, but Gene would have to turn to view it. Ron saw his partner's discomfort and said, "Hey, Wild Bill, I'll take care of the door this time. Let's get the ducks in a row for talking with Thor."

"Hmm."

"Last time we told him we needed time to check the alibis and do more interviews on the suspects, particularly the two without keycards."

"Yep."

"So what do we have that's new on either of them?"

"We have the interview with Beauchamp's wife. Her information indicates that whatever he did that night might have something to do with Abbate's death. Doesn't clearly implicate him, of course. But it makes it possible. Plus, we didn't have the manpower to do a twenty-four-hour tail."

"Good story, Gene. However, the emphasis last time we briefed was to decide about the non-keycard holders. On that front, we do have your experience running to the building and back to his house, but we have to deal with Thor arguing that the man didn't have a keycard to get in. That's the weakness in those data."

"I think we need to push the narrative that we have four individuals with motive and two of them have connections to people who have keycards. We cannot take them off the list until we are certain they could not have obtained a card somehow."

"I'll try that angle, but I doubt we will get away with it. In that same vein, our discussion with Raganathan and his alibi about that illegal gambling game downtown didn't get much traction with us, either."

"Still the manpower issue. Push that, partner. We can't be everywhere, and doing these interviews is time-consuming.

"I believe we will get out of Thor's office this time with approval to keep going only if we bring something new to the discussion."

"And you're worried because we don't have anything?"

"Right."

Gene nodded and pursed his lips. "It might push you a little," he said, "But you could always put that mystery compound stuff on Thor. When he understands these doctors are shading their stories and trying to get hold of that compound for fame and fortune, maybe he will see things more our way."

Ron nodded, made a few notes in his notebook, and then slipped it back inside his jacket pocket. "I'm going to freshen this cup and get one for Thor. Then let's go," he said getting up and heading back for the barista bar.

Gene liked everything about that idea and followed him.

Ron sat Thor's coffee cup on the corner of his desk. When the Captain looked up, Ron asked if they could sit. Approval was granted, the cup was moved in front of the Captain, and Thor looked at the two detectives blandly. "How're you doing?" he asked.

"We're pushing, Cap'n," Looney said. "We have generated probably more questions but we have what the doctors at New City think is a whole new way of looking at motive."

"Huh."

"Yes, sir. You recall that we had narrowed our list of suspects to four individuals on the basis that each of them had a motive to dislike either Abbate or Donaldson and might have been good for a frame-up. We have some issues with each of those individuals that are obvious and difficult for us to get around right now. One of the suspects is a drug salesman. He shouldn't have a keycard to the Railway Building and his alibi for the night of the murder is that he was playing in an illegal gambling activity downtown. For obvious reasons, we have not yet run that alibi down.

"Huh."

"Another suspect is a machine technician without a keycard. He has a stronger motive; he believes a family member died because Donaldson refused to care for her. You recall his alibi is a six-week-old infant he was babysitting. Well, Gene ran the course from this guy's house to Railroad, did the floor visitations to mimic the murder, got out and back to the guy's house in … What was the time, Gene?"

"Just over 90 minutes. An hour and a half."

"Huh."

"Right. While Gene's great work there shows that it is physically possible for Overhart to get there and commit the murder, it all begs the question of where would he get a keycard? Because we either can't prove an alibi or because we can disprove a different one, we have to put these two suspects at the bottom of the list for now."

Thor nodded and sipped at the coffee.

"But just yesterday, Tom Bolling gave us information that he thinks is somehow related to Abbate's death. It seems there was a mystery compound in the blood of all three of these patients we are thinking are at the center of things. This mystery compound, according to Dr. Song the pathologist at New City, may be something like a wonder drug. She thinks it caused these sick patients to recover from deadly infections."

Thor raised his eyebrows and his hands, palms up.

"Apparently, everybody expected them to die, but they recovered and she has reason to think this mystery compound was responsible."

"Huh."

"Well, it's a mystery because no one knows what it is, and there's no information in the medical record about anybody administering it. Whoever gave this compound to these patients is a mystery, also."

Thor nodded and looked down at his desktop. Ron gave him a few seconds to ponder the issues and then spoke up again. "So, you can see the problem here. If this compound is so effective, it's a big breakthrough in medicine. If Abbate was giving it to the patients and someone found out, they might have a motive to kill him and obtain the compound."

Thor started to raise his hand and Ron continued without pause, "But, if someone else was giving the drug to the patients and Abbate found out, somebody might think Abbate had to die to keep the secret," Thor's hand went down.

Everyone paused and looked at each other. Ron said, "You recall I found Abbate's research notes and I'm still trying to figure out what his Italian exclamations mean. Still could go either way. So we need more time."

Thor started to frown, and Gene interrupted, "Remember, Cap'n, we have the evidence that Donaldson was framed. If we don't press on now to find the murderer, the case falls back where Rocky left it. And any defense attorney will chew that up."

Thor nodded, looked at Gene sideways, and then asked Ron, "Want me to get Rocky to check out the gambling alibi?"

"I don't think so, sir. If Dr. Bolling and Dr. Song are right about this mystery compound, I think our murderer is a clinical person. I'm getting a list of all keycard holders for Railway, and I've got to spend more time on Abbate's notes and the hospital records for those patients when they recovered from serious infection."

They left the office. Gene asked quietly, "And what do you want me to do?"

"Get with Monique and try to figure out what this mystery compound is."

"Right. I have a minor in Chemistry."

"I know. I read your record."

"Now is it time for a séance with J.J. and John?"

"It's getting close. I think we may now have the data we need."

CHAPTER 51

Monique and Gene sat in the hospital cafeteria, weary from their efforts of the morning. They had examined, probed, rerun, and doodled with the information from the mass spectrometer concerning the unknown compound Monique had previously identified in the blood of the three patients they were studying. Gene's slightly more recent experience with spectrometric analysis of unknowns as part of his degree allowed him to take the lead in the initial attempts to calculate the mass and the chemical formula of the unknown.

After a few hours, they confirmed they were dealing with a short-chain alcohol with interesting chemical properties. Monique's original supposition that the compound contained halide ions seemed a good bet, but their mass calculations seemed too high initially. Now, as they finished their lunch, Gene seemed interested in getting back to the laboratory.

"Remember, I said I would buy us coffee at the Green Bean after lunch," he said, pushing his empty plate toward the center of the table.

"I recall," Monique said, paying attention to the last of her salad. "And, I am looking forward to it."

"I have an idea about this mystery compound, and I want to get our data into the NIST Library search engine."

"What's your idea?"

"I think we, and I really mean I, have been thinking that the attached halide is a single molecule. When we calculate the mass for the compound, the number comes out so high it can't be a halide in the Table of Elements as we know it. But it could be a multiple."

"Yes, I wondered about that, too. What's your intent?"

"Let's feed the data into the NIST Library using all possible combinations of halides that fit our previous calculations."

Monique pushed her bowl to the center of the table and said, "I agree. We should have thought of that maneuver hours ago."

"Don't be so hard on us. We hadn't had our Red Eye yet."

Nick, the barista, smiled at Gene and asked, "Where's your partner today?"

"Probably goofing off somewhere, letting me and the doc do all the hard work."

"Want your usual?"

"Yes, please. And one for the doctor. She needs to keep up."

"Maybe I should fix you two drinks so you can keep up with her."

Monique set up a pair of synchronized screens for their afternoon sessions. Gene started with locating and opening up New City's copy of the NIST Mass Spectrometry Library and Search Program following Monique's instruction. They had previously decided to set the Retention Indices at the default setting of two; if they found their mystery compound, further searches would be necessary anyway. Gene imported the Mass spectrometer spectrum from the serum samples and highlighted the sample they were studying. He clicked the mouse and the program began to hum.

Information from the NIST program slowly accumulated, and the researchers added it to the data they had previously collected. Shortly, they had complete identification of the compound and a chemical formula: C6H12Br2O4. Further connection to various databases supplied a chemical name.

"It's mannitol," Monique exclaimed.

"And you're going to explain to me the medical aspects, right?"

"Of course. Mannitol is a sugar, well, really a sugar alcohol. It is a sugar that is not well metabolized by the body. It can be taken by mouth to clean out the gut or intravenously to act as a diuretic."

"So, could this have been given for medical purposes?"

"I don't think so."

"Why not?"

"For two reasons. First, there was no reason for mannitol, and second, this mannitol is different."

"The two bromides, right?"

"Exactly. This is not your father's mannitol." Monique turned to another nearby computer terminal, signed in, and typed her access into the PubMed database of the National Library of Medicine. She entered the chemical formula of the compound and hit 'search'. The screen quickly segued to announce, "no results were found".

"Hmm," she said. "I was afraid that might happen. Gotta know the name to get the information."

"I know that feeling," Gene commented. "Anytime I asked my Dad a question, he said, 'Look it up' but I had no idea where to start looking anything up. Like trying to find the correct spelling of a word by looking in the dictionary."

"You learned to look things up, didn't you?"

"Well, yeah."

"And so did I. I'll just use words for this compound instead of a formula."

"I thought the words were what we are looking for." Gene said.

"Completely true, my friend. Just like looking words up in the dictionary, you had to start with a letter, right?"

"What're you gonna call it?"

"Mannitol-bisbromo." The PubMed screen announced another lack of results.

"Try 'dibromo'," Gene suggested and she typed it in. No results.

They each stared at the screen. Then Monique tried 'mannitol bromide' and the screen returned 12 pages of results. "Okay, Gene said, sitting down beside her. Monique quickly scrolled through several pages and their enthusiasm fell quickly.

"These are just references on mannitol," she noted.

"But, we're closer. We got some references. Try putting the words in backward."

Monique squinted at him, and he said, "You know what I mean."

She entered 'bromide mannitol' and got the same results as when using only mannitol as a search term. The term 'bibromide mannitol' yielded only two references, but each of those referenced a 'dibromo' compound. Monique typed in 'dibromo mannitol' and hit the jackpot.

The PubMed search engine returned 17 references regarding the use of a compound, dibromomannitol, in the treatment of chronic mycloid leukemia, and Monique said, "Detective, we just hit the lotto. We need to read all these references and look into their citations. There's got to be something here."

Two hours later, the pair burst into Tom Bolling's office.

"Hold on, here. What's up?" he asked.

"We know what the drug is. That mystery drug," Gene said.

Monique spoke, her head bobbing quickly, "It's called Mitobromitol. It's an older therapy for CML. Not as effective as the newer drugs. Alex may have been using this all along."

Tom looked a little overwhelmed, and he held up both hands. "All right. Settle down and tell me what you have learned. But also tell me what it means."

Monique and Gene looked at each other and Gene admitted, "We don't know what it means right now." Monique went on," The compound is called dibromomannitol, and is marketed under the name Mitobromitol. Twenty or more years ago, it was tried in the treatment of CML, but it turned out to be ineffective, and was replaced by more effective drugs."

"So, why did someone give it to our three patients?"

"That's not clear." Monique confessed.

"And why would anybody give them a drug proved to be ineffective?" Tom pressed on.

"Tom, we have been asking ourselves this for the past hour. We don't have those answers. What we do have is the name of the drug." Monique gestured with both hands in the air and then sat heavily in his desk side chair.

"A good starting place." Tom said trying to placate the obviously frustrated Monique.

"We found out that it is manufactured in Italy and distributed by a small pharmaceutical distributor in upstate New York." Gene said.

"You two made a lot of progress today, didn't you? Gene, what do you think Ron will have to say about all this?"

"First, he will make a derogatory comment about the chemistry part of the investigation, then he'll ask how our information moves the case forward. When I say I don't know, he'll nod knowingly and ask if I intend to take a day's pay for my efforts."

CHAPTER 52

M eg fixed her famous fried chicken for supper that night. Looney loved fried chicken – the homemade kind, not the 'extra crispy' commercial stuff. When he opened the front door and smelled the dinner preparations, his mood improved nearly one hundred degrees. He hung up his jacket and made his way into the kitchen where he found Meg at the sink. He came up behind her and gave her a big hug.

"How did you know?" he asked into the hair at the back of her neck.

"Seriously? After all the staring into space and mumbling answers to my questions for the past week, I'd have to be a pillar of salt to miss the signs."

"Well, it smells just wonderful. Can I help?"

"Absolutely not. I did the shopping and I'll finish the cooking. I even made it by the library to pick up the latest James Patterson. You go get ready for your meeting with JJ and John."

Meg referred to the later part of the evening, an activity that Ron Looney brought into their marriage and that Meg soon decided needed to have her blessing. The practice developed seemingly by accident before he met Meg. Ron had been single and living in off-base housing while stationed at Sembach AFB in Germany in the late 1970s. He and another AP rented a room in Kaiserslautern and they had found

303

a small bar around the corner from his lodging where U.S. Airmen frequented, and the band played mostly blues and jazz. Looney realized late in that posting that he had often spent the hours between supper and closing sitting in that bar, nursing one or two beers, listening to fair renditions of trombone duets of Kai Winding and J.J. Johnson or Miles Davis wannabes wailing on their trumpet into the wee hours. He also recognized that the following morning he seemed to have unusual clarity about whatever case he was engaged in, often being able to synthesize facts into a tenable theory that had seemed impossible the day before. This activity became known as the 'consultation with JJ & John'. Once he recognized the value of the practice, Looney began to make the 'consultation' a habit whenever cases became too convoluted.

After they married, Meg resented his going to jazz bars to work on difficult cases, so they had developed the current approach: Ron's favorite dinner and a solo evening with JJ & John in the living room. Ron turned their living room into a perfect listening studio. Not being a complicated man, Looney had developed his refuge simply. It had a plain turntable, a Denon DP-300F, with both 78 and 33-rpm settings. Looney's home system had a built-in pre-amp and two JBL EON615 15 inch speakers that he had placed in the corners of the living room. Plus, Looney had a collection of jazz vinyl going back three decades. The combination of a fried chicken dinner followed by a quiet evening surrounded by jazz greats was Looney's highest joy. He decided, for about the hundredth time that year, that he had definitely married up.

The reason Meg spent this much time and effort on this particular meal came when she learned fried chicken was one of Looney's comfort foods. Whenever he was sick or just troubled about something, fried chicken seemed to settle him down and help him repair. And, she discovered in addition to properly cooked chicken parts, the fried chicken entrée had to be served with the appropriate sides: mashed potatoes, green beans, and cornbread. Without the sides, the whole function of the meal would be disrupted. Over their years, Meg had learned when best to prepare this meal by being attuned to her husband's moods.

In Looney's opinion, 'fried chicken' was shorthand for "deep-fried chicken parts" with lots of rich fried crust and skin covering the moist and meaty parts of the leg, breast, and thigh. His mother had always fried chicken that way and Meg learned that the technique and results were the only way Looney was happy with fried chicken. So, Meg had 'gone to school' to learn the deep fry technique. It wasn't as simple as it looked, after all. There was the danger of dropping chicken parts into the frying grease – things that splashed out were painful and dangerous. Plus, there was the necessity for reading the chicken just right; too long in the grease and the meat was tough and the outer crust would begin to flake away. And if the parts were not left long enough then the crust was doughy and the meat not fully cooked. Meg had also learned the trick of testing the frying oil before starting – sprinkle a little flour into the liquid to see that it sizzles but doesn't burn. She also learned to set the frying oil temperature so that the first piece into the cooking pot sank and properly rose back to the top; pieces that wouldn't sink indicated oil too hot for cooking and pieces that sank and never rose were in oil that was too cool for proper cooking. Meg remembered thinking who knew there was this much science to dinner? Or to just frying up some chicken. Meg was especially glad she could just hike down to the SuperMart and buy the chicken parts — she knew that Ron's mother usually killed one of their hens for dinner and Meg was definitely not interested in the gutting and skinning part of fried chicken meal preparation.

After setting up his records, Looney went and changed into jeans and a sweatshirt and came back down to the kitchen just as the meal was being put on the table. Everything was there, the mashed potatoes, the green beans, and the iron skillet full of cornbread. The dinner conversation was intentionally aimed away from Ron's concerns at work. Ron wanted to hear about Meg's day, get second-hand information about the kids, two time zones away, and talk a little about their plans to build a deck out back. Ron could almost feel tension and tiredness leaking away from his body. And then, Meg set in front of him a piece of hot apple pie covered with a thick slice of cheddar cheese, and a fresh cup of coffee.

"Really, hon, how'd you know?" Looney asked.

"Last couple of days you have been too quiet and kinda moody, honey. And I know you get that way when you have a case that's bothering you."

"Am I really staring off in space?"

"Sometimes. Other times you look right through me like I'm not there."

"Whoa, that doesn't sound appropriate. Do I really?"

"Well, I know how to fix that, don't I, soldier?"

"Yes, M'am." He tucked into the pie with relish.

Later they stood side by side, washing and drying the dishes in one of their little rituals. Meg understood that Ron was about to sink into a reverie about the case and profoundly ignore her, hence the trip to the library. Their habit was to stand side-by-side, actually touching at the hips and shoulders while cleaning every last dish and pan from the 'comfort' meal in the sink. Their pattern, developed over several years, ignoring the automatic dishwasher, allowed him slowly to withdraw from her and the world for some time and ponder various inscrutables while allowing her to feel loved and not neglected. They would signal the end of the ritual with a second cup of coffee at the table sitting across from each other and making inane small talk until the coffee was gone. Then, Meg would take the cups, rinse them in the sink and go upstairs to read and sleep and leave him alone with his case.

This night he selected a pair of discs featuring Art Blakey and one of his favorites, Chet Baker and Russ Freeman. He set the volume low enough to keep from bothering Meg and started sorting papers on the coffee table while the music quietly rolled behind him. Ron carefully re-read the folders on each person involved in the case, including Tom Bolling and Monique Song. He read the interviews with all four of the major suspects and reviewed the documents sent by Bev regarding all keycard holders and their business in Railway. After reading each folder, he would consult his notebook, flipping back and forth to find every instance of a note concerning the individual he had just reviewed. Then, he would stare at the wall over the fireplace, conjuring up a timeline and trying to fit things into place.

After an hour, he went into the kitchen, opened the refrigerator and took out a bottle of beer, opened it and resumed his seat on the couch, and picked up the next file.

Somewhere around two in the morning, Looney had read every file and all his notes and had a timeline in his head but no real answers. He was still stumped about "why?" and therefore couldn't get close to "who?" And now, after three beers, his eyes were dry and burning and his head was aching and he felt hungry and sleepy at the same time. Without really planning to do so, he lay down on the couch and rested his head on the arm and closed his eyes "just to help me think a little" and then he was asleep.

Just after four in the morning, Looney felt a call of nature and got up to pee. Coming back from the bathroom he circled by the refrigerator and got a piece of leftover fried chicken to eat. After carefully cleaning his hands he picked two other records for the turntable; he had made a couple of changes earlier in the night, and now he went back to closing favorites: Coltrane and Brubeck.

Now semi-awake, he began sorting through his notes to identify the key elements that he did not yet understand. For some reason, Ron found himself leafing through the list of keycard holders again. When John Coltrane launched into his solo on Giant Steps, Looney just leaned back, closed his eyes, and let the staccato sounds aid him in conceptually putting pieces of the puzzle together and rearranging them on a large mental whiteboard.

With the rapid scaling of the notes echoing in his head, the individual pieces of Looney's mental puzzle were floating into their places did not require even virtual hands. The process was initially what only seemed to be a repeat of his scrutiny for the past several hours. Then, as he was about to open his eyes one of the pieces began enlarging and dancing to the rapid beat of the solo.

Eyes closed, and with sleep lapping at the edge of his consciousness, he noted that the dancing piece was pulling his attention away from the timing of events and putting more emphasis on the cause of events. Before he could sit up, the darkness at the edge of his mind became a closing circle around the whiteboard in his mind. As the darkness inched forward the center of Looney's vision was focused on a couple of key pieces of his puzzle . . . the list of keycard holders and pages from Abbate's research notes. They almost made sense . . .

Then, he slept.

Chapter 53

Looney felt so good the following morning that he went to the coffee shop on his way to the office. He smiled at Gene as he put down a cup of Red Eye and a morning bun in front of his partner. Under other circumstances, Gene would have been suspicious of such a gesture and produced a fountain of questions. This morning, however, he took one look at Ron's grinning face and said, "You had the session!"

"Is that a question, or have you developed a new way of saying, 'Thank You, Partner'?"

"Not a question at all. And, thanks, partner. I want to hear all about it."

"Not much to tell," Ron commented as he circled to his desk, sat down his coffee, and hung up his hat. "Read all the papers, drank some beer, listened to some good oldies. Went to sleep."

"Yeah, that's what you say every time. But you always come away from the consultation with an insight. What is it, man?"

"You know how sometimes I tell you it looks like a jigsaw puzzle with some pieces missing?"

"Yeah, right. I know."

"This time the big picture looks more like cheese."

"Didn't you eat before the consultation? You're always telling me about this great dinner that Meg makes for you. Did you forget to eat or something and now the case looks like food?"

Ron grinned at Gene. "You know, Gene, you are the one that is always thinking about food, not me. This is a strange practice for me. I think I need a little time to savor the experience of having a food image help me understand a case."

"What are you going on about? What kind of cheese are we talking about here? I'm thinking maybe a very large Brie, something with a resistant outside but a soft and tasty inside."

"Yeah, that sounds like something you'd conjure up."

"Is that it, then? Brie?"

"It is not." Ron took a long sip of his coffee, replaced the cup on his desk, and put his hands behind his head. "Rather than wait for you to run through a likely large litany of cheeses, I'll just tell you straight up. It looks like a big flat slice of Swiss cheese from twenty years ago. Lots of holes and they're all the same shape: round."

"Swiss cheese?"

"Yep. Full of holes."

"Your way of telling me that JJ & John didn't come up with an answer last night, and it's Swiss cheese?"

"I thought you would appreciate the irony more if I made the discussion about food."

"What's with the cheese being twenty years old? Is that a hint about something in the far past leading up to this murder?"

"No. It has to do with my mental Rembrandt of a slice of Swiss cheese. I remember them from childhood with big holes and medium holes and small holes …"

"Yeah, me, too. Why go back twenty years?"

"Perhaps you are not aware that the holes have been disappearing from Swiss cheese in recent years. Fewer holes and smaller ones, too."

"You are making this up." Gene said, crossing his arms.

"Am not." Ron finished his coffee and tossed the cup. "Fact is, the Swiss have figured out the cause and are fixing it, so you don't have to worry."

"I wasn't worrying. Why are the holes smaller?"

"Mostly fewer. It seems the cause of the holes is not related to bacteria in the cheese as was originally thought. They are caused by microscopic flecks of hay dropping into the milk buckets. With the advent of cleaner barns and less contamination, the cheese holes started to disappear."

"How'd you know this?" Gene probed, unconvinced.

"Read it in the newspaper. Point is, I see the case as having some holes in it. I think I have a new appreciation about some things, and we'll see how they play out."

"Swiss cheese."

"Old-timey Swiss cheese."

"I think I'm getting hungry."

"That's why I brought you a morning bun. Now I want to hear about your day with the erudite Dr. Song. Anything turn up?"

Gene leaned back and put his feet on his desk. "There actually was something that I was able to help her out with."

"Were you holding her coat?"

"I knew you would make some crack like that. No, my background in chemistry allowed me to work with her on the database and figure out the chemical composition of the mystery compound."

"Good for you. Is it important?"

"Is it important? You must have had the jazz too loud last night and can't hear properly this morning. I said we found the mystery compound."

"Perhaps I wasn't clear. Please tell me the importance of that finding."

Gene went quiet and sat back in his chair. Twice he opened his mouth to speak and thought better. At last, he said, more subdued, "We know it was once used as a treatment for that blood disease the three men had."

"Once? Not currently?"

"No. It wasn't effective. Only used now by vets."

Now Ron stopped all motion and stared at Gene. "Tell me more about that," he said.

"Don't know much. We read a dozen or so articles about this compound. Laboratory work initially suggested the compound would kill the cancerous white cells and would not affect the red cells. But in the clinical trials there didn't seem to be any real effect."

"Not that. What did you say about vets using it?"

"Yeah. I meant veterinarians, you know. Not guys like you who were previously in the Army or …"

"I knew what you meant, Gene. Tell me what the vets do with this drug."

"We read in the medical literature that it does work on this blood cancer in dogs, ah, big dogs."

"What else did you discover?"

Gene drew himself up slightly and said, "We found the manufacturer and the distributor here in the States."

"Where?"

"Distributor is in upstate New York. I've got the 800 number for the headquarters."

"Great! That's good work. Where's the Manufacturer?"

"Italy."

"Italy?" Ron was disappointed to hear that.

"Yeah, we looked it up. It's near the city of Bolzano. That's way up north."

"I know. Bolzano is in the Tyrol."

"I thought it was in Italy."

"It is. Tyrol is a region that was German until after World War One. The Allies split the country, and half went to Austria and half to Italy. The German Reich reclaimed it, but it went back to Italy after the war. This manufacturer may be German in lineage. What's the name?"

"Bozenhaus."

"Hmm. House of Bozen, or Bolzano. Not helpful. But you've got their number, right. Let's call."

"What's the time difference?"

"Uh, six hours, I think. So, it's not quite four o'clock there."

Looney made the call, and, with poor broken Italian on his end and limited business English on the other was able to talk with the Director of the manufacturing facility. The Director, impressed that he was being asked for information in a murder investigation, agreed to go through his files and provide names and dates of orders for dibromomannitol from veterinarians in Cincinnati, Ohio. Looney was profuse in his thanks for the Director's help and accepted his personal invitation to visit the plant if he were ever to find himself in Bolzano. He demurred from taking notes on driving directions, however, and hung up.

Ron gave Gene the thumbs-up sign, and they agreed to an early lunch.

"What was that all about, partner?" Gene asked as they headed for the door.

"Just filling in holes in the cheese," Ron replied.

CHAPTER 54

Back in the office that afternoon, Gene called the New York office of the distributor and procured the names of four veterinarians in the Greater Cincinnati area who had ordered dibromomannitol in recent years. Looney stuck his head in the Captain's office and gave Thor a brief report on the new findings. When he returned to his desk he found a sticky note on his desk phone listing two of the names for Ron to contact. He looked at Gene and saw him already in conversation with the first of his own calls.

Looney listened to one side of Gene's conversation and noted that his partner had apparently gotten in touch with a friendly and talkative veterinarian. Gene's attempts to ask follow-up questions routinely took interrupting the other end of the conversation. Ron smiled to himself, knowing that Gene would complain about his phone call for several days but he had assigned himself the call and could not cast blame anywhere else.

Looney looked at the two numbers Gene put on the sticky note and decided he would call them in the order written, the number at the top of the sticky note first.

He spoke initially with a receptionist who quickly made up her mind to assist him. She asked him to hold, and within fifteen seconds the veterinarian was on the line.

"Hello, This is Dr. Arman."

"Doc, my name is Ron Looney. I am a homicide detective with the Cincinnati Police and I would like to ask you a few questions if I may."

"Certainly, Detective. What is this about?"

Ignoring the question, Ron asked, "Are you familiar with the use of ah, dibromomannitol to treat leukemia in dogs?"

There was a pause at the other end and then Arman said, "What a strange question. Are you investigating the homicide of a dog?"

Ron answered, "No, our case involves humans, but this drug was present, and I understand it is now mostly used for dogs."

"Your information is correct, Detective. The drug is known as Mitobronitol. The term dibromomannitol is the correct chemical name, but it is marketed as Mitobronitol."

"Good information, doctor, thank you. And you are familiar with the drug, right?"

"Familiar, no. Aware, yes."

"What's the difference?"

"Well, I am aware that Mitobronitol has a place in the treatment of CML in large dogs. I have never used the drug and cannot say I am familiar enough with it to talk about dosing or anything like that."

"I see. Do you know about any side effects?"

"Not really. I would have to read much more about its use and outcomes before recommending it for a patient."

"How come you know about its trade name and what it is used for?"

"That is the strange part of this conversation for me, Detective. Until several months ago I was not aware of either the drug or its use. Then a man showed up with a Golden Retriever that had CML. He asked me if I could get this particular drug for his dog. I looked into it briefly and found a source and ordered some." He paused.

Ron asked, "Do I hear a 'but' in there, doctor?"

"Yes. I ordered it and have it on the shelf in my pharmacy. I called the man to tell him we had the treatment available, but he said the dog was moribund, and he wasn't going to put him through treatment. So, I have some of the drug, but I'm not really familiar with it."

"I see. I was also told that this drug was tried on the human disease but was not effective. Is it effective for dogs?"

"Well, the literature indicates that if given early in the course of CML there is often a remission for several months, but the drug is not curative."

"And the disease comes back?" Ron probed.

"Yes."

"All right, then. Thank you, doctor."

"Glad to help."

Ron hung up and made some notes on his legal pad, then looked to see what progress Gene had made. His partner was now poised leaning over his desk, holding his head with both hands, the left also cradling the telephone receiver. He was slumped forward, elbow on the desktop, barely moving. Ron had seen this posture from Gene previously and recognized it as the Bored but Stuck posture. Gene moved his right hand from his head, picked up a pencil, and made a note on the pad in front of him. The hand then went back to supporting his head. Ron didn't know if Gene was still on the first call or whether he had arranged to call two long-winded interviews.

Ron turned the page on his legal pad and dialed the office of the second veterinarian he was assigned.

The phone was answered by a peppy voice, "Doctors office."

Ron grinned and asked, "May I speak with Doctor Lingus, please?"

After a brief pause, the voice responded, "Uh, she's not here anymore."

"Oh, is this still a veterinary practice?"

Back to peppy, with questions she could answer, "Oh, yes. Dr. Lingus just retired, that's all. Dr. Bellingham took over. Do you need an appointment?"

"Ah, hmm, no. I would like to speak with the new doctor."

"Doctor Bellingham?"

"Yes, please. Is he there?"

A giggle, "Doctor Bellingham is a her."

"I see. My apologies. Is she available?" Ron thought he was just getting old.

"I don't know. Who are you and what's this about?"

"I am a homicide detective and I want to talk to her about a murder."

A brief pause, then, "I'll see. Hang on."

This time he waited over a minute before hearing a young woman's serious voice, "This is Dr. Bellingham."

"Doctor, my name is Ron Looney, and I am a homicide detective in the Cincinnati Police Department. May I ask you a few questions?"

"About what, detective?"

"Are you familiar with a drug called … Mitobronitol?"

"I don't think so. What does this have to do with me or this practice?"

"I'm not at all sure, Dr. Bellingham. We are working a murder investigation where some patients got this drug, Mitobronitol and …"

"What? Is it a veterinary drug?"

"Yes, it is, but formerly this drug was used on humans."

"Oh. Go on." She said brusquely.

"We think these patients were treated 'off protocol' with this Mitobronitol and we, that is, I, need to know more about it."

"I have not heard of it before."

"Used for leukemia in large dogs, I understand."

"You seem to know more about this drug than I do, detective. Why are you calling me?"

"Your practice, or more likely, Dr. Lingus' practice, ordered some of the drug from the distributor a while back. I wanted to know why."

"I cannot help you with that, Detective. I bought this practice from Dr. Lingus three months ago. As I understand it, she and her husband retired back to Scotland. I have no idea what you are referring to."

"I see. Did you retain her staff?"

"Yes."

"Could you ask them about this?"

There was a pause where Ron thought he heard someone breathing loudly through his or her nose. "Yes, I suppose I can. Tell me the name of that drug again."

"Mitobronitol. I appreciate your help, Doctor. Here's my cell phone number if anyone remembers anything. Thank you."

Ron hung up and made final notes. When he looked up, he faced Gene who was staring at him. Gene said, "I suppose you had two very good conversations and have learned everything we need to know to solve this stinking case!"

"Easy, Tiger. I just called the people you assigned. Didn't learn much. How about you? Your conversations seemed very, uh, intense."

"I'll say. I couldn't get a word in edgewise. I think those guys have spent their lives talking to animals and not expecting to have someone carry the other side of the conversation. And you talk about free association, these guys couldn't finish a single thought without remembering three other things to bring up."

"Anything of value?"

"Read my notes, I gotta go pee."

Gene headed for the toilets, and Ron reached across the desktop to get Gene's notepad. Several notations occurred under each of the veterinarians' names, but most were doodles. One doodle looked like Gene had been playing hangman. Ron could not decipher the notes before Gene came back, looking refreshed.

"Did you read my notes?"

"Did you win the hangman?"

"What? Oh, yeah, I did. I added a piece every time he said, 'besides'."

"What did they say?"

"You know, I think I memorized everything. Let me give you the hour-long saga."

"Please, no. The two-minute story, please."

"Probably not two minutes of usefulness in there. Both of them know the drug, each one has treated a single dog in the past five years. Dogs seemed to get better for a while, but then die."

"What caused the death?"

"They said the disease came back, the MCL or something."

"CML."

"That's it. Came back and dogs died shortly."

"Did they die from bleeding?"

"Nope. Just went to sleep and didn't wake up."

CHAPTER 55

They spent almost an hour at the coffee shop arguing about whether the veterinary findings had anything to do with their case. Gene was particularly skeptical at first but Ron's arguments concerning the surprise use in humans persuaded him they needed to keep that finding in their case. By the time they had walked back to the office, however, Ron had almost talked himself out of any connection at all.

Ron said, "You're right, you know."

"Often am. What about this time?"

"The lack of actual connectedness. I have this idea but I can't quite thread the needle and put the two together."

"Are you doing that stupid thing on me?"

"What thing?"

"The old 'circling back' thing. Remember, we said that only sounded like someone was circling the wagons or retreating."

"I am not 'circling back'. I'm just admitting that the thought I had after the consult with JJ and John just isn't connecting with reality now."

"Just don't 'circle back' on me," Gene said as he opened the door to the back stairway.

They sat at their desks and looked at each other, wondering what next steps they should be taking. Ron thought maybe he could call Dr. Barrington to see if she had located the record of the treatment they had discussed, but before he could pick up the telephone he heard the Captain call from his open office doorway, "Walker. Novalchek."

Thor was motioning for them to come to the office. Gene said, under his breath, "This can't be good. Didn't you brief him yesterday?"

"Yep. Something's up, all right."

They entered the office and found Rocky Knudson sitting in one of the chairs at the front of Thor's desk.

"Hey, Rocky," Ron said, trying to be cheerful at this uncomfortable turn of events.

"Hey."

Gene just nodded at the other detective. He and Ron remained standing, each unwilling to take the one remaining chair.

"Sit down," Thorason said, staring at them.

Ron shrugged and spread his hands, indicating the single chair.

"Go get one," was the terse reply.

Gene left and returned with a straight chair, and everyone was seated. Thorason looked at Rocky, who picked up the hint and said, "The ADA is all over me about Donaldson still sitting in lockup without arraignment."

Ron nodded that he understood but made no comment. Everyone stared at each other for several seconds before Rocky blurted out, "You guys have been mucking around for days now, and you got nothing. I'm the one that looks stupid in front of the ADA. I keep saying there's more information coming, but I don't got nothing."

"Huh," commented Thor, looking steadily at Ron.

"Uh, sorry, man," Ron said to Rocky. "I briefed the Captain, and I should have come to you."

"About what?"

"Our findings and conclusions."

"You got conclusions?"

"Well, some. For instance, we can be fairly certain that Donaldson didn't do it."

"What! This I don't believe. You gonna sit there and tell me you got proof I put the wrong guy in jail, and you don't tell me? Cap'n what is going on here?" Rocky appealed to Thor.

Ron answered, "Look, Rocky, it's not exactly all that clear, and …"

"If it isn't clear, then I should push for arraignment. ADA says we may have to let him go by tomorrow if I don't formally charge him."

"He didn't do it, Rocky."

"Why do you say that?"

"He doesn't have a motive."

"Yeah? What about that ethics charge the dead guy was talking about? You don't think that's a motive?"

"Rocky, They settled that argument days before. There's a legal document the hospital lawyer drew up signed by them both where they agree there was no ethical violation."

Rocky appeared stunned by this news. "Where did this come from?"

"Tom Bolling told me about it after you arrested Donaldson and he told us what you thought the motive was."

"Why didn't nobody share that with me?"

"Again, my fault, Rocky. We have been operating on a theory that the real killer thinks the frame on Donaldson is working, and we may trip him up."

"Real killer, eh? You know your guy was the only one in the building, right?"

"Again, Rocky, I'm sorry we haven't been briefing you daily. I can prove that almost anybody could have been in that building without their presence showing up on the keycard track."

"How would they do that?"

"The system is not very smart, Rocky. Anyone who uses his or her card to open the door from the inside is tracked as having left. All anyone has to do is stand there till the door closes with them inside."

Rocky did not take long to think about Ron's disclosure before saying with emphasis, "That doesn't clear Donaldson."

"No, it doesn't and we recognize that. But with the evidence against any motive …"

"I see. What you've done is destroy my case. You're working for the defense. I knew I shouldn't have listened to you." Rocky came to his feet and pointed at Thor, "You did this! You said I should let him try."

Thor didn't move except to say, "Sit down."

Rocky stood, shaking, for another few seconds while everyone held their breath. Then he sat down, gritting his teeth and glowering.

Thor said, "I have heard the evidence. Listen."

Rocky slowly relaxed his jaw and then nodded slightly.

Ron tried again, "Rocky, I should have briefed you earlier. I'm sorry. Gene and I found out from Dr. Bolling about the lack of any real motive early on, and that's been pushing us since. We believe Donaldson was framed with the keycard trick, and we've been closing in on a few suspects ever since."

Rocky stared at Ron, then shifted his gaze to Gene. They each met his stare with open eyes. Rocky said, "Okay. Maybe so, but you've left me with a cloud over my head if it's the wrong guy in jail."

Gene said, "Even if we have to let him go, you can always arrest him later."

Ron jumped into the conversation, "Wait a minute. We wanted him left in jail so the real killer would drop any defense. We don't think you'll need to be arresting Donaldson later."

Thor spoke again, "Tell him why."

Ron nodded and said, "We're close but maybe not by tomorrow."

Rocky interrupted, "Then I will have to let Donaldson out, and I'll be the laughingstock."

"No, you won't," Gene said.

Ron tried again, "Look, let me tell you why we think this was a setup to get Donaldson."

"Try me," Rocky said, folding his arms and leaning back in his chair. "I'm outvoted on this, anyway."

There was a knock at the door and Thor, annoyed at the interruption, said, "Come."

The door opened to reveal one of the young uniforms staffing the front desk. She said, "Sir. I have a fax for Detective Looney."

Thor's face started to cloud, and Ron was about to intervene and tell her to put it on his desk when she added, "I thought it might be important. It's from Italy."

Ron stood and stepped to the doorway. He took the sheet of paper and quickly glanced over the contents. As he finished reading the body of the message, however, his shoulders slumped and he started to shake his head. Then his eyes fell to the bottom of the page where a footnote was appended. He read the footnote twice, his shoulders straightening and a large grin coming across his face.

Ron waved the paper at the room and said, "We got him." Then, he turned to Rocky and said, "We will have everything by tomorrow. Thanks for your help."

Gene asked, "Are you going to share?"

"Oh, yes. Definitely. But, first I have to see a woman about a dog."

Ron ran from the room, grabbed his jacket, and left the building.

CHAPTER 56

Tom Bolling and Beverly Hancock had secured the Executive Conference Room for the meeting. Tom and Ron had discussed particulars on the previous evening, and Tom had contacted everyone Ron requested for the meeting that morning. Immediately after the Morning Meeting had ended, Beverly and Mary Brighthouse had set up the room with notepads and bottled water at each seat. Jacob Perkins and Lena Wilmette brought the medical and research records and placed them at the head of the table. Diane Ruttiger, secretary to the Director, gathered the attendees in the outer office and reminded them there would not be coffee, encouraging them to visit the Green Bean before the meeting began.

Ron Looney had arrived an hour before the Morning Meeting and quickly briefed Tom about the findings and the aim of the meeting. He slipped through the back door into the Conference Room during the setup to meet with Dr. Perkins and Mr. Wington, the in-house attorney for New City. When he finished that short meeting, he asked Mary to bring in the remainder of the meeting attendees.

Ron had specifically asked Tom to invite these individuals, and he had a reason for each person's presence. Mary placed name folders in front of their assigned seats, and everyone quickly found their place. Since Tom had asked them to attend, he opened the proceedings.

"Good morning. I appreciate you each making time for this meeting at such short notice. I do not think we will hold you very long. Detective Looney will explain the purpose of this gathering." Tom indicated that Ron was now in charge, and sat down.

Ron stood and introduced himself, "I believe I have met all of you but one. I am Detective Ron Looney of the Homicide Division of the Cincinnati Police Department. This is my partner, Detective Rocky Knudson." Rocky had quietly entered through the back door and now took his seat near the front. Ron continued, "As you all are aware, we are actively investigating the murder of Dr. Alex Abbate in the Railway building a short time ago. Our efforts have collected many facts, and the purpose of this meeting is to assist my partner and me in assuring we have those facts correct and in proper order. I thank you in advance for your assistance and cooperation."

"The first item involves the care of a patient with CML. Dr. Kindall, if you please."

Kindall opened one of the medical records in front of him and said, "This sixty-nine-year-old man presented with weight loss, anemia and a white count of eighty-eight thousand, all immature forms. He started treatment with Imatinib, 400 milligrams a day by mouth. He had increasing shortness of breath and was seen in the infusion unit to receive red cell transfusions. He developed severe right upper lobe pneumonia, and treatment with intravenous penicillin was initiated. A few days later, his pneumonia cleared, but his platelet count dropped to below 6,000 and he developed rectal bleeding. The bleeding worsened, and he died."

Ron asked, "Dr. Beauchamp, do you still think this patient's shortness of breath was due to his anemia?"

Beauchamp said, "Yes, I do."

"And you think the transfusions were appropriate?"

"Yes."

Ron asked, "Dr. Wannamaker, what do you make of the recovery from pneumonia in this patient?"

Wannamaker shrugged, "It was unexpected but gratifying."

"Do you think penicillin was the correct choice?"

"Yes. The organism was sensitive, and he recovered."

"Thank you."

At a signal from Ron, Kindall opened the next medical record and reported a very similar course in a seventy-three-year-old man, diagnosed with CML. This man also died from rectal bleeding.

Ron asked, "Dr. Kindall, what did the families of these men think about their illness?"

"The men had no families. They were homeless before admission."

At this point, the hospital lawyer, Mr. Harold Wington, interrupted to ask, "Why are you presenting these medical cases? I thought we were here to assess your findings in a murder case."

Ron nodded and answered, "Good question, sir. The answer is we think these cases may be related."

Kindall presented the third case and noted the differences. This man did not have pneumonia but instead had developed sepsis from a urinary tract infection. He was started on intravenous antibiotics and was improved the next day. Because of the experience in the other cases, close monitoring of his platelet count occurred, and he received platelet transfusions when his count started to drop. Unlike the other two patients, he did not develop bleeding. However, days later, he slipped in the bathroom, struck his head on the corner of the lavatory, and died of a cerebral hemorrhage related to a low platelet count.

Ron again queried Beauchamp and Wannamaker about their specialties, and their answers were the same as before: the treatment recommended was appropriate, and the survival from infection was unexpected. After the case reports were concluded, everyone relaxed.

Ron stood up again, asked for everyone's attention, and asked Dr. Perkins, "Sir, as the Research Director at New City, did you have cause to review the research notebooks of Dr. Abbate after his death?"

"I did. It appears from Alex's notes following the death of the third individual that he was aware of all three cases."

"Why do you say that?"

"He wrote "terzo" in Italian, meaning "third".

"Did he write anything else?"

"Yes, he wrote "chee".

Ron looked around the table and said, "I initially thought the word was not capitalized and considered it was another Italian idiom. Only recently did I realize it meant something else. Dr. Perkins, what do you believe Dr. Abbate meant by that word?"

"I think it means he intended to speak with Dr. Chee, chair of the Research Committee."

"Thank you, Dr. Perkins. Dr. Chee, did Dr. Abbate speak to you about any of this?"

Sonja Chee, a tall full-figured woman, flipped her shoulder-length black hair and said, "Alex did send me an email indicating he wanted to talk with me. But he did not mention what the subject was."

"Dr. Chee, as the chair of the Research Committee, do you also serve as the chair of the Research Ethics Committee?"

"Yes, I do."

"Is it possible Dr. Abbate wanted to discuss an ethics issue with you?" Ron asked casually.

"Of course. But, as I said, Alex did not tell me the subject of his concern."

"And the date of the email was?"

"Wednesday a week ago."

After a slight pause, Ron noted, "Dr. Abbate was killed the next night. And didn't have time to follow up on that email, did he?" Everyone looked to Sonja, and she shook her head.

Ron looked around the room and summed up the discussion, saying, "Our working theory, then, is that Dr. Abbate found something unusual about the treatment of these three patients and uncovered what he thought was unethical treatment. Possibly that was because of the homelessness and lack of family for these unfortunate men receiving some form of treatment without permission. Or maybe there was another reason, but whatever it was, it got him killed."

Ron had everyone's attention. He went on, "This exercise helps us understand the sequence of events and the relevance of the treatment each man received. Thank you all for your assistance." Ron dismissed the group.

CHAPTER 57

The assembled cast of clinicians looked stunned for a moment at Ron's dismissal. Everyone sat quietly and made no movement toward leaving. Most of them had thought there would be some 'reveal' before the end of the meeting and they were surprised to be dismissed. Ron smiled and indicated they should use the door into the Executive Suite for their exit. One or two individuals got up and hesitantly moved toward the door, and this movement encouraged others to do the same. Ron stood near the door and thanked each of them as they left.

Rocky stood up but made no move toward the door, positioning himself so he was actually blocking Drs. Beauchamp and Wannamaker from easy access to the exit. As the crowd thinned, he shifted his position to be out of their way, and they moved to the doorway, as well. Ron shook Beauchamp's hand and then turned to Wannamaker and held out his hand. They shook and Wannamaker turned to the door, the last to leave.

Ron stopped him by asking, "Say, Dr. Wannamaker, could you help me with one more detail?"

The doctor paused, halfway out the door, "Uh, sure, I guess so."

Ron motioned him to come to the table, and turned his back to Wannamaker, and started shuffling through a stack of papers. After a brief pause, Wannamaker stepped up beside Ron, as he did so Gene slipped into the room carrying a small backpack. Rocky closed the door behind him.

Ron said, "Here it is," and turned to hand Wannamaker a copy of the printout from Monique's mass spectrometer. Wannamaker looked at it and shrugged, "I don't know what this is."

"Oh, right. That's just the identification peak of a mystery compound we found in these three patients. I meant to show you this," he said as he handed Wannamaker the chemical information sheet Gene and Monique had connected to the mystery compound.

"What's this?" Wannamaker asked, dismissively.

"That is the mystery compound we found in these three patients. Do you know anything about it?"

"What is it?"

Ron leaned over and tapped the top of the sheet, "Says here its chemical name is dibromomannitol. Know anything about that compound, Doctor Wannamaker?"

"I don't think so. Doesn't really ring a bell." He turned and started back toward the door and stopped when he saw Gene and Rocky standing in his way. From behind him he heard Ron speak.

Ron said, "I thought you might remember the name of the drug that you recommended your veterinarian give to your dog. Don't you recall that?"

Wannamaker swallowed hard and said semi-nonchalantly, "Oh yeah. I forgot that was what it was."

"Really? You forgot the name of a drug that seemed to have miraculously cured your dog."

"Well, it wasn't that big a deal."

"That's not what the veterinary clinic notes say. The doctor wrote that you were concerned when your dog, which had leukemia, by the way, got pneumonia. You recommended this particular drug by name and told the vet it could work wonders."

"I don't remember saying that."

"She wrote it all down in the record. She gave the drug and your dog recovered from pneumonia. With leukemia. The vet was highly impressed."

"Yeah, we were both happy. So what? That dog died a few months later from the leukemia. Game over." Wannamaker shrugged his shoulders glibly.

"That's pretty dismissive, doctor. From what I understand, and you just agreed in front of all these other people, patients with leukemia don't often recover from infection like that."

Wannamaker stared at Ron who continued, "Unless they get dibromomannitol, eh, Doctor?"

"What do you want?"

"I want you to tell me why you gave those men this drug."

"I never said I did."

"Well, I want you to tell me that, too. And before you try to tell me that you don't know anything about it, let me show you a copy of the order you placed with the Italian manufacturer. A Rush Order two days before the first of these three men began miraculously to improve."

"That doesn't prove anything."

"Oh, actually, it proves a lot. But the more important proof is what Detective Novalchek found in your office desk."

Wannamaker spun to stare at Gene, standing at the door, holding a bottle of tablets he had removed from the backpack.

Wannamaker turned back to Ron, "What I did wasn't that bad. I was helping them recover. They were almost certainly going to die from that infection if I hadn't given them the drug. I knew it would work because it worked on my dog. They would have lived if they hadn't started bleeding …"

"Well, that was a described side effect of the drug when it was given as a primary treatment. Maybe you should have read more about it before pushing it on these unsuspecting men."

Wannamaker argued, "Look, I did read about it. I found that article about a man with CML recovering from pneumonia while he was on dibromomannitol. That article showed the immature cells were killing bacteria. I knew it was going to work. And it did!"

"Why didn't you tell Dr. Abbate what you were doing?"

"I was trying to help them, and Alex got all wound up about it."

"So, he told you he was going to make an ethics complaint?"

"Yes. Alex said I could turn myself in, or he would do it. He planned to talk to Sonja this week."

"So, he had to die, then, didn't he?"

"Wait, I didn't intend to kill him. I went to talk to him and see if we could come to an agreement."

"I don't buy, that, Cole."

"No. No, it's true. I was just going to talk with him, and Alex said no deal and turned his back on me. I lost my temper."

"Nice try, Cole. That story won't hold up in court. Your little trick with the keycard and waiting until you could frame Donaldson speaks volumes about planning and preparation. This case will be Murder One, no doubt. Detective Knudson, would you do the honors?"

Rocky stepped behind Cole Wannamaker and said, "Cole Wannamaker, you are under arrest for the murder of Dr. Alex Abbate. Anything you say, can and will be used against you. If you cannot afford a lawyer, one will be provided for you. Do you understand?"

Wannamaker, whose hands were cuffed behind him, seemed in a daze, and made no response.

Rocky repeated, "Do you understand?" and twitched the handcuffs.

"Yes," croaked Wannamaker, and Rocky frog-walked him out.

After a moment's silence, Tom asked, "What would you have done if he had decided to bolt and not show up after I set up this meeting this morning?"

Ron grinned at Tom, "Come on, General. You know I wasn't going to let him get away. Right after he arrived this morning, I booted his car."

ACKNOWLEDGEMENTS

I want to thank my wife and children for their encouragement during this writing process. Their feedback, support, and encouragement were positive factors in me finishing the original manuscript.

I also want to recognize Elle Murray for her faithful and frequent efforts to clean up the manuscript and to assist me in getting to the right place in decisions about format, artistry, and pagination.

Any errors that escaped these screening activities are mine alone.

Galen Barbour
Alexandria, Virginia
January 2023

Want more G.L Barbour medical murder mystery?
Turn the page for an excerpt from *Montana in the Rearview Mirror*.

Walt Dell is a young Irish American growing up in Northern Montana after World War II. His high school years, decision to join the military and involvement in the growing field of computers plus his marriage and move into civilian life are remembered as Walt tells high school seniors about those times in interviews for a political science project. Walt's memories stimulate both some serious thinking by the students and some memories for Walt; not all the reminiscences are comforting.

As Walt recalls 'the old days', the memories cut closer to the bone than he intended and he begins to share other events from his teenage years with another confidant, including the background and explanation concerning a mysterious death in his hometown just before he left for the military.

Walt's recollections of events in Basic Training were colorful but turned out to be very few. His explanation was, "I was sleep deprived! For two months! I didn't pay a whole lot of attention or take notes or anything. But, there was this one time …"

Walt did remember those long eight weeks, and he did so proudly. He might join a conversation later in his career where old soldiers were swapping stories. He would hold back, though, and not push to tell a story until things seemed to slow down. Then, he would say, "Well, there was this one time …" and follow up with a story so funny and ridiculous that his hearers laughed until they cried. When asked why he didn't tell his stories earlier, Walt's explanation was simple and straightforward. He would explain, "My Daddy told me the first liar doesn't stand a chance."

Asked about specifics, Walt often said, "It was like in the movies, lots of dirt and mud, people yelling at me to do something faster, jerked out of sleep at 0500 hours every morning. The only good part was the shooting range. I liked that." With some prodding, Walt told the group that most of the guys from Midwestern and Southern states were already proficient with rifles.

All-in-all, Walt made it through Basic Training without compelling harm to his psyche and a host of funny stories that he rarely brought out. When he was given his choice of Military Occupational Specialty (MOS), Walt went with the Signal Corps (MOS 25) even though that decision committed him to additional Basic Combat Training and Advanced Training of 16 more weeks. Later in life, Walt would share stories about these training periods as times when he forgot the outside world existed and was at his most calm, especially on the Firing Range.

PFC Walt Dell blossomed in the Signal Corps. After completing his Advanced Training at Fort Gordon, he was assigned responsibility for coding in multichannel transmission systems and quickly established himself as a leader and productive member of his platoon. The work assigned consisted mainly of keyboarding on the base; Walt wanted to gain competency in fieldwork and pushed his platoon Sergeant to help him transfer to Signal Support within the first quarter after he became permanent party at Gordon. His request was finally approved almost five months later and explains why PFC Walter Dell was engaged that winter with Signal Support for a nighttime battalion infantry exercise with light infantry from the 1st Infantry Division out of Fort Benning, GA.

The planning for such exercises was supposed to be secret, but nothing spreads faster in the Army than an exercise rumor. So, on that cold night, Walt was not surprised when the horns began shrilling their mournful single-note alert. Already half-dressed, Walt was first out of the barracks and into the rear of the truck his platoon would load and ride to the edge of the firefight. Their responsibility would be to maintain contact with the field command officer and report the effects of his efforts in enemy territory. Walt was excited about the exercise, his first field-level action; he wanted it to get going quickly and decided to help his platoon load their truck.

Walt jumped out of the tarp-protected truck bed and started handing boxes of equipment into the rear until became obvious there was more need for him in the truck bed. He jumped up on the rear bumper and started grabbing material from others, and placing boxes in the truck in the order needed. Everyone was eager to get to the field, and the truck driver was particularly hyped. When the truck was about three-quarters loaded, the driver jumped into the driver's seat and revved the motor.

Bare moments later, with Walt trying to wrestle a large monitor over the rear bed edge, the driver's foot slipped off the brake, and the truck lurched forward a foot or so. This forward motion caused Walt to lose his footing and fall to the ground from the truck bed, pulling the large monitor down on himself.

Medics were immediately summoned. Other members of the Signal Support team got the monitor into the truck, and it pulled away to join the exercise. The medics stabilized Walt on a gurney in the ambulance heading for the base hospital. On arrival, Walt was semi-conscious and obviously in pain; he was administered several doses of morphine and lapsed into a stupor. A radiographic study revealed the injury that changed Walt Dell's career ideas forever: the fall and heavy monitor had created an unusual circumstance: his pelvis was fractured on both sides.

The fractures made Walt's pelvis unstable, and he faced immediate surgical intervention to obtain stability; in the operating room, his fractures were stabilized by internal pins and an external wire across his abdomen. Walt woke up in recovery with considerable pain, and no memory of anything about the accident. His pain was intense for the first few days he was given morphine for pain control which left him with general narcosis helped to confuse him further.

His platoon leader visited him at the bedside and explained how the injury occurred. He also explained the injury was declared line of duty (LOD), meaning Walt would get some disability for the accident at retirement. Walt had no real concern about his retirement at that point and became suspicious of anyone who suggested he should take his recovery more slowly; he thought they might be pushing him toward leaving the Army. Resisting the advice to take his therapy slowly, Walt thought *I need to complete this rehab as soon as I can. I can't be shipped back to Montana.*

Throughout his hospitalization, Walt was most troubled by his post-operative restriction on weight bearing. He was allowed to sit on the side of the bed for meals but otherwise, except for bed baths, remained on bed rest for almost four months with some passive physical therapy. Walt had not completely adjusted to the restrictions on his movement when his commanding officer came to his bedside one afternoon.

Walt knew that such visits were unusual and feared he was about to be discharged.

The Captain took off his cap, sat in the only chair in the room, and asked, "How are you doing here, Private?"

Walt thought *I remember others saying that officers would ask the stupidest question,* but he said, "Just fine sir. Looking forward to getting back to work."

"I'm glad to hear that, for sure. But, I didn't come to encourage you to early recovery." He paused and looked at his lap.

"What is it, sir? You're not going to let me go, are you, sir? The doctors say I'm going to be well and will recover in time. I can still work in the shop here on base, I promise."

The Captain reached over and took one of Walt's hands. He squeezed, smiled wanly, and said, "I'm not here for that, soldier. Everyone says you are expected to fully recover. I'm here for another reason."

"What's that, sir?"

"I just received a telegram from the Army. Your parents were involved in a major automobile accident last night, Private. Both of them were killed!"

Walt felt his chest crumpling and being unable to breathe. He had a feeling of becoming very large while the room and its occupants seemed to be floating away and shrinking. One of the tiny figures raised his hand to touch Walt, and it seemed to grow larger as it approached his vision. Walt said, "Killed? You mean, dead?"

The Captain said, "Yes, son, that's what I mean. I know this as a shock."

Walt thought, *A shock? Really?* but said, "Yes, sir. Can you tell me what happened?"

"It seems they hit a patch of black ice at a turn. The driver lost control, and they went over a railing and rolled the car."

After a brief silence, Walt swallowed hard and asked, "Thank you, sir. What's going to happen next?"

"Are you asking about burial plans?"

"Yes, sir."

"I don't know what's going on at that end. But I would imagine soon. And you are in no position to return home to ..." The Captain paused to re-read the telegram, "to, uh, Peck, is it?"

"No, sir."

"It's not Peck? What is it then?"

"It's definitely Peck, sir. I was agreeing that I would not be able to attend." *And I don't want to be back there, anyway. That's why I didn't give Whealton as home address.*

"I see. I'm very sorry this happened, son. I will keep you apprised of the circumstances." The Captain stood, and said, "Well then ..." before turning to the door and marching out.

The nurse who had accompanied the Captain came to Walt's bedside and took his hand. She said, "Were you very close to your parents?"

Walt looked at her, thinking *here's another fount of wise questions,* and said, "I guess so."

She said, "Look, if you have trouble sleeping tonight, I'll get you something to help." She patted his hand and left.

Walt felt it difficult to cry. The event was not completely real in his mind, and he tried to guess which turn in the road was involved. *Can't do that because I don't know whether they were coming from the North or South, or why they were out so late. The Captain said black ice, must have been after dark. Oh, yeah, he said it was after dark. He also called me 'son'. But, I'm not a 'son' anymore, I'm the oldest. Now I'm going to have to start acting like an adult.* That did make him cry.

When he woke the following morning, Walt felt some chest pressure and breathlessness when he considered he was the 'adult' of the family now. He waited for assistance sitting up for breakfast and considered his new relationship with the world. He remembered many of his father's pithy sayings and his advice on how to get along and succeed. He had a new 'family' now - the Army. He decided he would work to regain his position with the new family, get along and succeed.

He knew he was the one to do it; after all, he was now an adult. *And this means I don't ever have to go back to Montana. That's good since I need to keep my distance from there anyway. Hell of a price to pay, though.*

From then on, Walt progressed so well with his recovery that his doctors thought he could start active physical therapy after three and a half months of bed rest. The physical therapy he most looked forward to was weight bearing, painful and uncomfortable as that was. After regaining weight bearing, Walt was most determined to get back to his assignment; he did every exercise as designed, not only in the clinic but also in his bedroom at night. He asked the therapist for clear measures of when he could leave the inpatient program. His approach to exceeding those measures was successful, and he was discharged back to the barracks on limited duty after five weeks of PT.

He still had a slight limp after discharge from Physical Therapy, so

Walt went back to PT to address it; three weeks later his limp was overcome. He had never been a sprinter, but by the time he was allowed to accompany the platoon on a five-mile run before breakfast, he became accustomed to finishing last.

But those physical limitations also led to a major career change: he was placed on Limited Duty (LD) at work and given only desk responsibilities. Walt was disappointed by this action by his supervisor but understood when quick movement or heavy lifting was needed he would be unable to perform. However, the deskwork he was given involved more and more coding, using the 88-column cards and a punch system. And Walt loved it; he was allowed to join the programming office to talk with the Army's satellite system. Everyone could see that digital electronic systems would be the technological breakthrough in future conflicts.

And Walt Dell was going to be there and involved.